REMEMBER MY NAME

DARA GIRARD

ISBN 13: 978-1949764215

Remember My Name

Copyright © 2016 Sade Odubiyi

Published by ILORI Press Books

Cover and Layout Copyright © 2016 ILORI PRESS BOOKS LLC

Cover Photos woman© Luminaimages/shutterstock; lake scene © Kattalina/ Dreamstime

Cover design by ILORI Press Books

This is a work of fiction. Names, characters, places and incidents are either the product of the author's imagination or are used fictitiously, and any resemblance to actual persons, living or dead, business establishments, events or locales is entirely coincidental.

ILORI PRESS BOOKS, LLC

PO Box #10332

Silver Spring, MD 20914

www.iloripressbooks.com

BOOKS BY DARA GIRARD

The Black Stockings Society

Power Play

A Gentleman's Offer

Body Chemistry

Round the Clock

Return of the Black Stockings Society

Playing for Keeps

After Hours

A Private Affair

Just One Look

Private Lessons

Henson Series

Table for Two

Familiar Stranger

Gaining Interest

Careless Rapture

Dangerous Curves

Duvall Sisters

The Glass Slipper Project

Taming Mariella

A Reluctant Hero

The Clifton Sisters

The Sapphire Pendant

The Amber Stone

The Emerald Ring

It Happened One Wedding

Unexpected Pleasure

Midnight Promise

Sweet Temptation

Always and Forever

Truly Yours

Novels

Illusive Flame

Honest Betrayal

The Daughters of Winston Barnett

Remember My Name

PART I

BETRAYAL

1

LAGOS, NIGERIA

"No one can know what really happened," Joscelyn Payton said in a low voice of both warning and demand as she stared at her two sisters. The sound of laughter, coming from their driver, who stood outside their window sharing a smoke with another man, pierced the tense silence of the room. Outside the expensive guest house, the sun melted slowly over the city of Lagos giving ample warning to those who needed to rush home before night descended—welcoming the dark elements that could grip the city and its residents in terror. But the three young women in the eggshell white room felt the icy fingers of darkness now, knowing that in a few moments they would have to face the consequences of what they'd done. "Am I clear?" she asked although she expected only one answer: Yes. At twenty and as the eldest, she'd grown used to getting her way.

Marie bit her lip, casting a nervous glance at the clock. In a few minutes their parents would return from visiting family friends of their stepfather who lived in a neighboring town. This had been their first visit to the land of their stepfather's birth and after five days in the country, he and their mother had been out a lot over the past two days having grown more comfortable leaving them alone. She rested her hands on either side of her as she sat on the side of the bed. At fifteen, and the youngest of the three girls, she had yet to gain her sisters' confidence. "But what if—"

Joscelyn shot her sister a cold look of rebuke. "Do I need to repeat myself?"

"No," Marie said, stumbling over the word. "I—I—it's just—"

Lorna giggled, nudging her younger sister with her elbow. At seventeen, she still enjoyed tormenting Marie who she saw as weak. "Now you've got her stammering."

"I knew you shouldn't have come with us," Joscelyn said, leaning back in her chair, a flash of annoyance crossing her pretty features. "You have no conviction. What's done is done. There's no going back."

"And it's for the best," Lorna added before Marie could protest, eager to agree with her older sister. She saw Joscelyn as her hero and was ready to follow whatever she said. "Don't pretend you didn't want this as much as we did."

Marie licked her lower lip. "I'm not saying that. It's just—"

"You think too much."

Marie swallowed and adjusted her glasses. "Are you sure there's no way it can be traced back to us?"

Joscelyn glanced out the large window as a spring sun settled over the city. "What can be traced to us?" she asked in a bored tone.

"You know the--"

She sent her sister a look of disgust. "That was a rhetorical question, dear. Try to keep up."

"Our problems are solved," Lorna said, reaching across Marie to pick up the TV remote left on the side table. "Just relax."

Marie jumped to her feet, wishing she could. Wishing she could be as mature and sophisticated as her sisters. Why didn't they care? Why weren't they worried? Why couldn't she feel happy about what they'd done? Lorna was right, this is what she wanted, but somehow it didn't feel right.

She glanced at Joscelyn, who looked as if she'd stepped out of one of the Nigerian lifestyle magazines her mother had lying on the coffee table. She had flawless cocoa skin, an elegant figure, and dark lashes and brows. Nothing bothered her. She was studying at the university and planned to be a neurosurgeon and nobody doubted that she would make it. Lorna was a smaller, slightly thicker version of Joscelyn, with Cupid's bow lips and laughing brown eyes. She kept her hair cut short and liked wearing dangling earrings to show off her neck. Marie felt like a baby giraffe next to them--all legs and neck. Not striking, but she wanted to be like them. She wanted to be like their mother, who'd given Lorna her figure and Joscelyn her face. She wanted to be like them. They were the Payton girls and that meant something.

Joscelyn came up behind her and rested a hand on her shoulder. Although the touch was light, it felt like a lead weight. "It's too late for second thoughts," she whispered, her breath brushing Marie's cheek, giving her goose bumps.

"I'm not having second thoughts," Marie lied, hoping she sounded convincing. She didn't like to upset Joscelyn. That was a scary sight. She would never admit out loud that Joscelyn scared her sometimes, that she feared her eldest sister's disapproval more than her mother's.

Marie shifted her gaze from the grassy courtyard to look at Joscelyn's reflection in the window. She saw a cool, satisfied smile touch her sister's lips. "Good, because there's no going back. Her fate is sealed."

Marie returned her gaze to the setting sun, splashing the

buildings in a brilliant array of red and orange. She nodded, feeling the impact of her sister's words and the decision they'd made. *And so is ours.*

2

___

She didn't expect her mother to scream. That wasn't the reaction she'd planned for. She'd planned for fainting, tears, even anger, but not screams. Screams that had the servants rushing into the living room where they all now stood. It was more drama than she liked and she truly didn't like the staff seeing their business. Her mother was really making a to-do about nothing. Catherine wasn't even blood related, just a stepchild her mother had acquired along with Dr. Emery Ojo's millions.

Joscelyn struggled to keep her tears in place, gripping her hands as she fought back anger. She wanted to cover her ears and tell her mother to stop it, but knew she had to act the role of distressed sister at all costs.

"Darling, sit down."

Joscelyn looked at her stepfather, relieved. *Yes, listen to your husband,* Joscelyn silently pleaded. *There's no need to overdo this.* She watched as her stepfather led her mother to the couch, instructing a servant to get her a glass of water. Joscelyn blinked her eyes, determined to keep the tears falling, she had to make sure that her mother saw how distraught she was. Show her how awful she felt.

Her mother stared up at her, her eyes wide with fear. "What do you mean you lost her?"

Joscelyn tightened her fist, wishing her mother didn't have to continue to shout. She glanced at the protective hand her mother rested on her rounded belly. Pregnancy hormones. That had to be the cause of this hysterical behavior. Her mother was usually much more calm than this. Maureen Payton was known for her decorum and reserved behavior. She hadn't even screamed when she'd learned her husband had been killed in a plane crash, leaving her nearly destitute with three young girls to raise. Others would have crumbled, but she'd survived, becoming a successful event planner before she met Emery Ojo who would change their lives. He was a successful dermatologist who owned a lucrative skin care line, toured around the world—and was paid hand-somely—as a speaker, he owned a concierge clinic where patients paid an annual membership, and also was a consultant. He was the perfect second husband for her mother. Unfortunately, he came with a daughter. "I just turned my back for one minute and she was gone."

Maureen shifted her keen gaze to Marie and Lorna who stood behind Joscelyn on either side. Joscelyn didn't dare turn to see their expressions, she just hoped it was as dejected and scared as she'd been able to manage. Her mother was smart; it wasn't just her beauty and charm that had caught her stepfather's eye. "And what do you two have to say?" she asked them, the stately Jamaican accent she'd perfected accentuating every word.

"I was looking at statues," Lorna said.

"And I was looking at a mural," Marie said. "I thought she was there."

Maureen pounded the arm of the sofa with her fist. "Why are you telling me this now?"

Emery rested a hand on her shoulder. "Take deep breaths. This isn't good for you or the baby. You have to be calm."

"How can I be calm when my daughters are stupid?" she said, waving away the maid who'd come into the living room to offer her bottled water and a glass.

"We didn't mean for it to happen," Marie said then fell onto a couch, tore off her glasses and dissolved into tears.

Maureen looked at her daughter, unmoved, then stared at Joscelyn. "Did you go to the police?"

Joscelyn wiped a tear away, pleased that more continued to fall. Her tears were real now, although instead of being the bitter tears of sorrow, they were acid with rage. She didn't like being called stupid, especially by her mother and for others to hear. "I thought maybe she'd show up here."

"An asinine and inadequate answer, but you already know that." Maureen narrowed her eyes. "You're not telling me something."

Lorna stepped forward, ever Joscelyn's defender. "It's the truth. She ran off. You know how she is when she wants something. It was just a minute and then she was gone. We searched all over and couldn't find her."

"She's ten, not five. What really happened?"

Lorna's voice rose with despair. "Why won't you believe us?"

"Because you don't lose a child in a market!"

Emery patted her shoulder, soothingly. "It's happened before. All over the world, especially--"

"I don't care."

"My dear, they're just as upset as anyone. There's no need to be angry with them."

"I'm not angry," she said slowly rising to her feet. "I'm furious. They should be too ashamed to even show their faces to me," she said, her gaze touching on each one of them. "How dare you come home without her!" She grabbed Joscelyn's arms and shook her. "You should have shouted 'thief!' to get the attention of others. You should have called us and told us the moment it happened. You should have had the police scouring the streets." She cupped Joscelyn's chin, meeting her gaze. "Now tell me what happened!"

"We just told you," Lorna said.

Maureen's mouth hardened. "Is that all?"

"Something may have happened," Joscelyn said in a soft voice, forcing her mother to lean in a little closer to hear her. "You're right. We didn't lose her in the market. We went somewhere we shouldn't."

Maureen released her grip and took a step back. "Where?"

"We wanted to see more of the city so we walked around a bit and got lost, but Catherine wanted to get something from a corner store she saw. It was down a side street. I let her go. I thought she'd come right back and I'll admit I was angry. I thought she was playing games. So I followed her and....and she was nowhere around. I asked the store clerk if he'd seen her and he said no. When I left that's when I saw them."

"Go on."

"I found her jacket and her shoe."

Maureen stared at her daughter for a long moment, then felt her legs give way. She would have collapsed to the ground if her husband and Lorna hadn't caught her. She didn't notice that Joscelyn made no attempt to help her. Her eldest daughter maintained her gaze, her brown eyes brimming with tears that strangely only fell intermittently. Maureen didn't remember walking back to her seat with their help or even sitting down. Her mind couldn't process what she had just heard. She shook her head when her husband offered her the glass of water the maid had left on the side table. Fear gripped her heart so tight she thought it would stop beating. Her precious child was lost. Possibly stolen. Maureen had lived long enough to know the dangers the streets afforded a young girl alone. Especially in a big city in another country.

She would not let that happen. She took a deep breath. She would find her. It was all just a mistake. She would get a call soon. The police had found her, she was scared but safe. Someone would find her and return her home. This wasn't happening.

She took a steadying breath, then said in a calm voice, "Get the car."

"You haven't said a word," Maureen said to her husband as they drove to the police station.

"What do you expect me to say?"

"Something. Aren't you worried?"

"Of course I'm worried."

"You can go ahead and blame me if you want to."

"I don't want to do that."

"Why not? I blame myself. I should have known better than to leave her with them."

Emery glanced at the three sullen young women sitting in the back seat. "They can hear you."

"Good. They should feel as guilty as I do."

"I'm sure she'll be fine."

"Is that what you keep telling yourself? Is that why you're driving like an old woman on a Sunday drive?"

"Do you see this traffic?" he said motioning to the chaos ahead of them, the crush of cars, motorcycles weaving in and out, pedestrians walking between cars—some trying to cross the streets, others selling goods. When one young man knocked on the window and waved a toy, she turned away. "We should have stayed at the guest house and let the police come to us."

Maureen glanced up at a building. "I couldn't wait."

"And it will be night soon."

"There's still plenty of time. Besides, you can always get an escort back if you need it," she said without concern. She couldn't tell him how desperate she had been to get out. She had to feel as if she was doing something. She looked through the crush of people coming in and out of shops, hoping to see Catherine. "You should have used the driver."

"I know how to navigate these streets."

"Then navigate them faster."

He sighed. "Getting there faster won't change anything."

"The first forty-eight hours are crucial. But as a doctor you know every minute counts."

"I also know that having a clear head is crucial."

"My head is perfectly clear." She glanced in the rearview mirror at her three daughters. "But obviously the minds of my offspring are as clear as mud. Or like something else with the same color and consistency but more stink."

"Tossing insults at them won't make their memories any sharper."

"Stop sticking up for them."

"Why are you getting angry with me?"

"Because your calm demeanor is more annoying than comforting. You seem resigned somehow. As if nothing can be done."

"That's not how I feel, but I can't tell you what you want to hear. I can't tell you that everything will be okay. That we'll ever see her again--"

"Shut up."

He gripped the steering wheel and his voice trembled. "We must face the possibility—"

"I told you to shut up. You're not making any sense."

Emery sighed. He knew more than anyone else the chances of finding his daughter were slim. "But I feel—"

"That feeling is wrong. That feeling is fear and it's something to be ignored. You can't look for something you don't expect to find."

"And what if we don't find her?"

"I don't plan to ever answer that question."

3

———

Sergeant Major Daniel Adeyemi liked fine bourbon, shiny rifles and pretty women, which was why he zeroed in on Joscelyn Payton the moment he saw her. It wasn't often that he was able to mingle with the upper classes. They didn't come to his station, let alone his office. Joscelyn probably got a lot of guys in trouble when she was younger. But it wasn't just her looks or overt femininity that caught his attention. She intrigued him and he wasn't sure why. With one glance she had the ability to make his office feel as small as a deck of cards and as accommodating as an outhouse. Through her gaze he saw his worn desk and dusty windows.

But as he spoke to her, he started to understand the lure. There was something not quite real about her, not mysterious exactly, but as if she wasn't of this world. Of all of the sisters, he should have chosen the youngest or the pudgy one to interview. They would have been easier to handle. But he always jumped at the thought of a challenge.

Unfortunately, she was proving to be a bigger challenge than he'd imagined because for some reason he didn't believe a word she said. He wouldn't trust her if she said water was wet. He didn't know why he didn't believe her story. He'd heard a lot of stories and most of them were as real as a fairy tale. As a cop he was used to getting lied to, but this young woman bothered him. She lied smoothly. Convincingly. He didn't even know why he felt she was lying, as there was nothing about her manner that hinted at it.

The tears that glistened on her long dark lashes were real, the slight tremble of her lips and the catch in her voice were touching, but he didn't like how she swung her foot. Her posture made it clear she wanted to be somewhere else, as if she had better things to do. Or maybe he'd become jaded. That was possible.

"You spoke to the shop clerk and he didn't see anything?" he asked again, pretending to look at his notes.

"That's right."

"Are you sure she went into the shop?"

"That's where she said she was going."

"And you didn't care to see if she'd made it inside?"

"I don't like what you're trying to insinuate."

"I'm not trying to insinuate anything, it just strikes me as odd that you would let your younger sister go into a shop in a place where you are unfamiliar without making sure she made it there."

Joscelyn shrugged. "I made an error in judgment. You're right, I should have been more careful, but it wasn't intentional."

He pretended to look at his notes again. "Of course."

"Are we finished now?"

"Almost. We'll look at the security cameras and see where she was last seen. Hopefully that will give us more information."

Joscelyn blinked and her trembling mouth tightened a fraction. "Yes."

She was annoyed with him or the situation, he wasn't sure, but she was anxious about something. He looked at her swinging foot again. He knew that the red sole was supposed to mean something, his sister had gone on about them. All he knew was that she'd never get a pair from him. But Joscelyn Payton likely had plenty. She had money and wasn't used to having her responses questioned. Maybe that was what he was picking up. An entitled little bitch or maybe he was just annoyed that she was wearing enough jewelry to pay for his mortgage for years. But he'd done something right. He'd made her nervous. There were no CCTV cameras. He knew that as far as security was concerned, law enforcement was gaining traction with closed circuit TV, especially in the UK, but it would take time to implement that level of security here, just the thought made people nervous and that was beneficial to him. He was used to liars, but outsiders like her weren't used to him.

"Is there anything else you remember?" he asked her.

"No, but if I do, I'll let you know. I really hope you find her."

Shit, why don't I believe that? "Of course."

"Thank you." Joscelyn stood and held out her hand. He shook it. It was slender and cold. He held it and met her lovely brown eyes. "And if there's anything you need to tell me, tell me now."

"I've told you everything I know."

"You'd better hope so, because if I find out you haven't...it'll make things very unpleasant."

She smiled. "I understand. Don't worry, I don't like unpleasantness."

That didn't surprise him. "Really?"

"Yes," she said, draping the strap of her handbag on her shoulder.

"Sometimes you can't avoid things you don't like."

She walked to the door, her shapely calves catching his eye. "You're right. That's why I

always get rid of things I don't like."

"That sister knows something," Daniel said when he met with the other officers in the main room.

"Unless you have evidence to back up that statement keep your mouth shut," Deputy Commissioner Paul Barewa, a squat little man with a pencil thin mustache, said. Daniel had briefly seen the DC speaking with the Assistant Inspector General. His presence made it clear that the case was to take high precedence.

"It's just a feeling, but—"

"Do I look like a man who cares about feelings? We have a tactical plan of action and we'll proceed by the book."

"She's not very...likable," another officer said tentatively.

Daniel cast him a dismissive glance. The younger officer had only recently joined the force, absurdly proud to be a constable, and Daniel had no interest in learning his name, although he did agree with him. "She knows something. I can feel it."

"That's not your instincts," Sergeant Perry said with a laugh. "I felt it too when her sister leaned on my desk and let me see down her blouse."

Daniel frowned. "That's not what I mean."

"They are pretty-pretty women."

"I'm not talking about her looks."

"And you have to deal with this carefully," DC Barewa said. "The family is very wealthy. We can't make any wrong moves. The parents are devastated. I don't think they're involved. We could be dealing with a kidnapping and ransom. From all that's been shared here, the three girls' stories fit. We're going to do whatever is necessary to find this girl."

Daniel felt his heart sink; he had a dreaded feeling that would not happen."We need to look into the possibility that they could benefit from the girl's disappearance," he said.

DC Barewa sent the Sergeant Major a stern look. "I'm going to pretend you didn't say that."

"You can pretend what you want. The truth is—"

"You're going to tip toe like you're walking on eggshells. You'll use kid gloves, no—silk gloves. I don't care. But you're going to put your suspicions aside and treat this like a *regular* case."

They didn't have 'regular' cases, everything depended on how influential and powerful the victim and perpetrator were, but Daniel decided to let the remark slide. However, what he couldn't let slide was his commanding officer's demeanor. He was too calm when he should be changing his pants after messing them. This was bad news. A powerful, rich man whose daughter's gone missing and they couldn't look at it too closely?

Then he understood. He'd been blind, but now the picture came together as he again thought about Ms. Payton's expensive shoes and haughty manner. He knew how life worked, that it wasn't always fair. One had to remember who buttered their bread. Once the meeting had ended, he followed DC Barewa into the hallway stairwell and waited for them to be alone before he said, "Your palms must feel rather smooth now?"

"What?"

"How much did she grease them for you?"

DC Barewa sent him a stern look. "I don't know what you mean."

"Or was it the father? Did he go to the Assistant Inspector General first? Maybe I should go to him—"

"No need for that."

Daniel's brows shot up, he'd only suspected, he hadn't thought it would be true. "So it was the girl?"

DC Barewa glanced around then lowered his voice. "This is between us."

Daniel held out his hand, pleased when he saw the crisp

green dollars, they would serve him well. The naira was considerably weak in comparison. "Yes."

"Good," DC Barewa said, putting the rest of the money away.

Daniel quickly counted the amount. "This will close my eyes, but not my mouth."

DC Barewa said something foul, but Daniel only smiled as he saw his little stack increase. "Thank you, sah." He tucked the notes away and went back to his office. Suddenly the office lights shut off, leaving him in darkness. A minor outcry of annoyance erupted from a receptionist due to the loss of computers and other electronics, but soon the generator picked up, and inside the office things hummed back to life again. But outside, only a few buildings had managed to regain their lights. Night had settled over the city with a heavy cloak and the sunlight was hours away. For many, darkness would be their companion until morning.

He sat at his desk and briefly thought of the missing little girl. He didn't know many things. He hadn't been one of the brightest at his comprehensive school and had gotten this position through the right connections. But he did know one thing: The girl wouldn't be found because she hadn't gone missing.

4

LONDON, ENGLAND

"Stop watching the phone, my dear, it won't change anything," Emery said when he found his wife sitting in the living room near the phone. She sat in front of a window where ash-colored clouds slowly moved past and a pigeon settled on the black balcony rail. She'd hardly eaten at dinner and hardly listened to what anyone said. She'd been preoccupied with any sound, rushing to the door if she imagined someone had knocked, when in truth it was likely the wind. He wondered if it had been wise to rent the London suite instead of returning to the States, but she'd been insistent. "I'm not crossing the Atlantic without her," so he and the girls had extended their holiday, but he wasn't sure how long that could be.

Maureen straightened the phone—a gaudy replica of something from the 1890s."I'm not watching it, I'm just sitting here."

"Waiting for it to ring."

Yes, she wanted to say. She was willing—praying—for it to ring. She couldn't bear to lose a child like this. She knew too much time had passed. That the longer it took, the less likely it would be to find her. But she had to try. She couldn't breathe, she couldn't eat or sleep until she knew where Catherine was. Days of not knowing if she'd eaten or where she'd slept. Was she tired? Was she crying alone somewhere scared? *Don't worry my darling, Mummy will find you.* If it took her last breath, every strength she had she would devote to bringing Catherine home. "It's still possible that someone may have news or someone may want money—"

Emery sadly shook his head and sat in front of her. "It's been over a month. If they'd wanted a ransom they would have called us by now."

"You're sure all the phones are connected?"

"Of course."

"And your new mobile is changed—"

"You mean charged?"

She waved a hand with impatience. "Yes, whatever it needs to be so that we don't miss any calls."

He released a heavy sigh. "It's been—"

Maureen ran a finger along the soft green damask trim of her chair. "You've already said that. If you're running out of things to say, stop talking."

He leaned forward, reaching for her hand. "I'm not the enemy here and neither are our girls. You've cut us out—"

"We have each other while Catherine is out there somewhere, alone, scared and hoping we'll find her." She brushed away an angry tear. "The girls must understand that. We can't give up. This is just the beginning. We can't lose faith. We must believe that we will see her face again."

Emery leaned back and sagged into the couch. "I can't keep doing this."

"You must try."

"I can't try any harder!" he said, shocking her with the force of his despair. "I've gone back seven times in one month! I've spoken to more generals, civilians, businessmen, and market women than I can count. Maybe I'm not as strong as you, but I can't go back one more time." He leaned forward, resting his elbows on his lap. "Can't you see that my heart is already broken? I have no strength left for hope. I can't think of her anymore. I can't think of how I am not able to protect her. That I've failed her."

"We will find—"

Emery surged to his feet. "Your words are like daggers to me. Empty words. I need you to think about your girls. I can't be strong enough for them. They need their mother."

Maureen's tone turned cold. "Are you saying that Catherine isn't my child?"

"You know that's not what I'm saying. Don't you see?" He fell to his knees, burying his face in her lap. "I miss her every second of the day," he said his voice shaking with tears. "I think of her with every heartbeat and it's killing me. No, I'm already dead. I breathe but I don't live."

"So you want me to be strong so that you can fall apart?" Maureen said in a quiet tone as she stroked his back. "Even though we need you? I need you? Is Catherine the only family you have? Was it a mistake to marry you?"

Emery shook his head in misery, but didn't lift it, as if afraid to face her. "My dear—"

"No, you don't think I didn't see it? Was it all for show? Not that you hid your favoritism very well. You didn't know how to be subtle, but I let it pass. I loved you and I loved the family we had, but now you've made it clear that was all a lie."

"It wasn't a lie. I love you and the girls."

"But not enough."

"I will provide for you, but don't expect more from me right now."

Maureen stopped stroking his back. "Don't make me hate you."

"How can I stop you from what you already feel?" he said, used to the stinging of harsh words and unfazed by them. His father had been a strict headmaster at an elite boarding school before becoming an education inspector. He'd been a man with a caustic wit who hated his son's soft-spoken, quiet ways and made his disgust known. His father demanded obedience and preferred to fire someone than ever admit he was wrong. Like his father, Emery could take his wife's anger, but not her delusions.

Maureen gasped surprised by the truth of his words. "I don't...I just need you to be strong. Forcing a child to carry the weight of your heart is cruel. How will Catherine feel when she returns and—"

He lifted his head and met her eyes. "Seven times—"

"May not be enough. Maybe it needs to be eight or ten or seventeen. We must try until—"

"She could be anywhere right now! Nigeria is a country of millions with more than 200 ethnic groups, numerous states and a topography as vast as three nations. And who's to say she's still there? How easy it is to leave and cross into Ghana or get to Benin or—"

"We can only hope—"

"Hope strips me bare each day and leaves me empty. I cannot face another day of hope that ends in heartache. How long are you going to keep the girls out of school? How long are you going to pretend that a tragedy hasn't befallen us? When will you allow us to grieve?"

Maureen adjusted the phone again. "When we have a reason to."

"We need to go home."

Maureen stared at his bowed head, hating him for his surrender. She wanted him to rage at her, to fight her. She turned away because she didn't want to be disgusted by him. She couldn't bear the sight of her husband falling apart. She wanted to pound his chest for stealing away her sanctuary. She wanted to find comfort in his arms, to shed her own tears and share her fears, but he would not be that rock for her. She would carry this pain alone. She'd forgiven him his doting ways on his only child, Catherine, because he'd been so kind to her daughters and they needed a male in their life. Someone who cared about them. But now he'd abdicated that role and she had to somehow protect them.

The acid tinge of anger coursed through her, leaving a bitter taste in her mouth. "Will you force me to bury another husband?"

He looked up at her. "I'm doing my best to get us through this, but—"

"Then be strong at least a little for me. Whatever love you have left over, whatever crumbs you have left to spare, give them to me. And I will ask nothing else from you until we bring our child home. Promise me at least that."

He stood. "I will try."

Maureen stood and poked him in the chest with her finger. "You will not try, you will do it and—" A surge of pain gripped her, causing her to gasp.

Emery looked at her alarmed. "Are you okay?"

No, she wasn't. After three daughters, she knew what a contraction was, but it was too strong and too soon. She took a deep breath. She had to be calm. She couldn't get too upset. She slowly walked over to a chair and sank down into it.

"Is it the baby?" he asked rubbing his hands together. "Should I—"

"I just need to rest."

"Yes, rest."

She gritted her teeth. Did he have to sound like a puppet? Couldn't he have a suggestion of his own? She took another deep breath, wishing his look of worry didn't annoy her. She wanted him to calm her, to tell her that everything would be okay. It was his fault that she even...she bit back a moan as another grip of pain swept through her.

Emery rushed to the intercom and hit the family room. "Marie, come! Your mother needs you."

Maureen rolled her eyes in annoyance. "You don't need to get them involved."

"You don't look well."

"I'm fine," she said through gritted teeth.

"Mom, are you okay?" Marie asked, rushing into the room.

Maureen released a long breath, then forced a smile. "Yes, my darling. I just need to go lie down. Help me up." She looked at her husband. "Get me a hot water bottle. I'll be in the bedroom."

On the stairs she gripped the railing, releasing a low groan.

"Is it the baby?" Marie asked, worried.

"I'm just tired," she said, her legs feeling like lead. The bedroom felt so far and she hoped she could make it without scaring her daughter. Marie was such a sensitive girl and easily frightened. She didn't want to do or say anything to cause her distress. She was just overly tired. She hadn't rested as much as she should have. Perhaps Emery was right and she had neglected herself too much. She had to remember she had another life that depended on her.

"Oh Mom," Marie said with a note of anguish. "If I'd known..."

"Known what?" she asked when Marie trailed off.

She shook her head. "I wish I'd looked harder for her. I wish this hadn't happened. I know all this has been terrible for you."

Maureen patted her daughter's cheek. She looked so guilty, as if it had been her fault. "It's been terrible for all of us. I'm sorry I'd forgotten that, but we will all make it through this and bring Catherine home."

But by the time Maureen reached her room and sank to sit on the side of the bed, finding Catherine was the least of her worries;

the contractions were too strong and too close together. She didn't feel right, something was wrong. But she didn't want Marie to know so she plastered on a smile. "Go my dear. I'll be fine."

Marie hesitated. "Are you sure?"

Maureen kept her smile in place, gripping the bed sheets in her fist behind her as another contraction hit. She couldn't speak, holding her smile in place so tight that she feared she'd crack her teeth, so she managed a nod.

Once Marie had gone, Maureen let her smile disappear and fear and worry battled within her. She rested her hand on either side of her belly and prayed. *Don't do this to me little one. Your time has not come yet.* She closed her eyes, breathed deep and tried to think of calming things like water crashing on a beach, a blue sky, the sweet taste of cotton candy. She imagined her heartbeat slowing and the tension in her fading away. And for a moment she felt she'd succeeded before another contraction seized her. She grabbed a pillow and screamed into it. More out of terror than pain. She'd lost Catherine. She couldn't bear to lose this baby too. She didn't think she'd be able to survive if that happened.

Emery knocked on the door then entered. "Here's your water bottle."

She grabbed the pillow and threw it at him. "You fool! Can't you see that I'm in labor? A hot water bottle can't help me!"

"You need to calm down and breathe deep."

"It's not working," she said with a note of panic, tears gathering in her eyes. She knew she was being unfair to him, he was a good man and was doing his best to help the family at this time of sorrow, but she needed a target for her anger. She needed someone to blame for how unfair things all seemed.

"It will," he said in a soothing voice. "Lie back. You can be angry at me later." He helped to lift her legs up on the bed.

"Give me the phone." She could take the pain, but she feared the moment her body urged her to push. It was too soon. Way too soon. She had another three months to go. Now wasn't the time. *Please don't come yet.* She dialed the phone with shaking fingers, relieved when her doctor picked up. She was a woman her husband had forced her to see when they'd arrived in England because he was concerned about how the shock of Catherine's disappearance had affected her and the baby's health. When Maureen told her the symptoms she said, "Have you called an ambulance?"

"No."

"Get one right away. I'll meet you at the hospital."

Maureen hoped that she'd tell her that under the circumstances with all the stress and strain this was natural. That all she had to do was relax and things would be okay.

She told herself that as she lay on the cot in the ambulance, the sound of the sirens seeming to block out the questions from the EMTs. She told herself it would be all right, even as her doctor examined her and the contractions grew stronger, even past the moment when there was nothing more they could do to stop the baby from coming, she believed everything would be all right.

She closed her eyes and left the pain of her body and mind, imagining it all as a nightmare.

Instead she saw herself sitting in the garden of their Maryland home, surrounded by well-tended pink and red roses, wisteria wrapped around their gazebo and daffodils trimming the stone foot path while the spring sun warmed her face. She felt Catherine's hand on her belly, lightly rubbing it for good luck. "Like Buddha" she'd teased.

"But I'm prettier."

"Yes," Catherine said, sitting down on the wooden bench beside her. "You're the most beautiful woman I know." She sighed and let her shoulders droop. "No wonder no one believes we're related."

"But we are."

"I'm not pretty like Joscelyn, Lorna or Marie."

Maureen cupped her chin. Catherine was a gangly child, but strong, with kind eyes and soft rather than striking features. She had honey brown skin and a humble, pretty look that could be easily disregarded. "No, you have your own special beauty." She kissed her on the cheek. "Don't you forget that." Maureen remembered how she'd initially been wary of dating Catherine's father. She wasn't sure of the rough-edged little girl she'd introduced to her more refined daughters. She'd expected her to pull some pranks to show her dislike over her father's interest in someone else. She seemed incredibly close to her father and probably didn't want anyone to come between them. But to her surprise, the young girl took to her immediately. Shyly offering her a bouquet of flowers when she and her father came over to Maureen's house to have dinner for the first time. But she knew that she wanted to be this girl's mother one day when she found her that same evening sitting alone on the front step of her townhouse crying. She'd gotten into an argument with her eldest daughter.

"What's wrong?" Maureen asked sitting down beside her.

"I want you to like my dad."

"I do like your dad."

"And I want you to like me too."

Maureen rubbed her back. "I do like you."

"Dad wants to marry you."

"I know."

Catherine took a deep breath then said in a rush, "I'm sorry I got angry. I'm sorry I shouted at Joscelyn. I'll be better next time. I'll try really hard to be good." She turned her tear stained face towards her. "Don't leave because of me like Mom did. Please."

"I don't plan to leave. But you must know that your mother didn't leave because of you."

Catherine sighed. "Yes, she did. She didn't want to be a mom. She wanted to be free."

"Well, I like being a mother and I would be so happy and proud to have four daughters." And since that day their affection for each other only seemed to grow. Maureen remembered that moment and looked at the young girl she'd adopted, her heart full of love.

As if sensing her affection, Catherine threw her arms around her new mother's neck. "You're my lucky charm. I love you so much." She sat back and smiled, swinging her legs. "Ever since you married Dad, my life has been so wonderful and now I think my life will be even luckier when he comes along," she said, mentioning the little brother she expected to have.

"You don't mind not being the youngest anymore?"

"No, I'll be a great big sister and now...now I'll really belong."

"But you do belong."

"Sometimes..." She bit her lip. "I try, but I don't think Joscelyn and Lorna like me that much."

"That's what having sisters is all about," Maureen said with a slight laugh, remembering the contentious relationship she had with her own sisters. "Don't take it personally. You were an only child and it takes getting used to. But never think you don't belong to me." She touched her chest, indicating her heart. "You were born to me, right here. In a place very special. You are my daughter and I am your mother."

"And you love me?" Catherine asked with childlike eagerness.

"Very much," she said knowing that Catherine still felt the sting of her birth mother's abandonment.

Catherine clasped her hands together. "I'm so happy sometimes it frightens me. It's so perfect. We'll all be one family."

"Yes."

The sight of Catherine's smiling face faded away as the sound of the doctor's instructions penetrated her mind, she heard the sound of the hospital monitors, felt Emery's hand holding hers.

"One family," Maureen whispered, tears seeping from her eyes as the baby she'd hope to carry to term left her too soon.

5
______

"We made a mistake. We shouldn't have done it. Not now," Marie said as the three sisters sat in Joscelyn's bedroom. Joscelyn sat at her desk with a large anatomy book highlighted with different colors and pages of notes. She'd taken a semester off of school to deal with the after-effects of what had happened but didn't want to fall behind. Lorna toyed with a perfume kit, delicately mixing scents. Marie sat on the bed, unable to do anything else. She should be in school studying, but she hadn't been able to focus. All that she used to like to do no longer seemed to mean anything. Before she would have delighted at the sight of the red phone boxes and the double decker buses, Covent Garden and the taste of trifle, but she felt too scared to even leave her room.

"How were we supposed to know this was going to happen?" Joscelyn said.

"We could have waited."

"Waited for what? We didn't have a choice. It had to be done. Don't pretend to feel sorry now, you wanted this as much as we did."

"No, I didn't."

"You hated when Mom married Emery and you were no longer the youngest one. You were no longer the cute one."

Marie turned away from her sister's accusation, feeling the guilt like acid in her heart. She hadn't liked Catherine taking her place and she couldn't deny the jealousy that seized her with growing intensity every passing month as she saw her mother's belly swell with new life. A new life that was getting all the attention that should have been hers. She'd hated the sight of the nursery and Catherine talking about how they'd take the baby to the park and teach it how to swim. Catherine didn't even like to play with dolls and all of a sudden this new baby was the greatest thing. And she'd watched her mother and Catherine giggling over the color of the pillows and blankets that would be in the baby's bedroom. And there was one moment when she'd caught them in the kitchen, Catherine's eyes wide after feeling the baby kick that Marie saw what she feared. Her mother's look of love. Her mother loved Catherine as if she were her own flesh. She saw a bond between them. Something strong and special. Catherine had come into their lives and stolen her mother's love away.

No, she couldn't deny her jealousy. She had wanted her step-sister gone. She'd wanted her mother all to herself again. She didn't mind sharing her with her sisters and stepfather, but Catherine was too much. She'd been relieved that the plan had worked. But she hadn't realized the cost. She hadn't thought of how much her mother would suffer. And for the first time in a long while, she thought of someone besides herself. She thought of her new brother, who was so small he could fit inside her step-father's hand. He looked alien and all the tubes connected to him in NICU made him seem even more otherworldly. But she didn't want him to die. For her mother's sake. She wanted him to live.

"This may kill her," Marie said with dejection. "We have to do something."

"There's nothing we can do," Lorna said.

"Maybe if we said—"

Joscelyn sent her a cutting look. "You will say nothing."

Marie pushed up her glasses and rubbed her nose, agitated. "I'm just saying that giving her hope may have been a mistake."

Lorna frowned. "Hope? When did we give her hope?"

"By saying we found her shoe and coat. We should have hinted at something else."

"Like what?"

Marie bit her lip then threw up her hands. "I don't know. That's she's dead."

"She might as well be dead," Joscelyn said with a sniff. "We'll never see her again."

Marie shook her head. "I didn't think...Mom..."

"You leave the thinking to me and remember what you promised."

"I won't forget."

"Because if you do, you know what can happen."

"Don't threaten me, Joscelyn."

"My my, have you developed a spine?"

"I mean it."

"So do I, don't forget—"

"I said I won't forget," Marie said, then stormed out of the room.

Lorna watched her go then shifted her gaze to Joscelyn. "Should we be worried about her?"

Joscelyn turned a page in her book and made a notation in the margin. "Do I look worried?"

"No, but if she were to say--"

Joscelyn lifted her head amused. "Do you think Mom would believe her over me? Who would really believe we did what we did?" she said with a slight smile of satisfaction. "And what proof is there?"

"You're right."

"We've gotten away with what we've done. Nothing can ruin that," Joscelyn said, more to herself than to her sister. It was really Catherine's fault that all of this had happened. If only she hadn't been so cocky and arrogant. She always thought she was special...

"I had the most amazing dream! I'm going to be powerful and richer than Daddy one day and you will remember my name," Catherine had told them one October evening as the three sisters sat in the living room. Joscelyn was watching TV, Marie doing her homework and Lorna writing a note to her boyfriend.

"So what?" Lorna said, spraying the paper with perfume.

"It means that I'm going to be great, someone remarkable that you'll all admire."

"Will you move and shut up?" Joscelyn said. "I'm trying to listen to the show."

Catherine shifted to the side. "But my dream also—"

"And how can I concentrate on my homework with you talking?" Marie said. "I have an exam coming up."

"But--"

"Mom!" Lorna said. "Catherine's bothering us."

Maureen's voice came down the hall. "Catherine, have you done your piano lessons?"

"No, but—"

"I don't want to hear the word no. Get them done."

Catherine headed to the door then turned and looked at them. "It will happen, you'll see," she said then left.

Lorna looked at her sisters. "I can't stand her."

"She's just a big mouth," Marie said. "Ignore her. She just wants attention."

"She's a brat and should be taken down a peg," Lorna said folding up her note. "Can you believe that? She thinks we'd think about her when she's grown? Why does she think she's so special?"

"Because she's Emery's favorite," Joscelyn said in a bored tone, staring at the TV screen but not hearing a word.

"He says he doesn't have favorites," Marie said.

Joscelyn looked at her amused. "And you believe that?"

"No, but—"

"And she's quickly becoming Mom's little darling too," Lorna said.

Marie sighed and returned to her homework.

"Personally, I wish she'd disappear," Joscelyn said. "We'd all be better off without her."

"I know. Wouldn't that be great?" Lorna said, warming to the idea. "No more strange dreams, no more flirting."

"She doesn't flirt," Marie said.

"You should see how she talks with Greg," she said referring to her boyfriend. "He thinks she's so adorable. She's not even pretty."

"But people like her," Marie said.

"Too much and that's not good for us," Jocelyn said.

"What do you mean?"

"What if something happened to Emery? Do you really think he'd divide the estate equally among us?"

"We'd always have Mom."

"What if that's not enough?"

"Emery is not going to die."

"Dad died and I remember how hard it was for us. I'm not facing that again." She drummed her fingers on the arm of the chair as the faint sounds of the piano came towards them. The house was well designed so that the music wasn't distracting with the door closed, but the thought of Catherine's clever, efficient fingers sliding along the keys without error annoyed her.

No, it was more than annoyance. Her mere existence bothered her. She hated her stepsister's face, the sound of her voice, how everything came so easily to her. She'd been her father's little princess after her mother left. She'd never known struggle or hardship. And the admiration Joscelyn had fought to gain from her mother was now lavished on Catherine with abandonment. What did her mother see? What did anyone see? She was a pest. A nuisance. Every day she wished that she would disappear.

And Joscelyn's anger grew as she sat and listened to Catherine tell their mother and father her dream as they finished dinner, the scent of coconut rice and jerk chicken still scenting the air. "And you will all remember my name," she said, wiping her hand through the air as if her name was to be written in the stars.

"And why wouldn't we remember it?" her father said with a smile. "How can we forget it when you're one of us."

Catherine shook her head. "No, it was bigger than that, Daddy. I was powerful and my name made my sisters shake with fear." She frowned. "Or was it joy?"

"Your dream is our nightmare," Joscelyn said under her breath.

"What?" Catherine asked, not catching the venom in her sister's tone.

"Nothing," Maureen said, having heard her daughter's words and choosing to ignore them. "Finish your food."

"I will. I just thought you should know."

"Nobody cares about your stupid dream," Lorna said. "I once had a dream that I was trying to ride a unicorn."

Catherine looked at her for a long moment, concerned. "Trying to?"

"Yes, it was wild and bucking and trying to throw me off."

"And you said it was a unicorn? Not a horse?"

"Does it matter?" Joscelyn asked.

"Yes," Emery said. "She's good with dreams."

"No, it wasn't a horse," Lorna said. "It was a black unicorn with a golden mane."

Catherine shook her head. "That's not good. You will be disappointed in love if you don't change your heart and keep to the man who is meant to be yours."

Silence fell as everyone looked from Catherine to see Lorna's reaction.

Lorna's eyes widened. "What? You don't think I have a good heart?"

"No, I'm not saying that. Your dream is. Your heart is... um...not happy."

"That's not true. I love Greg and he loves me."

Catherine shrugged. "I'm only telling you what the dream meant."

"It was a stupid dream," Lorna said. "It doesn't mean anything. Nothing you say means anything. You're just trying to sound more clever than you are. Marie skipped a grade while you were held one back."

"That's enough, Lorna," Maureen said.

Catherine shrugged again. "I know I'm not as smart as Marie, but I do know dreams. You don't have to listen, but what I said is true."

Lorna pushed her chair back. "May I be excused?"

Maureen looked at her daughter's half-eaten plate, shared a look with her husband, then nodded. "Yes."

"I didn't mean to make her angry," Catherine said once Lorna had gone. "If she'd told me about something else—"

"I think it's best to drop the topic," Maureen said.

Catherine fell quiet for a while, then said, "I'm going to be a great person one day. Very powerful."

"Yes, dear we know that," Emery said in an indulgent tone. "Lorna said those things to you just because she's upset."

Catherine shook her head. "No, that's not what I mean. I feel as if my dream was a warning. That you'd better be nice to me," she said, glancing at her two remaining stepsisters.

"Catherine, I said that's enough," Maureen said, her patience thinning.

But Catherine ignored her stepmother as she looked at her two sisters. "Or there will be consequences."

Joscelyn remembered leaving the dinner table with a burning hatred. Some kid was going to tell her how to behave? Was going to try to manipulate her with a dream? No, she looked sweet, but she was dangerous. She may not have Marie's book smarts, but she was clever. A threat.

But it was only when she overheard her parents speaking one evening that a plan began to form in her mind.

"Lorna's still upset by what Catherine said," Emery said worried.

"She's a teenager," Maureen said in a flippant tone. "She'll get over it."

"They haven't taken to each other yet."

"It's only been a year. There will be growing pains and this is how girls can be, don't worry."

"You're right," he said with a laugh of relief. "I have others things on my mind. I didn't want to tell you, but remember that grapefruit scented scrub Catherine made for your birthday? I decided to test it at a small boutique to see if it had potential. It's been selling steadily for weeks. I'm thinking of making it a permanent new item."

"That's wonderful. She'll be so happy when you tell her. She's already started working on two new natural scrubs that she wants me to try."

"Yes, that's why I'm thinking of introducing her to the business a little earlier than expected. I think that next year she should be in charge of this new line and start shadowing some staff and learning more of the business."

"At eleven?" Maureen said taken aback. "None of the others

have been given a privilege like that. You've not even let Marie look at the business yet."

"Marie will head off to college and have a successful career at whatever she chooses. Joscelyn's path is set and Lorna will probably marry and focus on having a family. However, we both know Catherine's not domestic material, nor is she academic."

"She just needs to study more and focus."

"No, I don't think that's the answer. Catherine may not be book smart, but she has a head for business. That's going to serve her well in the future. I see her taking control of the company when she's older."

"It doesn't seem fair to start her so young on that path."

"None of the others have shown the same amount of interest, besides, they will always have their investments so they'll be well provided for."

"I still think she's too young, but she does have a knack for coming up with innovative ideas and if you feel this is right, I won't stop you."

Joscelyn felt her heart grow cold. It was just as she feared. Catherine would inherit everything, she would continue to get special treatment. As much as Marie worked, she would be passed over by Catherine who would waltz into a position of power before she even hit puberty?

Joscelyn continued to think about her problem at school the next day. "You've hardly said anything," her friend Gloria said as they sat in the lunch lounge on campus. Gloria was as dark as an ink blot with big teeth as white as salt and had an uncle who was a board member at the university. She was smart and connected— very useful. The best kind of friend to have.

"Sorry."

"Are you ready for your first family holiday together? Is that what's bugging you?"

"Yes," Joscelyn lied. "We're going to visit my stepfather's family in Nigeria."

Gloria shivered. "I had an aunt who always threatened to send me to family over there if I misbehaved."

"What?"

"Oh, yes. I know you'll be in the more cosmopolitan areas, but there are still a lot of places that are like the end of the world. No electricity, potholes as large and deep as wells. In some parts you could disappear and no one would be able to find you."

"Really?" she asked, suddenly very interested in everything her friend had to say.

"Oh sure, and you always have to be careful of kidnappers. Only flash your gold," she gestured to Joscelyn's earrings, "in the right places, but I'm sure your stepfather knows all that. I don't mean to scare you."

"No, you're not scaring me. This sounds interesting. What about the police?"

"Which ones?"

"What do you mean?"

"The real ones or the fake ones? Most have been bought, the rest can be bribed. But with your stepfather's connections he'll get top of the line security and you'll never have to deal with any of the thieves, kidnappers, or deal with bribes."

"No," Joscelyn said unable to stop a smile. "What if I wanted to?"

"Wanted to what?"

"Learn how to bribe someone to do something for me."

"I have a cousin who knows some shady people. Is this for a paper or something?"

"Yes," she lied. "My own research."

Gloria wrote down her cousin's information.

Joscelyn put the paper away. "I think I'll really enjoy this trip."

And she did. She enjoyed visiting Victoria Island, dining at a private golf club, the posh hotel they'd stayed at when they'd first arrived before going to the guest house, and she'd been able to handle the police beautifully.

Joscelyn walked to her window and stared at the London traffic. She'd thought of what she'd done and felt no guilt, no remorse, no unease. Her conscience felt clear. And she slept well every night. Better than ever. It had been such a liberating feeling when they'd boarded the plane, the bright glittering lights of Lagos twinkled beneath them as they rose into the dark sky and left Catherine behind. She'd never escape. There was no way she'd ever see her again, she'd taken the steps to make sure.

It was a shame about her mother and the baby, but casualties happen in battle and she'd just won one. A battle for her and her sisters' futures. It hadn't been a selfish act, it had been one necessary for survival. And she knew how to survive.

Yes, Catherine's words had been foolish and her supposed 'vision' had all been a silly dream. Joscelyn had already proven it was a lie because she'd never remember her. She'd already started to let the girl's name slip from her mind.

6

———————

Lorna set her perfume kit aside and picked up a magazine, wishing she could feel as calm as Joscelyn looked. She wanted to be able to trust that Marie wouldn't say anything, but she wasn't so sure. She didn't regret anything, but it was still too soon to feel safe. She looked at the email Greg had sent her. He'd kept in touch every day. And to think that she'd almost lost him...

"I think we should start seeing other people," Greg suggested as Lorna placed her hand on his thigh in the car, an autumn breeze tossing leaves past the window. They hadn't done more than heavy petting, but she wanted him to know she was up for more.

But she hadn't expected his response. She paused. "What do you mean? I don't want to see anyone else."

"I'm going away to school soon and—"

"I don't care. We can keep in touch and see each other on breaks. Please, Greg," she said, lightly touching his cheek. She couldn't imagine life without him. She'd committed every aspect of him to memory from his bronze skin to his deep dimples and crooked smile. "I love you so much."

"Lorna, I just--"

"Have you met someone else?"

"No, it's just my heart isn't in it and Catherine said—"

She stiffened, her mouth going dry. "Did Catherine say something to you about me?"

"No." He shook his head. "Forget I mentioned it."

"No, I won't forget. What did she say?" It wasn't fair. Catherine was ruining everything! First her stupid dream and now this! Greg had always had a soft spot for her. For some reason, a lot of the guys from her school did when she invited them over to study or hang out. They liked to listen to her interpret their silly dreams. She couldn't believe how some girl in elementary school could capture the attention of guys in high school? Once, she'd overheard Greg tell a friend that Catherine was cute now but in a few years she'd be beautiful. Beautiful! How could that lanky, stupid girl be anything. *She* was the one who was beautiful. He should have been talking about her.

Greg was her first real boyfriend and she didn't want anyone to steal him away from her. She didn't ask for much. She didn't care about her mother's marriage, she didn't mind sharing her mother with her, or living with her, but Greg was hers. All hers and she didn't want him thinking of anyone else but her.

She still couldn't get Catherine's silly words out of her mind about not having a heart of love or something stupid like that. She did love. She loved a lot and she wouldn't let anything happen to it.

"This is my decision. All mine."

"What did she say?"

He briefly rested his head back. "It's personal."

"I don't care."

"And it won't change anything."

"I think I have a right to know why you want to end something good. Why you're even bringing my stepsister's name into it."

He sighed. "Lorna, this has nothing to do with your sister."

"*Step*sister."

"Right, stepsister. It has to do with you and me. I think you're...you can't keep giving me notes every day."

"I'll stop."

"And calling me three times a night."

"I'm just checking to see if you're okay."

"And telling my friends where we'll live when we get married."

Don't you see us together forever? "I was kidding."

"It's too much."

"I'll slow down if you want." She took his hand. "I love you."

He pulled away. "I know, but we need space."

"What did Catherine say?"

"I told her about a dream I had."

"She's a liar. She can't interpret dreams. She just says it so that people pay attention."

"Maybe, but some of the things she's said have come true. You'd be surprised, your sister has a gift."

"And she told you to break up with me," Lorna said in a hard, flat tone, her eyes burning with tears.

He threw up his hands. "See? That's the problem with us. You don't listen to me. You only hear what you want to. I said my decision has nothing to do with your si--stepsister," he quickly said before Lorna could correct him. "I feel like life is just starting out for me and I don't want to—"

"Feel tied down?"

"I wasn't going to say that."

"But that's how you feel."

"I just need space. That's all." He dropped her home and Lorna watched his car drive away. She stood in the driveway until his headlights had disappeared, feeling as if her world were crashing down around her.

The slap came as a total surprise.

Catherine stared up at Lorna as she sat on her bedroom floor, a hand to her stinging cheek. "What was that for?"

"What did you say to him?" Lorna demanded.

"Who?"

"Greg! What did you say to him? Tell me!" She grabbed the collar of Catherine's shirt and shook her. "Tell me now!"

"What is going on in here?" Maureen asked, coming into the room.

"I don't know," Catherine said.

Lorna slapped her again. "Yes, you do and I hate you."

Maureen grabbed her daughter's wrist. "Calm down. You know better than that."

"But Mom, she's ruined everything. Everything! My life is over!"

"No, it's not."

"It's not fair."

"Catherine, what happened?"

The girl slowly shook her head. "I don't know."

"Yes, you do," Lorna wailed. "You told Greg to break up with me!"

"Did you say that?" Maureen asked.

"No, I told him—" Catherine stopped and bit her lip, chagrined.

"Go on."

"I'm not sure I should. It was a private dream."

"What are you, a damn priest?" Lorna spat out. "You can't keep secrets."

Maureen nodded. "You don't have to tell us his dream, just what you told him."

"I told him that he needed to prepare for a different life and in order to do that he had to be free."

Lorna pointed at her like a victim pointing out a perpetrator in a police line. "See! She told him to dump me."

Maureen shook her head. "No, what she said could have been interpreted a number of ways. A man makes up his own mind."

Lorna tapped the side of her head. "But she planted the thought there."

"It was already there," Catherine said. "The dream told him."

"Your lies always ruin things."

"I didn't lie. Besides, you're meant to be with someone else if—"

"I love *him*. I love him so much I could die."

Maureen touched her shoulder. "Lorna, calm down."

"No," Lorna said, yanking away from her mother's touch. "You don't know how it feels. He loved me too. I know he did, but she slowly poisoned him against me. I saw you giggling and smiling with him, acting all innocent."

"That's enough. You know she's too young to think like that."

"Is she?"

Catherine shook her head in remorse. "I didn't mean to make you angry. I was just trying to help."

"I know, dear," Maureen said, "but you have to be very careful what you say."

"Lorna, I really didn't mean—"

"I'll never forgive you for this!" She left, slamming the door behind her.

Lorna thought about her anger back then amazed by all that had changed since then. Now Catherine was gone and Greg was back to comfort her. He'd sent her an email. She hadn't lost him. He promised to stay with her through this and she'd make sure he stayed for a long time. She'd never let him leave her now.

Joscelyn really was brilliant. In hindsight she'd made it all seem so easy. Lorna hadn't suspected a thing that fateful day. She'd been as ignorant as Marie about what would happen to Catherine not long before it did.

"I know a way to get rid of our mutual problem," Joscelyn told them as they sat in the living room of the guest house, Joscelyn had been able to briefly distract Catherine by telling her of the mini garden the chef had. She now happily chatted with the woman in the kitchen.

"What?"

"We all know that our lives will be better without Catherine in it. So I've decided that we have to do something."

"There's nothing we can do," Marie said.

"We can make her disappear."

"How?"

Joscelyn grinned. "What if she got kidnapped?"

"Oh that sounds like a good idea," Lorna said rubbing her hands together.

"And then she'd never be our problem again."

"Kidnapped?" Marie said with a frown. "You can't force her to be kidnapped. Plus, kidnappers ask for ransoms and we know Emery will pay and—"

"She won't really be kidnapped. That's just the story we'll use."

"Then how are you going to make her disappear?"

"We'll have to work together to make this work. And only we

can know about this so we have to do it when Mom and Dad aren't around."

"What are you thinking?"

"I was thinking of a shopping trip. Mom trusts me so I'll take us all to the marketplace."

"And what will we do at the marketplace?"

"We're going to sell her."

7

———————

LAGOS

The market bustled with life as Catherine went through the crowded aisles with excitement. She saw a basket filled with huge snails and another brimming with yams. Women and men carrying various stacks of baskets on their heads—one filled with lemons and another with chewing gum. She smelled smoked fish and the day was hot, but she'd grown used to it. She saw rows of bronze jewelry, wooden sculptures and fabrics in an amazing array of colors and patterns.

It had been a wonderful day. She was so glad she was having such a good time with her sisters. Lorna had forgiven her—after not speaking to her for days after Greg broke up with her—and was actually being nice! She'd even treated her to a sweet, ripe mango! She planned to buy them all something really special. But she wasn't sure what. She didn't know how to barter the prices as she'd seen her father and Joscelyn do with many of the market sellers, but she'd try.

She thought it was strange that her sister Joscelyn wanted to go to a place outside of the marketplace. It didn't look as friendly as the other place. There wasn't as many people either, but maybe it was a secret place few tourists knew about. Joscelyn always liked to be adventurous. Catherine saw a man with things inside the back of his van, which had been painted a bright assortment of green and orange with the words 'God is Good' scrawled on the side.

"Go and choose something inside," Joscelyn said.

Catherine frowned as she peered at the assortment of items sitting on either side of the hollowed out van. "But I don't like it."

The man held up a pretty necklace. "I have more of these. Wouldn't your mummy like it?"

Catherine touched the necklace with hesitation. It did look nice. She could just see her mother wearing it and the smile it would bring to her face. Maybe there was something else there she could get. She looked up at the man. He was of medium height with a big forehead and fat lips, but a very warm, smiley face. However, something about him bothered her.

"Go on," Lorna said. "Mom would love that."

"Here, you'll get special things no one else can find," the man continued.

She did want to get her sisters something special. She walked towards the van.

"Go on, get in," Joscelyn urged her.

Catherine stopped at the back of the van then turned to her. "Come in with me."

"I will once you get in. Stop being a baby."

Catherine hesitated then did. She crawled inside and looked around unimpressed. It was just as she'd thought, only the necklace he'd shown her was of any value. The rest of the items looked cheap and ugly. She turned to her sisters to tell them that, but when she turned she saw them all staring at her. None had entered. She started to crawl back to them when Joscelyn looked at the man and said, "We're done here," and the two doors closed.

"What are you doing!" Catherine cried, pounding on the

door. She tried the handle, but it didn't open. *What was going on?* "This isn't funny. Open up."

She went to the side window and saw Joscelyn getting—or was she giving?—something from the man. She looked at Marie, who was looking away at something in the sky. Lorna stood with her arms folded and a smirk on her face. *Why weren't they helping her? Who was that man?* She saw the man leave, then felt the van start. *No, no. This can't be real!* She screamed and pounded harder. She looked at Joscelyn and her sister looked back at her as if she didn't see her at all.

As the van bounced along, she crawled into a corner, curled herself up and cried. Where was he taking her? How would she get back home? She didn't know how long she was like that before the van stopped and the back doors opened.

She squinted against the light, the man a silhouette in the doorway. He held out his hand. "Come."

"No."

"I said come."

"No."

He crawled inside the van and grabbed her arm. She gripped the back leg of the seat in front of her. She held on tight and he pulled her. He said something in a foreign tongue and another man appeared. She struggled to fight them both, but they overpowered her and dragged her out. She went limp, causing one of the men to stumble. He swore and used his other hand to get her to move. She bit his hand. He released her and swore again, startling the other man, who loosened his grip. She slipped out of his grasp and ran.

She didn't know where she was going. The landscape was so unfamiliar. Large trees and a long dirt road and one large house. She ran towards the stone fence then stopped when she saw the shards of glass that lined the top of it. 'To keep burglars out' her father had told her, but now they kept her in.

She turned and saw the two men following her and when she turned to her other side she saw more men had appeared. She had to get free. She ran towards the fields. Her skin scratched in the bushes. Then something fastened around her arm. She looked up and saw the face of the man from the van. His hand covered her mouth, stopping her scream.

They took her to a room where another man looked her over. A man with small eyes, a flat wide nose and bushy beard. He wore a shiny gray suit, black shoes and a tilted black hat and large gold rings on three of his fingers. The man she'd bitten whispered something in his ear and he nodded.

"You're a fighter," he said.

"I don't belong here. Take me home."

"This is your home now."

"My father is--"

"Of no importance to me."

"You're going to be in so much trouble when he finds me."

"No one will look for you." He sat down. "Because you belong to me now."

She gripped her hands into fists. "Take me home now."

"You will do as I say if you want your family to stay safe."

She stiffened. "What?"

"I will kill them if you disobey me."

He was a kidnapper. That was it. He wanted money. That's why Joscelyn was talking to that man. But then why did it look like he was giving her something instead of the other way around? Maybe they were instructions. That's why her sister didn't do anything to help her. They were scared. Maybe the men had guns, although she didn't see them. But maybe they were out of sight. She'd heard about kidnappers taking kids for money. Her parents would come up with enough to get her back. She wouldn't have to stay here long.

"You want a randsom?"

"Ransom," he corrected then laughed. "There is no ransom for you."

"My father will pay."

"Take her away."

Once she was out of sight, Valentine Ejo walked into another exquisitely decorated room where four men sat in overstuffed chairs, looking through the one-way mirror. "Did you see that?"

"Yes," Michael Ayodeji said, a dark, bald man with brown eyes that seemed to shine like gold. He made money easily and made decisions with the same facility, which was why Valentine enjoyed doing business with him. It always proved profitable.

"It was a risk getting an American," Edwin Agboola said, removing lint from his sleeve. He wore a crushed blue velvet suit and matching shoes. No matter how high the temperature, he was never bothered by the heat. "She may take longer to break."

"American-born," Valentine assured him. "Her father is one of us. So she'll know enough of our ways."

"Plus she's young and she's strong and will fetch a good price," Ayodeji added.

Adam Rich, an English name he'd given himself, pressed a handkerchief to his small, brown forehead. He was a man constantly sweating, although he'd spent most of his sixty years on the continent, he should have been born in a cooler climate. "She'll scare my clients."

"Drug her enough and she'll be compliant."

"Too much of a risk."

"I'll take her," Ayodeji said. "She's got a lot of good years in her."

"She's yours."

One of Valentine's handlers rushed in before the men could shake hands and seal the deal. "I'm sorry, sah."

"What is it?" he snapped.

"She's escaped again."

"Do you think that's news I want to hear! Get her!" Valentine sat back in his seat.

The man nodded, then disappeared.

Rich pressed his soggy handkerchief to his neck. "You don't look worried."

"I'm not. She can't get far and the running will tire her out and make her more amenable." He sent a nervous look to Ayodeji. "Have you changed your mind?"

"No," he said, his golden gaze seeming to be brighter than before. "I like a challenge."

PART II

CAPTIVITY

8

———

"Stop running, sista, and de beatings dey will stop too."

Catherine didn't reply. The sun sat high in the cloudless blue sky, but fortunately she found some reprieve under a tree. A lizard scurried past along the red dust path of the property and a bird landed on a tree branch. She envied them. Both were small enough to escape the metal cage where she'd been kept the past few days since trying to escape the second place she'd been sent to. The square cage gave her enough room to sit, but not to stand or lie down. She didn't know how long she'd been in there. She also didn't know how long it had been since she'd last seen her family. She glanced at the cage next to her, filled with puppies who ate and pooped in the same place-—much like her, but at least she was let out to use the toilet. But that didn't stop her from feeling like an animal—dirty, discarded. How could this girl ask her to stop running? Why hadn't her ransom been paid? What was she still doing here?

"It's best to accept what life hands you," the girl continued.

Catherine didn't reply, but she was glad the girl was there. She was one of the few girls she liked. She'd learned her name was Helen. "But you don't use names here," the girl had warned her in a soft voice.

Catherine knew names didn't mean anything here. A place where they toiled the land from sun up to sun down and lived in a shack with bunk beds. No one spoke in sentences. There were just shouts and orders. Demands and commands.

The girl held out a bowl of pounded yam and greens. "You have to eat. If you don't, I'll get into trouble. Do you want to eat or drink?"

Catherine was too tired to speak. She hesitated, then twisted her hand once. It was the gesture that Helen had taught her— twist your hand twice if you want something to drink, once if you want to eat.

She took the food and ate letting her gaze study Helen.

She was the fattest girl she'd ever seen. Catherine tried not to stare, but couldn't help herself. She'd never seen a girl who looked so strange with such skinny arms and legs and such a big belly as if she'd swallowed a beach ball. Catherine wondered if Helen was somehow deformed, the way she waddled around when she walked, but she was a good worker and one of the few who managed to smile at her. She had a pretty brown face with round cheeks, braided hair and lashes so long they didn't look real.

There wasn't much to smile about as they worked day and night digging a tunnel, to where she didn't know. She'd tried to escape her handlers twice but had gotten caught. It was this strange girl who'd first approached her with food when she was first kept in a cage for three days as punishment. Catherine wondered if Helen was a little person, but she didn't seem to be.

"I won't be able to see you soon," Helen said.

Catherine paused with a handful of food to her mouth. "Why not?"

"Dey say dey're going to confine me."

"Con-what?"

"Put me away."

"But why? What did you do? Is it because of me?"

"No, it's because of this." She pointed to her belly.

Catherine hesitated then said, "What's wrong with you?"

"Nothing, silly. I'm going to have a baby."

"But you can't. You're too small. I'm bigger than you are."

"I'm eleven."

"See, that proves it. You can't have a baby. Only women have babies."

"You get a baby if it comes."

Catherine frowned. "If what comes?"

"You not learn how babies come, sista?"

"Of course," Catherine said, offended. " But kids don't have babies."

Helen's gaze fell away and Catherine felt guilty, knowing she'd said something wrong. She was always saying the wrong thing when she didn't mean to. But it didn't make sense. She didn't know that little boys could make little girls pregnant. She thought only adults did that. But she wasn't smart and there was so much she didn't know. Maybe Helen was one of those child brides she'd read about in the third grade when she'd learned about pioneer women. Women in the past married young and had babies, but all those girls were at least teenagers. Not a year older than her. And why was she here?

"Your cycle come yet?" Helen said in a quiet voice.

Catherine knew what she was talking about since her step-mother had explained. "No."

"Den you're lucky. You betta hope it doesn't come for a long-long time."

Catherine licked her lip. "Is your husband looking for you? Were you snatched too?"

Helen shook her head. "No husband. I nah snatched. I was sold just like you."

Catherine stiffened. "I wasn't sold, this is a mistake."

"You get used to it."

"I'll never get used to this. I will escape--"

"You're dumber dan you look. Nah talk dat way. You can think it but never say it." She moved a little closer. "You wan' feel it?"

"No." Catherine clenched her hand and briefly thought of her stepmother. She was going to have a baby and she wouldn't be there. She wondered if they were still looking for her or if they'd given up.

Helen suddenly gripped the bars. "I'm scared. I'm scared of what will happen to me."

The look on the girl's face frightened her too. She'd been good to her and she would help her too. "When I get out, I'll look after you."

And Catherine did her best to take the extra load that Helen couldn't. No matter her state, they treated her without care, but Catherine slipped Helen her ration of water and food.

Then one day they were awoken in the middle of the night. "Come, we're leaving." When Helen stood the man said, "Not you."

"I'll look after her," Catherine said. "She's strong."

The man paused and stared at Catherine, clearly not used to a child speaking without permission, but it was too late to pretend she hadn't said anything. She'd seen him about, not one of her handlers, always watching. He had fine features, thin, almost non-existence brows, and calloused hands.

"Fine," he said.

But to her horror, everything wouldn't be fine. They were loaded into the back of a windowless van along with a group of other girls with their legs and wrists chained to the floor. In the dark, they bumped along on the road. Some of the girls felt sick as if they'd been tossed into a boat on a raging sea, others fainting in the stifling, dark confinement.

"Catherine," Helen said in a panicked voice.

"Yes, I'm here."

"I wet myself."

"That's okay. It happens."

"You daft?" another girl said. "She means the baby's coming."

She didn't understand how that could be the same thing. "Helen?"

"Yes, she's right."

Catherine couldn't see Helen in the darkness, but knew she had to do something. She pounded on the back of the cab, using all her strength to make as much noise as possible.

"Stop that," the other girl said. "It won't work."

"We have to do something. She needs help." Catherine ignored the other girls' warnings and kept making noise until the van stopped and the back doors opened. "She needs help!" Catherine said with a feeling of relief. "The baby is coming."

The light from the moonlight swept into the back of the van. The man looked at Helen for a long moment. Catherine couldn't understand his behavior. Her friend was clearly in pain, her shirt soaked with sweat, her body twisted in agony, she was about to ask him what was wrong when he left. "It's going to be okay," she said pulling against her restraints wishing she could be by her friend's side. She was about to say more when she heard the man's footsteps again. He appeared at the opening with a thick rope. He wrapped Helen's legs together then tied her hands behind her. Once he was through, he looked at Catherine and said, "Now the baby won't come." He closed the door and moments later started the van.

Horror filled the air.

"I told you not to say anything!" the girl said.

Catherine's voice turned hoarse. "I didn't think he'd—"

"She shouldn't have come with us anyway."

This was all her fault. She shouldn't have forced her to come, she shouldn't have expected them to help her. She'd been stupid and now her friend could die. She struggled, fought against her restraints. She had to reach her. She had to set her free, set the baby free. But she couldn't. She screamed. Her screams mingling with Helen's.

"Hold on, Helen, please."

"I'm meant to die. It's my fate. Don't blame yourself."

"No, you can't die. Please!"

But the sound of her pleas were drowned out by the sound of Helen's screams. And in that sound she heard her friend's fear and agony and could do nothing. An agony that lasted hours until a silence fell. A silence so loud it made her ears ring, pounding against her eardrums.

Finally the van stopped again and the doors opened. Catherine looked at the man who'd opened them. He had a face she'd remember and hate for the rest of her life. Such a pretty face on such an awful man. He stepped in and undid Helen's chains, dragging her limp, bloodied body along the floor of the van before lifting her in his arms. She saw her friend's eyes flicker, a relief touched her heart. She was still alive, although barely.

"Where are you taking her?" Catherine asked, unable to stop herself.

"You ask too many questions," an older girl spat out.

The man nodded. "Yes, but that will end soon." He glanced down at Helen as if she were a slab of beef. "Let this be a lesson to you."

He turned and another man closed the door, leaving them in darkness once again.

9

———

Dr. Eunice Davis draped her stethoscope around her thick neck and sighed as she stepped back from the girl laying on the bed. A heavy-set woman with brightly rouged cheeks and purple eye makeup, she ran her small, box-shaped clinic as efficiently as she could. "The baby's dead," she said in a flat voice.

Booker stared back at her unmoved. "Will the girl live?"

"Yes, if we act fast. I'm surprised she's lasted this long." Dr. Davis shook her head in sympathy. "Poor thing was too small to give birth I gather?"

Booker shrugged as if he didn't know about such things.

"You should have gotten here sooner so we could have done a C-section. Never mind. Let's get her into surgery now."

He nodded, then left.

When he returned to the van, he saw Pakimi taking a smoke break. He was as skinny as the cigarettes he liked to inhale and edgy as a hen in a fox den. "Gold or brass?" he asked tossing his cigarette on the ground. He crushed it under his heel.

Booker knew the question referred to the girl's worth. She was golden if alive, brass if not. "She'll live, but the baby's gone."

"Why did you do it? The baby could have fetched a nice price."

"She can't afford to have a baby like that."

"What do you mean?"

"Anderson got to her."

"Shit. Isn't this the third one?"

"Yes," he said in a grim tone.

"Doesn't the bastard know what these girls are meant for? We can't have them popping out babies. That's what the baby mill's for."

"I know."

"He's becoming a liability. There's plenty of sweet ass for him to taste, why does he keep messing with our girls?"

Booker sighed. "He said this one came on to him."

"And you believe that?"

"I can pretend to."

"What will you do if Chief finds out?"

"He said if I took care of the problem, he wouldn't do it again."

"So that's why you did this? You should have unloaded her. She shouldn't have any connection to us."

"Relax, I had my reasons."

"Your brother is going to ruin things for us."

"I won't let that happen. I'll make sure he learns his lesson this time."

Plenty of husbands had threatened to chop off Anderson's balls. He was a handsome, charming man of twenty-seven who liked to take what wasn't his. His mother had named him after an English author she liked to read. But her son hadn't opened a book since leaving school and preferred to use his charm to get what he wanted.

But when he woke up and felt something pressed against his most delicate area, he knew charm wouldn't help him. He became instantly wide awake, adjusting to the brightness of the room as his gaze fixed on the gun.

He didn't dare move, he was even afraid to breathe. He swallowed as he let his gaze trail up the gun to the man who held it. "What the hell are you doing?"

"I'm here to ask you the same thing."

"Put the gun away."

"No."

His older brother Booker could be crazy, but this was taking things too far. "I'm serious."

"So am I."

Anderson swallowed again, licking his lips, trying to figure out what he'd done wrong this time. He was always getting into trouble for something.

"I brought you a gift." He nodded to something on Anderson's left.

Anderson slowly turned his head, then yanked back when he saw the dead baby. He glared at his brother. "Have you gone mad?"

"Perhaps."

"Stop it."

"This is your fault."

"Put the bloody gun away and get that thing out of my bed."

"I thought you should take care of it since it's yours." Booker put his gun away before sitting on the side of the bed. "Now do you know why I'm here or do I need to continue to press your memory?"

Anderson scrambled to sit up. "It was an accident."

Booker shook his head. "No, it wasn't."

"It won't happen again."

"You've said that before."

"I mean it this time."

"You've said that before too." Booker stood. "I don't think I'm getting through to you. I should just tell Chief how much you've cost him."

Anderson jumped out of bed and fell to his knees. "No, please. I didn't...I won't...please..."

Booker blinked, looking bored, then sighed. "You stay away from the merchandise. Is that understood?"

"Yes."

"I don't care if you see a girl that makes you rise so high it hits you in the face. You don't touch her."

"I won't."

"Good." He stood, turned and opened the door.

"Wait, aren't you going to take...it?"

"I meant what I said. It's your problem now."

"You're a sick son of a bitch."

Booker flashed a cold smile. "You're starting to catch on."

11

—————

Michael Ayodeji was a man who hated to wait for anything so he wasn't pleased that his inventory arrived nearly two days late.

"What was the delay?" he asked when it finally arrived at his headquarters, a grand palace with imported marble floors and columns. His family residence was twice the size, and the church he owned three times bigger. He sat in a large white chair while all the others were grey and smaller, making visitors very aware of their station in comparison to his.

"Some trouble on the road, sah," Booker said.

Michael nodded; he prided himself on being a reasonable man. It was a valid excuse, he had to bribe a lot of key people in order for his business to operate unmolested in the day. At night it was even more dangerous. Booker watched one of Chief's associates look over the girls to count them. He'd told them how many he was shipping and he'd notice if one was missing. Fortunately, Booker was wise enough to compensate for his brother's mistake.

Chief looked over the suitcase filled with money. Booker

waited. He knew the amount was enough so that no questions would be asked. His boss knew his merchandise well and could spot a cheat from a mile. Booker made sure to make the amount a shade more than his boss would expect.

After a long moment he closed the suitcase, nodded to a man to take it away then stood. "Good job."

Booker nodded. "Thank you, sah."

He walked down the line of ten girls, his face giving nothing away. His smooth ebony features were as hard as granite, his golden gaze intense. He walked with a limp but refused to use a cane. He stopped in front of the Mosquito. Booker had given the new girl the nickname because she irritated him, but he wouldn't dismiss that she couldn't be dangerous.

Chief lifted up her chin and turned her face so that her cheek faced him. "What is this?"

"Sah?"

"I see bruising. Why does she have bruising?"

"She's a little wild and needs a little extra handling." He knew better than to mention any details. After they'd left the hospital they'd stopped and allowed the girls to get out and given them some food. They lined up against the van and ate like starving dogs. As he'd passed her, she'd said in a low voice. "Beware the snake."

He paused then continued to walk away, but couldn't ignore her words because for the past year he'd had a recurring dream with a snake in it. A green and black snake that slowly coiled around his arm before biting him. She must have overheard him when he'd complained to Pakimi about it. He wasn't used to a dream repeating itself like this one. He sighed and returned to her. "Go on. You have something to say, so speak."

"Misfortune is headed your way," she said in a quiet voice, keeping her gaze lowered. "You will suffer." She slowly lifted her gaze and a bright, wide smile spread across her face. "And I'm glad."

He slapped her with the back of his hand, harder than he'd ever hit anyone, even his second wife and that cow deserved every strike. But this girl...that smile...it enraged him. He rarely lost control but she'd pierced him. Something about her terrified him. A cold dread enveloped him. Her eyes were too knowing. As if she could see into his thoughts, as if she'd been inside his dream. If he were truly mad, he'd imagine her as the snake.

She was just a child, but her gaze had the wisdom of someone much older.

But he couldn't fear her. She was nothing. If she were truly powerful, she wouldn't be here. If she had a gift she'd been warned about her fate. That she'd end up living lower than a goat. He immediately felt ashamed that he'd allowed her to get to him. He prided himself on not being superstitious. He didn't believe in juju, he didn't even give God much thought. But something about his dreams did disturb him. Pakimi rushed over to him. "Have you gone mad?" his voice high in panic. "Chief will notice a bruise."

Booker flexed his fingers. His hand actually stung and that was rare. He felt as if he'd smacked a stone. The girl was powerful in a strange and haunting way. "It should be healed by the time he sees her." But unfortunately it hadn't. It had even swollen as if to mock him. The girl defied him at every turn. He'd be glad to see the last of her.

"I don't care how wild she is."

He bowed his head in contrition. "Sorry, sah."

Chief frowned. "How many times have I told you to leave the face alone?"

Booker wisely kept his head lowered, his heart pounding. Chief could be unpredictable. He could leave unscathed or be punished.

"The price goes down with damaged goods and I hate losing money."

Booker swallowed feeling slightly sick. This could be the end for him. If only she hadn't made him lose his temper. He bowed his head in contrition. "Sorry, sah."

"The suitcase wasn't as full as I would like."

Shit, he wanted more money. Money he didn't have. He searched his mind for a suitable reply.

A female voice broke the silence. "It can be covered with makeup."

Booker resisted the urge to lift his head and see who had spoken. Whoever it was, was now his angel. If only Chief believed her.

"You're certain?"

She nodded. "Ehen. I can."

"Then do it. You have ten minutes before they arrive."

12

It was like something from a dream. A room filled with fine ladies and a gentleman, sweet scents in the air, marble floors and large white columns, a place for princesses. Catherine looked around the room in awe. It reminded her of the hotel where her family had stayed before settling in the guest house. Had her family finally come to get her? They'd been told they were going to new homes. She looked around the room, but she didn't recognize anyone.

She soon realized that no one was smiling. Why was she here? What did they want? One woman stood up. A fine figure of a woman draped in silk, chocolate dark skin and dark eyes. She slowly walked down the line, then stopped in front of Catherine then nodded to the man.

"Step forward," he said.

Catherine shook her head. "I can't."

"Why not?"

"I don't want to be adopted."

The woman laughed, but the man grew angry. He gestured to another man, who grabbed her arm. "I'm not supposed to be here.

I have a family." She looked at one of the fine ladies and gentle-men, wondering why they had turned their eyes away. Surely, they knew this was wrong, surely they knew she didn't belong here. Why wouldn't they help her go home?

Booker shoved her into a room.

"What is your name?"

"My name is—"

"Six months and you still don't understand?" He poked her in the forehead. "Are you stupid? You don't have a name. Not anymore. And you will do as you're told if you want your family to live."

"My family lives far away from here."

"But you have a grandmother and aunt who don't. What about them?"

She felt her heart grow cold. They'd never mentioned them before. How did they know? Would they really hurt them? She thought about Helen and knew they would.

The man nodded, pleased by her silence. "Good. Now you're beginning to understand."

"But--"

"You don't speak unless spoken to, don't think unless the thoughts are shoved into your brain. You are no longer a person, but a thing. The sooner you accept that the easier it will be."

She sucked in her lips and boldly stared back at him, silently saying the words of her heart, *I'll never accept that.*

He narrowed his eyes and his mouth thinned. "I should gouge your eyes out. You will look down, you will do as your told or you will suffer more."

She kept her voice soft. "Snake. Bite."

He raised his hand.

"Not the face!" a woman said, entering the room. "I just finished fixing your mistake, don't force me do to it again."

"This one is worthless. We should tell—"

"And why would the sun worry about a mosquito? Don't worry." The woman who'd spoke up earlier, sat down and smiled at him. "Let me talk to her."

"You won't get far."

The woman kept her smile in place and waited for Booker to leave. Once he was gone, she turned her attention to Catherine. She was an attractive woman with dusty skin, high cheekbones and eyes as hollow as caves. Catherine knew the woman could smile, but doubted she'd ever had a genuine emotion of kindness in her life. As she'd put makeup on her face, her touch was cold, her look even colder and that same look pierced her now.

"You've had it easy up 'til now. But if you're not careful that could end."

"I don't belong here," Catherine said. "If you want money I know my dad will pay. Just..." she let her words fall away because it was clear the woman wasn't listening. Instead the woman stared out the window as if Catherine hadn't spoken at all.

"How old are you?" she asked in a soft voice, her gaze still focused on the window, a russet colored cloud slowly sliding past.

"Ten."

"And have you ever been touched?"

"Touched?"

A cynical smile twisted her lips. "No, you haven't." She turned and fixed her hollow gaze on Catherine. A look so dark and deep, Catherine felt as if she were dragging her inside to an awful place. "Creatures like you rarely have a choice, but here is your last one. If you don't behave, you'll end up with men like that—" She nodded to the door, referencing to Booker who'd left. "Breathing down your neck and thrusting himself between your legs—every moment of the day—and at night. And they'll rub you raw until you feel dead inside. Do you want that?"

Catherine thought of Helen and what a man had done to her. "No," she said wanting to sound brave, but her voice cracked.

"Then you will follow directions and do what we say. We're better than most. You're lucky to be with us. Now repeat that."

"Repeat what?"

"How lucky you are to be with us."

Catherine took a deep breath. "I am lucky to be with you."

"Good. Now smile."

Catherine plastered on a grin.

"That's better." She patted Catherine's cheek, then pinched the bruised flesh under her fingers, making Catherine wince until tears of pain filled her eyes. "And don't make me ever repeat this. You will behave. Understood?"

"Yes."

She released her and smiled. A genuine smile, as if she were a teacher and Catherine her star pupil. "Now make me look good. Or you will see the bodies of your grandmother and aunt scattered along the roadside before I slit your throat."

13

———

SIX YEARS LATER, MARYLAND, UNITED STATES

The moment she saw the police, she knew. She'd been enjoying a lovely luncheon at the club that winter afternoon when they approached her table. Maureen had seen that expression before. Although she'd been dreaming, hoping, praying for years to have the police show up at her door. She didn't expect them like this. That glint of pity and sorrow in their eyes. They came with news of death.

It was already two months into the new year; it still didn't feel fresh as it carried the battered, ash soaked remnants of the previous year—2001. She lived in a nation that would never be the same again after the horrors that had happened in Pennsylvania, Washington, DC, and New York. She was still trying to come to terms with the new world in which to raise her son who asked so many questions she couldn't answer and now this...

"Just tell it to me fast," she said. "Where did you find her?"

She'd expected a call from the embassy, since Catherine's disappearance was an international issue. One of the officers hesitated, an older man with a scruffy brown mustache that seemed to move on its own. "May we speak somewhere more private?"

She took a breath, although her lungs felt like they would burst. She'd give Catherine a wonderful funeral. She'd give them a chance to say goodbye. Maybe this would help them feel like a family again. In the last six years she'd felt as if she were sleepwalking. And that even though they were together they were apart. Perhaps now she could feel as if she could live again. "Of course."

Once she'd lead them to a private suite and they were seated she waited.

"Ma'am, it's your husband."

"My husband?" No that was wrong. She must have misheard them.

"Yes."

"Has he been in an accident? Is he injured? How bad?"

"Is there someone who can be with you?"

Oh God she'd heard those words before. "Tell me what happened."

"The doctors tried everything—"

"What happened?"

"He was involved in a single car collision. It appears to have been a heart attack, but we won't know everything until the ME's report."

"We're sorry," the other officer said. "But we need to ask you a few questions."

Maureen sat, feeling numb. His heart. The heart he'd turned from her the moment Catherine went missing. The heart she'd never been able to reclaim. He'd died years ago, only now she would bury him.

"Emery's dead," Marie told Joscelyn over the phone from her dorm bedroom, where her roommate—a senior studying Childhood Education—was passed out on her bed after a night of partying. Marie didn't particularly like her, but although she could commute from home, she wanted the freedom of living on her own. But her mother wouldn't let her get an apartment no matter how many A's she'd earned as a junior at Georgetown, so she'd moved onto campus. "They think it was a heart attack."

"Pity."

"Pity? That's all you can say?"

"Yes. He was unhappy and making Mom miserable so I guess it's for the best."

"That horrible."

"But it's true."

"What about little Aaron? He'll have to grow up without a father."

"Maybe. Mom still has her looks. I don't see her having much trouble snagging another man."

Marie cringed at her sister's callous words. "He's not a pet you can just replace. Didn't you feel anything for Emery at all?"

"Aside for pity and occasionally contempt? No. And don't pretend your heart is broken. I remember how nervous you were when Mom started dating him. You were so afraid he'd steal all her love."

"That was a long time ago. I was a child then. Emery was a good man. I'll miss him."

Joscelyn sighed. "Yes, he was good to us. I suppose there will be a funeral?"

"Of course."

"Then you tell Lorna."

"Why?"

"You'll see," she said with a smile in her voice. And twenty minutes later Marie found out what her sister was talking about.

"Are you kidding me! This is so unfair!" Lorna wailed. "How could he do this to me? I'm supposed to get married in six months. Who's going to walk me down the aisle? Who's going to make the speech at my reception!"

"Lorna, that's not the big problem right now."

"Not the big problem? Do you know how much planning goes into a wedding? And I wanted that day to be perfect and now it's ruined."

"Uncle Walter can walk you down the aisle and give the speech."

"Uncle Walter? He clashes with everything! First of all he's shorter than I am and he has buck teeth that he should have gotten fixed years ago! No, it would be a disaster."

Marie shook her head. "We'll come up with something. Right now we have to be there for Mom and Aaron."

"Aaron was going to be my ring bearer."

Marie pushed up her glasses. "He still will be."

"I sound selfish, don't I?"

"The fact that you even have to ask is rather sad," Marie said, glancing at her roommate when she interrupted the silence with a loud belch. She absently scratched her bottom before turning her head. Marie turned away; her roommate liked to drink and at times smelled like a brewery, but she never got sick, at least not in their dorm room.

"I guess I'd rather be upset about the wedding than Emery. I'm sorry he's dead. I'd rather be angry at him than sad that he's gone."

"I know."

"I won't get my father and daughter dance, I won't get—"

"I know." Marie bit her lip. "Do you think sorrow can kill?"

"What do you mean?"

"You heard me. Can sadness kill someone?"

"How would I know that? You're the one studying psychology."

"Yes, and there's scientific studies about death and depression."

"I don't know what you're trying to get at."

"I'm trying to reconcile myself with the fact that we killed him."

Lorna lowered her voice and said firmly, "We didn't kill him. Why would you say that?"

"Because of what we did."

Lorna's tone grew hard. "We didn't do anything, remember?"

Marie glanced at the stack of textbooks on her desk and paperbacks by Carl Jung, Erich Fromm, and Oliver Sacks stacked on the ground near her bed. She was searching for answers she'd probably never find. "He died a little every day."

"That's not our fault. People disappear. It's not the end of the world. Horrible things happen. You move on. You'll be a terrible psychologist if you don't tell your patients that."

"Psychiatrist."

"I know you keep telling me there's a difference, but I really don't care. But let me give you a little advice. Guilt gets you nowhere, regret is for losers. Physician, heal thyself."

She knew her sister was trying to be funny, but she wasn't in the mood to laugh. "So you never think of her?"

"Not when I can help it. Unless..."

Marie sat up, did her sister possibly feel some of what she did. "Unless what?"

"I wonder what Emery's will says."

14

———

*S*he couldn't tell anyone what she'd seen. Michela Lopez quickly gathered her few belongs in the small apartment she shared with two other women, desperate to leave.

"Where are you going?" Harriet Winstrom said, passing by the younger woman's room. She was the house manager at the Ojo house where they both worked and made sure everything ran smoothly from the kitchen staff on down.

"I'm quitting," she said stuffing her bag.

"But you need this job," Harriet said, knowing Michela was sending money to her parents in Florida and a son she was supporting who lived with them.

Yes, but I can't stay. Not after what I've seen. What she suspected she'd seen. Maybe she was wrong. She didn't want to find out either way. "I'll find another one."

"Don't do this. Tell me what happened?"

"Nothing. I just...I have to leave." She couldn't let any of the household see her, they couldn't suspect anything.

Yes, she'd seen it and it was so awful. It would follow her. How could a daughter do that to her father? This house had suffered so much, but now she knew it hadn't been a heart attack. She knew that evil lived there. Evil she didn't want to face.

"Please—" Harriet said, reaching for her hand.

"Let me go," Michela said yanking away. "I'm sorry," she said with regret. She didn't want to go and hated the thought that she would leave everyone else to have to do extra duties to cover for her. And Harriet had been kind enough to hire her in the first place. "Truly," she said before she zipped up her bag and ran out of the room, not daring to look back.

15

Joscelyn sighed at the sight of her stepfather's closed coffin decorated with a large casket spray of larkspur, roses, carnations and Stargazer lilies complemented by the lush green of ivy vines. She sat surrounded by the sound of soft crying, people blowing their noses and whispering among themselves in agreement to the eulogy. She didn't dare look at her mother. Although she knew what she'd see. Her mother would be stoic, just as she'd been at the funeral of their father.

Joscelyn cast a glance at Lorna and her fiancé, Greg. Her sister dabbed at her eyes, determined not to ruin her perfectly applied makeup. Marie looked a mess, her eyes and nose were red and she'd already gone through nearly a box of tissues and the service was only halfway over. She felt for her. She knew how much Marie admired Emery. She didn't remember their biological father since she'd only been one years old when he died.

It was all such a pity. Such a waste. If he hadn't kept digging, she wouldn't have had to do what she did. All these years, he just wouldn't let it go. Why not just accept Catherine was gone? Her plan was flawless. Nobody needed to know anything. Especially her stepfather and it would have worked if that damn Sergeant Major Adeyemi hadn't found Jesus. Of all the women the man had to fall for, it had to be some preacher's daughter who turned his heart to God.

Joscelyn sniffed with displeasure. He'd likely found an easier way to make money. Marie handed her a tissue, misinterpreting her sniff. Joscelyn took it, even though she didn't need it. Damn. Why did it have to come to this? Why hadn't the officer just asked for more money like a proper Nigerian? But he'd tried to ruin things.

It was only by accident that she'd seen his number on her stepfather's cell phone, which he'd left on the kitchen counter. He could be so absent-minded. She'd gone to make herself a snack to eat on the way to the hospital, glad to be in her final year of medical school. Now she got to focus on doing real work instead of studying the likes of inorganic chemistry, pathology and medical ethics. She initially thought of ignoring the ringing phone, but then grew curious when she saw the foreign number. The moment she'd picked up, Adeyemi had started talking before she spoke. "Sah, I have news that I think you should know. It's been on my heart for years. My wife convinced me to call you. She's a woman of God and I am working towards being worthy of her and Him. Chief Dayo told me you are still looking for your Catherine. I don't mean to take up your time, but your daughters know something. They paid the Deputy Commissioner—"

"Did they indeed?" Joscelyn said, glad to have gotten the information she needed before anyone else did.

He paused. "Who is this?"

"I'm disappointed in you. Spreading lies is so beneath you."

"Ah... *you*," he said, giving the single word a world of meaning. "You will pay for your sins, to God be the glory. "

"How much to make my sins go away?"

"No earthly money can—"

Joscelyn rolled her eyes and let out a long breath. "Why do men who turn to God become so boring? I don't need a sermon."

"You need to tell your father what you know. He will find out from someone."

"A wire transfer will be quick."

"I don't want your money."

"Then we're through." She disconnected then swore. She hadn't considered this. Nigerians were known for their love of money and corruption. Why did this ridiculous lowly man have to be different and change? Her stepfather couldn't know the truth. But he'd tricked her. He'd tricked all of them. That quiet, calm way of his had blinded her to the truth. None of them suspected he was still searching. All these years he'd seemed so resigned. She'd actually admired him for it. But that had been a lie. She shouldn't have underestimated him. A man like him hadn't built a lucrative business by luck. If Adeyemi told him anything, that could be a problem and cause him to doubt their story. But perhaps he wouldn't believe it. Truly who would? She could lie and say that he was getting back at her because she hadn't given him sexual favors. But the timeline was wrong. Why would he wait six years and the fact he was now married to a woman who'd encouraged him to confess gave his story credence. How could she fight that?

She could use tears. But even if she got Emery to believe her, there would still be that element of doubt. That's all Adeyemi had to give him and that would ruin everything. Her stepfather would approach the Deputy Commissioner, maybe even others.

And, if he started talking to her mother...her mother who suspected there was more to their story than they were telling... no, that would be disastrous. Joscelyn licked her lip, fear and anger knotted inside her. She had to do something.

"What are you doing?"

Joscelyn spun around at the sound of Emery's voice. She saw him in the kitchen doorway. It took her a moment to realize she still had his cell phone in her hand. She had to think fast and give him a good explanation. "You just missed a call."

"You don't usually answer my phone."

Why had he assumed she'd answered it and not just checked the number? Had he overheard her talking? "No, but it looked urgent because it was from Nigeria."

He rushed towards her, his gaze sharpening. "Who was it? What did they say?"

"It's not good news," she said feigning pain.

"At this juncture, any news is good news to me."

At this juncture? Joscelyn thought trying not to smile. He could sound so formal sometimes. "They found a body. They think it's Catherine because it was wearing her other missing shoe and the clothes we'd described."

"Why didn't you come get me? Why did they hang up?"

"The line got disconnected. I was thinking about how to reach them again when you entered."

Emery held out his hand. "Let me call them now."

"He said he was leaving."

"I can reach him. Who was it? Not too much time has passed."

She reluctantly handed him the phone. She watched him dial with growing anxiety. She couldn't let him hear what Adeyemi had to say. She couldn't let him uncover her lie. She'd lose everything then. He'd disinherit them, their lives would be ruined. If only he'd just trust her. Why didn't he just trust her? "I just remembered something," she said.

Emery looked at her startled. "What?"

"He was going out, but would be back in an hour. You should try then."

"I want to try now."

Joscelyn gripped her hands as he dialed. She heard the phone ring. Once, twice, three times.

"You're right," Emery said after the fifth ring. "He's not there." He disconnected.

Joscelyn held back a cry of relief and nodded solemnly.

"I have an appointment, but I'll speak to whomever called later." He turned and left.

No, she couldn't let that happen. That's when she spotted his thermos. He always liked taking his coffee with him before he had a meeting. She went to the medicine cabinet and took out one of her mother's prescriptions. She knew it would have an adverse affect on him, especially with his high blood pressure pills.

Slipping the medicine into his thermos had been easy. What was hell, was waiting to see if it had worked. When Marie had called her that afternoon, that's when she knew they were all still safe.

The ME's report had been inconclusive, but no one wanted to bother her mother with an investigation, so that crisis had been averted. A heart attack was sad, but simple and clean. It really was too bad. She hadn't minded Emery and he'd been a good father to Aaron. Why couldn't Aaron have been enough for him? A son to rear and love. Why had he left his heart in that wretched country? Always talking about it as if it were some Shangri-La when it was filled with corruption and dirt roads. No, that was unfair. She'd seen some pretty places, the guest house, the hotel, but she'd seen Guyana, Brazil, and Spain too and felt no tug to anything or anywhere. She couldn't understand people's attachment to places or things. She could live anywhere, with anyone.

If only he'd accepted the new life he had. The new family. If he hadn't looked back, tried to hold on to the past, he would still be alive. The future. That was all that mattered and she'd do everything to protect it.

She glanced at her brother Aaron, who was pulling on his bottom lip and trying to keep still. He was a good little boy, inoffensive, not rowdy and annoying like most boys. He'd be useful when he was older. She'd take care of him and make sure to take his father's place.

Now she had to find a way to make sure Adeyemi stayed in line, otherwise she'd make sure he found out if heaven existed.

16

———

"This is payment."

Maureen froze as she stood staring at Emery's grave site, the sound of the rain tapping against the canopy above her. She hadn't heard the woman approach. She wished she had, then she would have been more prepared. It was never wise to let a snake sneak up on you and she knew better than to have her guard down. "Not now, Mum."

Tamilla Goodfield was not a woman who liked being told what to do. She did exactly as she pleased. At sixty, she carried herself like a woman half her age, although her pinched features made her face look a decade older. She'd never been much to look at, so her daughter's beauty had come as a surprise to everyone, especially her. A daughter, who had once been a source of pride, now only gave her pain. "It was bound to happen. You didn't think you'd be able to get away with your deception forever, did you?"

Maureen adjusted the veil of her black hat. "I didn't do anything wrong."

A sour grin touched Tamilla's mouth. "Yes, keep telling yourself that. But no matter how many times you say it, doesn't make it true. You were selfish and cold and that hasn't changed."

Maureen pulled up the collar of her grey cashmere coat. "I said, not now."

Tamilla continued with enjoyment. "Two husbands buried and you're barely past forty. At least you have only one child to worry about this time with the youngest girl in college."

"She's not my youngest. My youngest is still missing."

"Joscelyn told me that she was dead. That some officer—"

"I don't believe it. Joscelyn has been working hard to uncover the truth. She told me she contacted the Nigerian consulate, the embassy, the police and host of other organizations to no avail. I think they told her Catherine's dead to get her to stop asking questions, because when I've asked to have the body shipped, she tells me they always have excuses. Catherine is still out there."

Tamilla's pleasure dimmed and her tone grew solemn. "Paying for your crimes no doubt. Poor child."

"I don't serve a God that cruel."

"I don't think you've ever served anyone but yourself."

"I can't change the past no matter how much you want me to."

"I want you to admit what you did."

"I didn't do anything." Maureen opened up her umbrella and headed to her car. She'd sent the girls ahead with Aaron so that she could be alone to say goodbye to her husband. She wished she'd been kinder and more patient with him, but she had no chance to make it up to him now.

Her mother followed her. "You stole your sister's life."

"What life?" Maureen said, wishing she could walk faster, but the wet ground was the enemy of her high heels. "There was nothing to steal."

"Except the man she loved."

"I loved him too."

"You loved his potential, not the man. Stop acting so innocent with me. I gave you life and know every shade of your heart. A heart that has more darkness than light. You can fool everyone, but not me. You knew exactly what you were doing. You stole the man and the destiny that should have been your sister's, but you couldn't keep it."

Maureen approached her car and motioned to the driver, who immediately jumped out and opened the back door.

"I haven't finished talking to you."

Maureen sat inside then closed her umbrella. "Yes, you have."

Tamilla slid in beside her and closed the door. "She's coming down to see you." Tamilla smiled at the look on Maureen's face. "Ahh...yes, that's a surprise. How long has it been? Fifteen years?"

"Why does she want to see me?"

"To gloat at your despair, I hope."

"That's not funny."

"I know."

"I was young. I fell pregnant. It was an accident."

"It was a miracle. What woman carries a child for two years?"

Maureen smoothed down a crease in her black skirt. "I told you I had a miscarriage."

"Right quick. And made sure not to get pregnant again until you were good and ready."

"I don't—"

"You were never pregnant. You trapped him with your lies. Admit that much."

"Why?"

"Confession is good for the soul."

"So they say."

But she didn't plan to confess anything. She didn't regret a thing. She'd known she had to find a way out of Jamaica and the poverty she'd been born into. She was not going to live the life her parents had. Especially her mother, a woman who'd borne more children than she could handle from two men she knew of and one she didn't. Maureen knew she didn't have school smarts like her sister...but she knew opportunity when she saw it.

"His name is Clyde and he has an uncle in America who wants him to work with him."

"That sounds exciting."

"I hope he'll ask me to go with him."

"I'm sure he will."

"He's ready to settle down."

"But what about your studies?"

"I hope he'll let me finish, but he doesn't seemed too bothered by them."

Maureen listened with envy. Her sister was going to leave and have a wonderful life away from this wretched life. She was already going to university. She would become a teacher and get a good job. Maureen had no such prospects.

America. She wanted to go to America. She wanted to live the fine life she saw on TV and in magazines. She hated having only three dresses to wear. Ones she had to wash by hand every week. She wanted to know what it was like to have a dishwasher and plates that weren't chipped and shoes that hadn't been bought at a jumble sale or out of someone's car boot.

Seducing him hadn't been difficult. She knew she was pretty and used her looks. Her sister's smarts couldn't compare. He didn't want to wait, and unlike her sister, she didn't force him to. They did it in his car. When she told him she was pregnant, he did the honorable thing. She knew he would because she'd chosen him with care. He wasn't like most men she knew who knocked a woman up, then disappeared.

"What do you mean you're getting married?" Robin said, stunned, as they sat in the small sitting room of their house.

"But I thought you loved me. I thought we..." She let her

words trail away as she stared at his bent head. "I don't understand."

"We didn't mean this to happen," Maureen said before resting a protective hand on her stomach.

Her sister saw the motion and her eyes widened in horror. "No."

"Yes."

Robin surged at her. "You bitch!"

Clyde grabbed her, but not before Robin tore the sleeve of Maureen's dress and scratched her arm.

"Go, both of you," Tamilla said. She'd watched the pair with distrust when they'd first asked to speak with her and now her expression was even less welcoming. "The deed is done so go on your ways."

After a fast wedding, Maureen would leave her life on the island and be free of her past. It would take her sister another ten years before she had the chance. She hadn't seen her since the wedding of a cousin a few years back. Why did she want to see her now?

"Because of me I got all of us out through sponsorship. We're all living better lives than we would have."

"It wasn't just because of you. I was blessed by God, although you think that you sit on his right hand side."

"I know I wasn't your favorite."

"Did you even love this last one?"

Maureen didn't misunderstand her. "I loved both of my husbands."

"Too bad that couldn't keep them alive."

17

—————

She'd changed a lot in fifteen years. Become more self-confident and assured of herself. The kind of woman who wouldn't have let the man she loved slip through her fingers. She'd done well for herself, managing to get a doctorate degree and become a professor. She'd never married. Maureen didn't know why, but suspected. She didn't know much about her anymore except what she heard from others.

"Oh yes, did you see the property she bought?", "Yes, I heard she's holidaying in Aruba this year.", "Of course I know she'd gotten another degree."

And now she was here, in Maureen's living room. What did she want? An apology? A chance to gloat as her mother said? She wouldn't make the first move. She'd let her come, her sister would have to do the rest.

"Beautiful home."

"Thank you."

Robin picked up a silver framed photo of Catherine. "I was sorry when I heard about—"

"Why are you here?" Maureen asked, unable to pretend

anymore. She could plaster on a smile about anything else, the loss of her husbands, her daughter's upcoming wedding, but Catherine was too raw a wound for her to pretend.

"I didn't come here to fight, if that's what you're afraid of."

"That's not what I asked you."

She set the photo down. "I've hated you for years. And envied you. But I got over it. No, that's wrong, I should say these last few years changed me. I lost fifteen pounds, changed my hair and decided to start thinking about the future instead of the past. I was offered a one-year tenure at a school in Ghana and that's why I had to see you."

"I'm listening."

"It's a long shot, I know, but the principal told me that a lot of students come from Nigeria. Many from top families. I may be able to make inquires and find out what the police in Nigeria know."

Maureen felt tears gathering in her eyes. Her sister would help her find Catherine? She'd forgiven her? Her compassion overwhelmed her. She covered her face and cried.

"I'm sorry for your loss."

"It's been a nightmare."

"I can't make any promises—"

"Just the fact that you're here, that you're willing to do something, means the world to me."

She took her hand. "Good."

"What made you change?"

"Does it matter?"

"Yes."

"In truth, it was Catherine's disappearance. Your loss took me back to mine. After Clyde died, I thought I'd moved on. I thought I'd gone on with my life and I'll admit a little bit of me was glad that you'd lost him just as I had. You stole him from me, and death stole him from you. But it was only after Catherine disappeared that I realized how much I was still raging inside. Raging that you'd married again and were living well with three children you'd had with Clyde. When Mum told me about the loss of Catherine, it made me realize how much nothing is guaranteed. That I wasn't living. I'd let my bitterness take over. No more. I'm done hating you and him. Or anyone. That's what made me change."

"I don't know how to thank you."

"I haven't done anything yet," Robin said.

"You've given me hope."

"She may not be alive."

"I know that, but even if I could give her a proper burial that would be something."

"I'll do my best to find her," Robin said, giving her sister a hug before she said goodbye. She believed Catherine was dead, but if her sister wanted to believe otherwise, who was she to stop her. *I'll do my best to find her.* Robin got into her silver Lexus and sped down the long driveway, her sister's mansion becoming a dot in her rearview mirror, unable to stop a satisfied smile, knowing she hadn't meant a single word.

18

---

*S*he wouldn't have had to beat the little termite *if she hadn't looked at her with such defiance.* Elsie tossed the whip she'd used to strike the girl and went into the bathroom to wash her hands.

Such pride had to be shaken, destroyed. She had no right to even glance in her direction, let alone stare at her with eyes so full of rage that she seemed to penetrate right through her. The girl was her property. Why didn't she understand that? She was nothing without her. Didn't she provide a roof over her head? Clothes? Food? Was it so wrong to ask for an honest day's work out of her?

Elsie sat in front of her vanity and took a deep breath. She couldn't frown, that brought wrinkles. She took another deep breath. In. Out. In. Out. One, two, three...She counted until she reached ten. She had to remain calm. She glanced outside the window. Today the sun peeked through the ever present English clouds, sending a hushed yellow glow to the lush blue carpet and assortment of pink roses displayed in a crystal vase in the corner, a gift from her husband for Valentine's Day.

She wasn't a cruel woman. Margarite liked to burn her girl with cigarette butts, Remi hardly fed hers, but she didn't do that. Elsie knew she was much more considerate. All she asked for was obedience and respect. No...she didn't ask for respect, she demanded it and the look that girl had sent her wasn't respectful.

But now she would. Now she would keep her gaze lowered to the ground like the flea she was. And if she dared to look at her like that again, she'd make sure the punishment made her remember.

THERE WAS no one to tend to her wounds; the blood soaked the back of her shirt—her skin sticky and raw.

Catherine had never felt so cold. A cold that gnawed at her bones, like a parasite that had seeped under her skin, eaten away her flesh and exposed her skeleton. The tiny space heater in the dark, dank room glowed against the darkness, but the chill of the room swallowed up any warmth, making her shiver beneath the two thin sheets she huddled under. She felt so numb with cold that her body didn't even have the energy to shiver. She'd shivered the first few days, but no more. And for a moment she thought of an aunt who was Catholic who raged against the sins of suicide and talked about the pit full of fire in glorious detail. For a moment Catherine thought of going there. Thought of how much better it would be to burn than to freeze. Her mind thought that it wouldn't feel so different when you feel like your skin was being peeled away. Frost or flame, the pain was the same. She was already living in hell.

She'd spent four years with Dr. Bandele and his family in Abuja and Berlin before being given to Mrs. Bandele's sister in England. England, with its grey streets and grey skies. Wet mornings and cold winters. Winters. Something she hadn't experienced in years. She once missed the sight of snow, now she feared it. From working for the Bandeles, she'd picked up how to behave in order not to get into trouble. Curtseying, saying 'yes, mah', 'no, mah' 'I'm sorry, mah'. She learned their manner and accents, keeping her words short. No one cared to listen to what she had to say anyway. She'd also learned from another house girl, who lived with a widowed grandmother in a hut out back and worked in the kitchen, who to avoid.

"Be careful of the master," she'd told Catherine during one rare moment when they had a chance to speak at the back of the house. "He's a carpenter."

"A carpenter?"

"Yes, de kind of man who'll rub his body against yours like sandpaper."

Two weeks later he tried, but didn't succeed. She got a lashing, but he didn't try it again and she thought she was safe. And she was, until the eldest son tried the same thing when he came home from university. Her resistance this time caused a bigger ruckus—especially when she scarred his face and arms with her nails—and her actions had caused her to be sent away.

In some ways, Mrs. Salako wasn't as bad as her sister. In other ways worse. She spoke in a soft voice and never shouted, unlike her sister, who seemed to say everything at the top of her voice, but she had an unpredictable temper. Catherine never knew what would make her angry. Mrs. Bandele never needed a reason. Catherine could always tell when she was in one of her moods. She tried her best to stay out of her way, but that wasn't always possible. Mrs. Salako ignored her most times, but had more of a nervous energy. As if she always expected someone to slight her. It was known in the family that her sister had gotten the better deal. She lived better, her husband made more and they had three homes and two properties, while the Salakos only had one house and no property to think of and a combined income in the low six figures.

Mrs. Salako hosted many parties, but never seemed to be happy. She was a very insecure woman, reminding Catherine of a girl in her school who did everything to get in the good graces of the teachers even though it made her unpopular.

She hadn't meant to look at her mistress. She knew she wasn't supposed to. It was her temper again. It always got her into trouble. But it had seemed so unfair. Emily was such an ugly little girl with her limp hair and round face but she liked her doll. Everyone knew it and her brother had pulled its head off and made her cry. So while cleaning his room, Catherine had made sure one of his prized action toys had shattered to the ground. "Mum! Look what she did. Look what the monkey did."

"Did you do this?"

Yes, with pleasure. "An accident, mah."

"It wasn't an accident," Michael said running into his mother's arm and burying his face in her arms. "I saw her."

Elsie patted the back of his head. "Don't cry. Mummy's here." She glared at Catherine.

"Say you're sorry."

"I'm sorry," Catherine mumbled.

Elsie whacked her on the back of the head. "Say it like you mean it."

"I'm sorry," she repeated a little louder. But that's when she'd made her mistake. She'd looked at her. A woman as lovely as her daughter was plain. But it didn't matter, she knew she was a monster.

"You will be punished."

So she beat her and left her in the dark for two days.

When Catherine saw light again, she could barely stand the sight of the sun, keeping her eyes half-closed against the glare.

"Do you know who I am?" Elsie asked when she found

Catherine in the sitting room wiping the table with a cloth in a slow circular motion.

"Yes, mah," she said taking her time to clean every inch of the table. She'd learned not to hurry. To make each motion mean something, that no matter what the task, it was better than being in the tiny room with one dull light bulb and thin sheets. At least above stairs was warm and she could see the sunshine.

"Not *mah*," Elsie said, bristling with irritation. "It's madam here. I've told you to call me 'madam'."

"Yes, madam," Catherine said, putting an extra emphasis on the second syllable. She hated her and every time she forced her to use the formal phrase, she added to it. Yes ma-*damn* you to the corners of the earth. Yes ma-*damn* all who come after you.

Elsie took a deep breath and started counting aloud, then stopped at ten and looked at Catherine. "Why do you enjoy making me angry?"

"I'm sorry, mah-damn," that I have to continue to hear your voice or have your stale breath in my face.

Elsie took a seat. "You're still young I suppose, and need more training. I'm very patient."

"Thank you, mah-damn."

Elise gritted her teeth. "Did you clean the kitchen?"

"Yes, mah-damn."

"Do it again." She stood, then left.

"You're getting upset for no reason," Howard Salako said as he massaged his wife's shoulders, the sound of her favorite Bollywood soundtrack playing in the background. Although she'd had a long bath, she was still fuming and tense.

"I don't know why I hate how she calls me madam. It sounds rude somehow."

"Don't let it bother you, you can't get everything after all. Does she do the work?"

"Very well."

"Then leave it at that. Good help is so expensive nowadays."

THE LITTLE GIRL approached Catherine with a brush and a ribbon. Catherine stared at the objects for a long moment. She wasn't good with such things. The strands of hair wouldn't stay together. But the little girl was patient. So while she sat, Catherine told her a story, remembering when her stepmother had done her hair. At times it seemed like only a day ago, other times it felt like decades. She knew time was an illusion. A minute could be a year and a year a minute. It still seemed only minutes ago that she was at home with her family. The girl jumped up when her name was called then turned and kissed Catherine on the cheek before she left.

Catherine wiped the kiss away, knowing it meant nothing. She'd seen the little girl kiss her dog with the same tenderness. They all saw her as a pet. But treated her with less dignity and her heart continued to grow cold. She no longer felt human. She didn't know the last time she'd laughed or smiled. She'd been caught trying to get past the alarm system. There was also a gate at the front entrance. Escape was futile and even if she did, where would she go? They had her passport. It was a fake. She hadn't even been able to see the name they'd created for her. She didn't have a name. Hadn't been called anything for six years.

But she'd had a family once and sisters.

Sisters.

She now only lived to see them again. They must be so worried about what had happened to her. They probably blamed themselves for leading her to the van, but they'd all been victims.

They had tried to pay a ransom, but the men had been greedy. But she would escape this somehow and return to her family. She'd see her father again and stepmother and hug her little brother.

How? The voice of defeat whispered in her ear. How can you escape here? Where will you go? Who will believe you? You are invisible, nothing.

But every night she let her anger warm her and kill that tiny voice until it became a whimper.

19

"**G**irl!"

Catherine paused. She'd been folding the clothes in the laundry room when she heard the command. She hadn't heard it in a while. She walked to the living room—making sure not to hurry—wondering what the madam would blame her for this time.

"Yes, mah-damn?" she said once she'd reached the room, where she found Mrs. Salako sitting on the brown leather love seat with another woman.

"Mrs. Leland has something to say to you."

Catherine didn't know the woman well. She'd seen her at a few gatherings hosted at the house, but like the other guests, she didn't mean much to her. She didn't stand out, although like many of the madam's visitors, she was impeccably dressed. Today she wore dark trousers and long black boots, a turquoise blouse and a long gold necklace. She had light chocolate freckles on her honey skin, and her long legs and her neck reminded Catherine of a flamingo. "I was just telling Elsie what a gem you are," she said, shouting at Catherine as if she were speaking to someone who didn't speak English.

Catherine cast a nervous look at madam. Nobody thought of her as valuable, let alone a gem. What was the woman on about?

Mrs. Leland clapped her hands together and beamed. "I listened to your advice and my son's life was saved."

Catherine gripped her hands behind her back. Mrs. Leland was a stupid woman. It was strictly forbidden for her to speak to anyone, especially guests. She'd only spoken to her because she'd seemed so distraught when she'd seen her alone at one of the parties. "I'm sorry, madam, me nah say nothing."

Mrs. Leland blinked. "But you did. At the last party I told you about my dream."

"No, mah," Catherine said lowering her gaze to appear appropriately subservient. "You must switch me with someone else."

"I didn't. I know it was you. I'm here to thank you, you silly girl."

Catherine shook her head. "I'm sorry, mah. I did nothing."

"But—"

"It's a harmless mistake," Elsie interrupted. "They tend to look alike. She hardly talks and is too stupid to offer you anything useful."

Mrs. Leland frowned. "Yes, well. I'm sorry to have wasted your time."

"A visit from you is never a waste," Elsie said with a smile. She waved a hand at Catherine. "You're dismissed."

Catherine nodded and left, inwardly releasing a sigh of relief. She hoped that madam truly did believe she was stupid and that her lie would pass. She had taken a risk talking to Mrs. Leland without permission.

At one of the parties one evening, moving around unnoticed,

she wanted to announce to everyone 'I was once just like you. I used to go to school, ride horses, swim in the ocean, play in the garden. Fly in airplanes.' But her life before seemed like a dream. In four more years, half of her life would have been lived as a slave.

Perhaps it was arrogance that had made her speak, as much as a desire to help. She wanted someone to see her. Really see her and need her. She didn't expect much, surprised that the woman had even listened, let alone followed through. She was glad her son's life was saved. But she'd put her own at risk.

"Was she really mistaken?" Elsie asked Catherine later that evening after Mrs. Leland had gone.

"Yes, mah-damn."

"I wonder why she confused you with someone else like that."

We all look alike, isn't that what you said? Catherine shrugged.

"Nobody else better mistake you for someone else."

Catherine bit her lip and nodded.

20

———

S he hadn't made a mistake.

Robbie Fraser waxed the Salako's black BMW as his mind ruminated over the conversation he'd overheard. He knew Mrs. Leland hadn't gotten the house girl confused with someone else because he'd heard the girl talking to her that night. He'd gone out for a smoke and eavesdropped. He hadn't thought much about it until now.

At eighteen, he had dreamed of being a star. He'd fallen in love with films and gotten his good looks and tanned skin from his mum, an Afro-Caribbean woman, and his name from his father, a Scottish man who'd died when Robbie was nine. Life had been hard after that, but he still dreamed of making it. But although he had the looks, plenty of girls had shown him how much so, he didn't have the drive, talent or the humility to admit to himself that he wanted something for nothing. So, by twenty-eight he ended up being a driver, still hoping that one day he'd be discovered and waiting for that special moment that would change his life.

However, Robbie could spot star quality in others. And he

saw it in the Salako's house girl. When he'd overheard her talking to Mrs. Leland he'd been most surprised at how certain she sounded—she usually sounded halting and unsure. But that night she had a con artist's smooth delivery. Either she was a superb actress or the real thing. He couldn't think what she could get out of scamming the woman. He hadn't heard her ask for anything. Maybe she just wanted to help. That kind of naiveté could be useful.

Later that night as he lit one cigarette with the butt of another, he couldn't stop thinking about the house-girl. That girl had a gift and the Salakos didn't realize the goldmine they had living under their roof. Then again, they had enough dosh that they didn't have to worry about it. However, Robbie had plenty of money worries that a girl like that could make disappear. He stubbed out his cigarette and called his cousin, Faye Randolph, a woman barely scraping by, reading tea leaves and crystals.

"I know a girl who interprets dreams," he said once she came on the line. "I think she could be of use to you."

"How?" Faye asked ever suspicious.

"Business is bad, isn't it?"

"It's just the location."

She'd been using the same excuse for years. "It's because people are catching on. But instead of having to con them, how would you like the genuine article?"

"I'm listening."

"Salako's got this girl working for her, yea. And she's good at interpreting dreams."

"Dreams are a hard sell, Robbie. I don't—"

"Come on, give us a listen."

She sighed heavily. "Go on then."

"This girl's spot on, she is. Mrs. Leland's been talking her up like the girl's the bleeding Virgin Mary."

"'Cause she's soft in the head," Faye said, unimpressed. She'd grown used to his stories about the women Mrs. Salako entertained. More money than sense most of them. "Besides, one reading isn't enough."

He sighed, annoyed that his exaggeration hadn't worked. "She's got the gift, I tell ya. As plain as the nose on my face, that girl's got it. You can't pass up an opportunity like this."

"What opportunity? She's not mine."

"I think she could be," Robbie said, glad she finally sounded interested.

"I don't have that kind of money. Unless you're planning on robbing a bank or something."

"Don't worry about money. I plan to get her another way."

"How?"

"You leave that to me. Just believe this. This girl is going to be our ticket. Just you wait and see."

"I think you're dreaming too much. Mrs. Salako won't let you have her."

"Don't you worry. I'll get the house girl without paying a thing."

"How?"

"By promising her what she desperately wants."

"And what's that?"

"Freedom."

"How much do they pay you?" Robbie asked Catherine when he caught her taking out the trash and recycling. He looked around to make sure they weren't spotted. He knew the mistress was away and the master at work. But he had to act fast. He tightened his red scarf and rubbed his hands together against the cold.

She shook her head, dumping the bottles into the recycling bin, letting them clatter together, sending a scared sparrow off into flight, and causing a striped stray cat to lift its head in interest as it lazed under the car. She turned to return to the house.

"They don't pay you anything, do they?"

She stopped.

That was good. "How would you like to get out of here?"

She spun around.

Robbie smoothed down his hair, knowing he looked his most dashing and trustworthy in his crisp uniform. "I can make that happen."

"How?"

She was talking to him, that was even better. "I have ways, but you'll have to do what I say."

"What do you want?"

He hesitated, doing his best to look confused. "What do you mean?"

"Why would you help me? I have no papers. I have no money."

"Don't worry about that. Things can be arranged."

"What do you want?"

"Nothing."

She turned.

He silently swore. Wrong move. "You're right. I'm sorry. I didn't mean to lie to you."

She slowly turned back to him and waited.

"I help you and you help me."

She measured him up and down; for some reason the assessment made him nervous. Although she didn't look older than seventeen, she had an unsettlingly keen gaze. "You're married?"

"Yeah," he lied, hoping she'd trust him more. He'd come up with a story of why he didn't wear a ring if he had to.

"Yet you want to sleep with me?"

"No," he said, waving his hands, and flashing his most charming grin. "No, that's not what I mean. Listen, I help you and you can help me. How would you like to get paid? Aren't you sick of being here? Don't you want a new life?"

Robbie held his breath, hoping she'd taken the bait. He saw the desire in her eyes but though she was young, she was still sharp. He had to be cautious.

"Yes," she said in a soft voice.

He fought not to look visibly relieved. Getting her to say yes was one thing, getting her out of there was another. "Good. Then you have to do exactly what I say."

Catherine didn't move, she just stared at him, making Robbie wait five excruciating seconds before she nodded her head.

21

Catherine couldn't sleep that night. Had it been a dream? Had the conversation with the driver really happened? Was he going to help her escape? What work did he want her to do? It didn't matter. She could earn money and find a way back home. The plan on how she would escape seemed rather simple and crude, but if it worked that was all that mattered.

Two nights later, Catherine crept through the silent, dark house and got to the alarm system at the front door. She carefully put in the numbers until it disengaged, then she used the key the driver had given her to get through the gate that covered the door entrance. Once she'd gotten past that she saw his car parked out front on the curb. She raced to it, jumped into the back seat as instructed and squatted low on the floor. Suddenly bright headlights lit up the interior of the car.

"Shit!" Robbie said as the headlights swept past then turned into the residence.

"What is it?"

He didn't turn to look at her. "Just stay down," he said then got out of the car.

Catherine heard the other car hum to a stop and then a door close. Mr. Salako had arrived home a day early. Would he notice the gate, the alarm?

Robbie put on a performance like none in his life. He smiled at Mr. Salako as he hurried and took his bags. "Allow me, sir," he said taking the keys and pretending to open the gate.

"Lucky she didn't set the alarm yet. Sir. Have a good evening."

"Thank you."

Robbie hurried back into the car and started it. It wouldn't take long for Mr. and Mrs. Salako to exchange stories and question his presence there, but he wouldn't be around to care. He sped down the street, knowing they wouldn't try to find them. What could they tell the police? *Somebody stole my slave?*

They would just get another one. He didn't have to worry, but he still didn't breathe until he was several miles away.

"Did you get her?" Faye asked, meeting Robbie at the door.

"Yeah, I got her," Robbie said, walking into the flat, which was crowded with more furniture than one woman—or flat—needed. He stretched over an ottoman and squeezed between two coffee tables.

"Then where is she?"

Robbie turned, surprised by the question, then realized Catherine wasn't behind him. He raced out the room, hitting his knee against the arm of a couch and swearing, before he reached the hallway. His heart returned to its regular rhythm when he spotted Catherine slowly shuffling down the hall like a patient in a mental hospital drugged up on pills. "Come on," he said, making sure to sound patient, although he wanted to yank her inside and not let her out of his sight. When she reached the doorway, he held his hand out to her, but she recoiled from his touch. That was a first, women usually liked an invitation from him, but he knew he had to be different with her. He opened the door wider. "That's right. You're safe now." He looked at Faye, triumphant. "See? No trouble." He closed and locked the door behind him.

"Did you tell her about me?"

"Only the basics."

"She's a bit timid."

"Only 'cause she's scared, but I'm telling you our fortunes have changed."

"And I thought she'd be prettier."

"She'll clean up fine."

Faye motioned Catherine towards her. "Come here, love. That's a girl. I don't bite and I don't have fleas so you needn't worry," she said then laughed at her own joke.

Catherine glanced at Robbie, then gave Faye a considering look. "What do you want me to do, madam?"

"Oh, aren't you keen," Faye said, pleased. "That's good. No, darling you don't have to clean up round here. We've got something else in mind for ya. Sit down and I'll tell you."

Catherine cautiously sat, keeping her gaze on the woman. She hadn't taken offense by her comment about her looks; she was used to being assessed then dismissed. She wondered how alike or different she'd be from her two last mistresses. Not that it mattered, she was to be free. She wondered how much the woman would pay her. In looks she was strikingly different, pale skinned with dark, curly hair, moss green eyes and wide shoulders. She looked several years older than Robbie, but every year looked good on her.

"I've heard you have a gift for interpreting dreams."

Catherine shrugged.

"That kind of service should be paid for. How would you like to earn some money?"

"I would."

"Good," Faye said, glancing up at Robbie and the two shared a private look before she returned her attention to Catherine. "Because from now on you'll earn a mint."

And she did.

But she never saw a pence or a pound.

Robbie and Faye treated her better than any other mistress or master. They dressed her up in fine clothes—silks, satins, cottons so fine it felt like air—fed her foods she'd smelled but never had a chance to taste—Greek kebabs, Indian masala—and gave her a room with a real bed and mattress. With sheets that kept her warm. But for all their care, they never let her have any money. They told her that they had to deduct the clothes, food, shelter from the profit, calling them unavoidable expenses. They talked about how they had to pay fees and were working hard to make sure that the business ran well and that with all the work they did there was hardly anything left, and when they started making more money they promised she'd get her due share.

It was after six months of their empty promises that Catherine realized she'd never see any money. That they were content to make money off of her and, like a prized horse, she was property they planned to profit from. She'd traded one cage for another.

She didn't have to work as hard as when she was with the Bandeles or Salakos and that was a relief. There were no foul moods, shouting and no beatings, but she was still weary and owned. Robbie and Faye made sure she was dependent on them. She never knew where they were—what city, what town they were in. Every few months they'd leave one town and settle into another. She didn't know how much money they made, but as time passed the accommodations became more appealing. From cold water flats underground to ones above ground with expansive views.

Her new routine was pure performance. They'd even given her a stage name—Epic—and a costume. She always wore an elaborate mask that covered her eyes.

"That's part of the appeal," Faye had told her. "People like the mysterious. Now you're the woman behind the mask who can interpret dreams."

The days were long for Catherine, with many clients, but after years of hard labor she found it manageable and for the first time in a long time started to feel human again. She felt that she had something of a life. She didn't take for granted her regular meals, the sight of the sun and the feel of it on her skin when they took her on drives in the new car they'd bought. Plus, she could talk to people and be of service. They didn't pay her, she knew she was still property, but they valued her enough not to mistreat her.

However, Robbie and Faye were clever enough to shy away from too much publicity. They didn't want too many questions about who 'Epic' was or where she came from. They made sure most of their clients were from the immigrant communities and kept their business mostly underground and by word of mouth.

They didn't let her be with anyone alone. Although they weren't in the room when she did a reading, they watched her on camera from another room. Even when she was outside they weren't far away; she could always feel their eagle eyes on her. Once they'd treated her to a strawberry ice lolly and as she sat on a bench and finished it, she saw a chocolate Labrador on a lead wearing a sparkly hat and bandanna. She smiled at the sight, until she saw her own reflection in a shop mirror and saw the clothes they'd chosen for her to wear. She was their pet— their goose that laid the golden egg, their cash cow.

But deep down she still felt that one day she would be free. The dream from when she was young still came to her every few years. The dream of being powerful, richer than her father, and her sisters trembling in awe. It seemed impossible...but the dream wouldn't die and she lived in quiet isolation under the control of Robbie and Faye for four years until she met a customer who would unsettle them all.

22

———

Something about him scared her. Brooding, dark energy radiated from him.

He was a strong presence, with a lot of dormant power. He couldn't be called a handsome man, he had skin the color of maple with eyes that were too penetrating, and a jaw so angular it looked as if it could cut steel. He was the kind of man who looked like he'd never been young, although she knew he couldn't be more than thirty. He moved in a restless manner that made it clear he didn't want to be there in the dimly lit room, surrounded by velvet drapes that covered the large windows and multi-colored candles placed at various heights around the room. He looked as if he'd just come from a business meeting, wearing dark trousers, a crisp blue shirt, a darker blue tie and black jacket.

Catherine sat across the circular table from him and wondered how anyone had been able to convince him to come. He looked like a man of his own mind and not easily persuaded to do what he didn't want to. Perhaps he was doing this for the sake of his friend's mother; she knew he was a referral. Or he was desperate enough to seek help wherever he could. She dared to meet his eyes again, briefly, and saw the light flare of anger and despair in his dark brown eyes. Yes, this was a man haunted by dreams.

He held out his palms. She blinked at their size. Although he was a tall man, somehow she hadn't expected his hands to be so large.

"What are you doing?" she asked, resisting the urge to lean back, although his large hands somehow called her to touch them.

"Isn't this what you do?" he asked.

Even his voice was dark with a raw gritty quality. "No," she said. "I don't read palms. I read dreams. Just tell me about it."

He sighed, resting his hands on the table with classic American impatience, which matched his tone. "Is there really a need? I don't believe in visions or dreams or..."

"Den why are you here?"

He lifted a brow, bored. "Does it matter? You'll get your payment whether I believe in you or not."

"I want to help you."

"No one can help me." He sighed again. "I'm disappointed."

"Disappointed?"

"I'd always wanted my palms read."

She wasn't sure if he was teasing or not. He didn't look like the kind of man to have a sense of humor. "How about dis? I pretend to read your palm, you tell me your dream."

"I have more than one."

"Tell me de most recent."

"Okay." He held out his hand.

Catherine took a deep breath then pulled his hand towards her, letting it rest in hers, his palm facing up. A shock of awareness coursed through her. His palm was so hot, she'd never felt this before and had to steel herself so that she would not pull away. Perhaps because she hadn't touched someone else in so long she'd become extra sensitive. She swallowed and took a deep breath, then lifted her gaze, ready for him to speak. Her words died on her lips when she found him studying her.

"What?" she asked, her heart starting to race.

He blinked then lowered his gaze. "Nothing."

"Go on," she said trailing a finger along a line in his palm with her other hand.

"I can't—"

"Yes, you can. Take your time."

A shadow of a smile touched his mouth. "Because time is money?"

He was in the mood for a fight and she didn't plan to give him one. She was used to those clients who were skeptical. She'd learned not to be provoked. Her past years had taught her a lot about how to handle people. "Close your eyes and relax and let the memory of the dream come to you."

A shadow of a smile touched his mouth. "Do I have to close my eyes?"

"Yes."

"Even though you're supposed to be reading my palm?"

"I'll read your palm, if you close your eyes."

He held her gaze for a long moment before he nodded and shut them.

Catherine swallowed, relieved to no longer be locked under his scrutinizing gaze, feeling as if she'd been released from a spell. "Now what do you remember?" she asked tracing a line in his palm.

"I'm climbing a white mountain."

"What is it made of?"

"How did you—?"

"Just tell me."

"It's made of sugar."

"Is it a steep climb?"

"Yes, very and I never reach the top."

"How do you know it's sugar?"

"I don't know," he said, shaking his head. "I just do and it's not a cold place. I need to get to the top, but no matter what I try, I can't..."

"You're not meant to reach the top. You're resisting a change dat is about to happen. You will keep climbing mountains until you accept this change. But it is hard for you. You're not a man who adapts to change well. You like permanency."

"Why sugar?"

"I don't know, what does sugar mean to you? It's your own private message."

"Hmm..."

"You don't believe me."

"No, that's what bothers me." He opened his eyes and studied her. "I do."

SHE DIDN'T EXPECT to see him again. Part of her didn't want to, was afraid to. He was such an oddly compelling man. But she'd learned not to trust people. Everyone had a hidden agenda. At twenty she was annoyed that she'd even noticed his looks, or the confident swagger of his gait. He was just another customer—or punter as Robbie liked to call them—that paid the bills and kept her bound to them.

She hadn't told him anything special and imagined him flying back to the States with a novelty tale to tell his friends.

But to her surprise, he returned a week later, this time casually dressed in jeans and a yellow T-shirt that had the word 'Aruba' in red printed across it.

"Why do you wear a mask?" he asked, after she'd interpreted another dream.

"Because I don't wish to be known."

He closed his hand over hers. "Tell me your name."

She froze. "Epic."

"Your real name. You know what my name is."

Yes, she did. Tytus Carter. He'd been insistent in letting her know his name as if it was to mean something to her. She quickly surveyed his size, assessing what she would need to do in case he decided not to let her hand go. "You didn't have to tell me. Most customers prefer not to."

"I wanted you to know." He rested his chin in his other hand and looked at her as if they were at a pub and she was a pretty girl he planned to get to know better. "So tell me yours."

She didn't know what to do, his manner wasn't aggressive so she didn't feel frightened, but she knew his behavior wasn't acceptable. "I don't have a name," Catherine said, careful not to glance at one of the hidden cameras. She knew Robbie and Faye could see her, but there was no sound so they couldn't hear what they were saying.

"You must have a name."

"There's no reason for you to know it," Catherine said, wondering the best way to handle the situation. She'd had other male customers hint at wanting more, but they were more to the point. His interest disappointed her, she'd thought he was different. "Let me go."

He glanced down surprised. "I'm sorry," he said, quickly releasing her hand. "I don't usually act this way. I'm not...I mean..." He sighed, then shook his head. "Is it so strange for me to want to know more about you?"

Yes. "Dere's nothing to know. I am here to serve you, dat is all."

"A slave to my wishes?"

She inwardly winced at his choice of words. "If you like."

"Then I wish—"

"This is not a game—"

"I know," he said, his gritty voice deepening with feeling, his eyes boring into hers. "There's something about you that's...I don't know...amazing."

He sounded sincere, which startled her and kept her spellbound. She knew she should make a sign to the camera to end the session. "There's nothing amazing about me."

"I slept through the night. The first time in weeks because of you."

Yes, he did look brighter than he had last time. *I'm glad.* "I did nothing."

"Do you like doing this?"

I don't have a choice. "Yes."

"I want to see you again."

"You can make an appointment."

"Outside of this," he said, glancing around the room.

"Dat is not possible."

"Why not?"

Robbie came into the room. "Your time is up."

Tytus reached for his wallet. "I don't mind paying for another session."

"We'll schedule it for another time."

He slowly stood, when he did he was nearly a foot taller than Robbie. "What if I want to extend my time now?"

"We have other customers."

"The waiting room is empty. I made sure to be the last one."

"She's tired."

Catherine watched the two men with growing concern. Tytus was going to cause trouble and she couldn't afford that. "Another time," she said.

He shot her a look. "I just want five more minutes." He handed Robbie a wad of notes then pushed him out the door and held it closed.

Catherine shot to her feet. "You shouldn't have done that."

He leaned against the door. "Are you afraid of him?"

Not afraid, just trapped. I have nowhere else to go and I can't trust you yet. I can't trust anyone. There are so many people with nice faces hiding cold hearts. "No, I told you. I like it."

"Just give me a name."

Why did Americans have to be so pushy? "No."

He folded his arms, widening his shoulders and making the room feel small. "Something doesn't feel right about all this."

She took a step towards him then halted. "You should go."

"You're frightened of something."

"I'm frightened of you."

He stared at her for a long moment then lowered his gaze and said, "Fair enough. I'll try to be less frightening next time." He opened the door and Robbie stumbled inside. "Bye," Tytus said before he left.

Faye came into the room. "What did you do?"

"Nothing." It was a silly question considering they monitored and watched every interaction she had with costumers.

"We have to move," Robbie said later than night after they'd eaten leftover Chinese, the cartons still scattered on the table. "We can't have him asking questions." They hastily packed their belongings and ushered her into their car.

Catherine's heart raced. Part of her was glad to leave Tytus's penetrating, keen gaze, but he'd also been a chance of escape. He was American and Robbie and Faye had mentioned that his referral also had a lot of money. But she'd only met him twice and couldn't trust him. He could trick her as Robbie had. If he knew she was helpless, he could use it to his advantage.

She'd never see him again. The one person she'd been allowed to touch in a long time, the one person who'd made her feel human again, if only briefly.

23

"What do you mean they're gone?" Tytus said unable to believe the words of the building manager, a woman who looked like she could hide the Titanic in her cleavage.

She looked at him bored as she sat behind her desk, chewing gum. "Just up and left, they did."

"And they didn't say where they were going?"

"Nope, left a lot of unhappy people, and they always paid on time, pity."

"They didn't say why?"

"It's not my place to ask, love, but they must have had their reasons."

Tytus felt as if someone had punched him. He'd finally met someone interesting, someone who seemed to understand him like no one else and she was gone. He didn't even have a name. Hell, he didn't know anything about her except her eyes and the shape of her fingers and the soothing voice she had. He swore. She was right. He hated change. He hated thinking that he'd never see her again, but he had to realize that was a distinct possibility.

"Just forget her," his friend Arthur said when Tytus returned to the car. He blew into a tissue, his eyes and nose red—from allergies, he liked to say, but Tytus knew his friend was still trying to get over a bad breakup and the sight of garden window boxes always reminded him of his ex-girlfriend. Unfortunately the building had several.

Tytus jumped into the passenger seat and slammed the door. "You think I haven't tried?" If only it could be that easy. From the first day she'd haunted his thoughts and he didn't know why. Female company had never been a problem, but just as she helped him, he felt that he could help her. Help her? Why did he think that? Her eyes spoke volumes, answering questions he hadn't asked. She had an accent he couldn't quite place. Not that he had much chance to listen. She didn't talk more than she needed to. Most women he knew could hold a conversation on their own. He didn't think she was happy. He didn't feel she was safe, but he didn't know why. Maybe that was her con. But the interpreted dreams were real. Or did he just want them to be real? It was a stupid infatuation. He'd allowed himself to be suckered.

"I need a drink."

"That's the ticket, mate. You're paying, right?"

Tytus put on his seatbelt. "Don't I always?"

"Just making sure," Arthur said putting the car into gear.

Tytus rested his head back and closed his eyes. He'd forget her with a nice pint or two.

A MONTH PASSED before Catherine felt she could forget the

touch of Tytus's hand and his insistent questions. It was two months before she pushed his face from her mind. After four months Catherine felt confident that a customer would never rattle her again as much as Tytus Carter had, but that was before her past walked into the room.

24

The young black woman in the expensive suede jacket and pixie hair cut offered her a shy smile as she sat. She spoke, but Catherine could hardly hear her over the sound of her pounding heart. She had the advantage because she wore a mask, but it didn't matter. She wasn't sure she could get over the shock of seeing Marie again.

What was she doing in England? What was she doing here in this nondescript side street building? Did anyone else know she was here? Catherine didn't know if she should rip off her mask and say, 'It's me!' and embrace her or stay still and wait to hear what she had to say. She didn't want to put her stepsister in danger since she knew they were being monitored. If Robbie and Faye saw Marie as a threat, as a way they may lose their cash cow, there was no way to know how they would react.

Catherine swallowed, begging her heart to return to normal. She would proceed with caution. She would hear what Marie had to say and then find a way to give her a message or a signal. Once she made her decision, she took the time to give her stepsister a more assessing look. Marie didn't appear as Catherine would have imagined her. Although she was only twenty-five, she had dark circles under her eyes and a miserable countenance. The faint smell of smoke and liquor clung to her coat. There were so many things Catherine wanted to ask her, but she would wait. Captivity had taught her to be patient.

"How can I help?" Catherine asked, hardly recognizing her own voice when she finally managed to speak.

"I don't know what I'm doing here," Marie said, flashing another shy grin. "I haven't believed in this stuff since..."

"Since..." Catherine repeated, urging her to continue when she fell silent.

She shook her head. "A long time ago."

"You're not British."

"No."

"Are you here on holiday?" *With your family* she wanted to add, but knew she'd already asked enough questions.

"An internship, but I have been to England before. My step-father had a place in the city."

"Had?"

"Yes, sadly he passed away."

Catherine's heart constricted with such force she feared it would stop. She couldn't breathe as misery so acute gripped her, causing her to think she was going to suffocate and pass out right there. The world grew hazy—expanding and constricting as if she'd inhaled a drug. Daddy was dead? Dead? She'd never see him again?

She fought back tears. "I'm sorry," she said in a near whisper, afraid if she spoke any louder Marie would hear the pain in her voice.

"Thank you." Marie let her gaze drop, giving Catherine a moment to wipe an escaped tear. "It was so sudden and at night I dream and see myself digging his grave. But I know what that dream means, it's just a guilty conscience."

Sister, I'm here! Just wait a little longer. "You mustn't blame yourself—"

Marie looked at her sharply, curious. "What do you mean?"

Catherine blinked recognizing her blunder. She'd revealed too much. "That your father's death...it couldn't be helped," she said quickly recovering herself. *Oh Daddy, I've missed you so much. Are you really gone? Why couldn't you wait for me?*

"I'm not Catholic and there's no one for me to confess to," Marie said. "But I have to get it off my chest to someone."

Catherine nodded. "Go on."

"I'm a fraud. I help people all day, people pay me and I can't help myself. My life is shit."

Catherine paused surprised by the coarse language and bitterness in Marie's tone. "I don't believe you."

"You should because it's true."

"You are pretty, successful and—"

"I haven't spoken to my family in over a year, I haven't seen them in two. I can't stand the lies."

"Lies?"

She nodded, pushing her glasses up. "Yeah."

"What is your family like?

"What family?" she said with a cynical sniff. "I've fooled myself into believing I had one for years. I did have one once, but I threw it away and I'll never forgive myself."

"How did you...what happened?"

"I can't tell you."

"Why?"

"I promised not to tell. It's our secret and it haunts my dreams."

But you came to me, you want to speak you just said so. "I'm good with dreams."

Marie couldn't help a smile. "I know. Maybe it's my conscience that led me here. When I heard about you, I thought what the hell." Her smile fell. "She was also good at this."

"Who?" Catherine asked. She barely managed the word, her heart pounding in her chest so hard she felt breathless.

"My stepsister."

"Oh, you said was...what happened to her?"

Marie closed her eyes and rubbed her head. "This is so hard. I can't tell you, I can't tell anyone because I promised but..."

"Because of what may happen to you?"

"Nothing will happen. There's no proof, nobody can touch us, we got away with it and it happened thousands of miles away."

Catherine paused at the unexpected words. *Nobody can touch us? We got away with it? That didn't make sense.* "What?"

"Years ago I lost a sister."

"She died?"

"She may be dead, but I don't know that."

"What happened to her?"

Marie bit her lip and shook her head. "I'm so ashamed at my cowardice that I let it happen."

"I'm sure it was something you couldn't have stopped."

"I could have. I could have said something, done something to stop them, but I went along with the plan."

"Plan?"

"Yes. My sisters and I were so full of jealousy that we sold our sister into slavery."

Catherine stared at her tongue-tied and stunned. *Sold!?!* She'd been sold? She hadn't been kidnapped for ransom? She hadn't been taken by strangers? She'd been sold like an animal? Her sisters were the reason for her years of captivity? They'd been the reason for her days of hell, the beatings, the hunger, the cold, the loneliness? They'd been the reason she'd never see her father again? Why? Why? Why?

"The moment it happened I regretted it," Marie continued, unaware of Catherine's eerie silence. "Especially when I saw what it did to Mom. She nearly lost our brother when she had him premature and hasn't been the same. Fortunately, he lived and she puts her heart into his well-being."

Catherine didn't know what to say. Her younger brother had barely survived? Did her mother even think about her anymore now that she had him? Did she know what her sisters had done?

"What's his name?" she asked before she could stop herself.

"Who?"

"Your brother?"

"Aaron."

She gripped her hands underneath the table. "And why did you hate your sister so much?" she asked in a cool tone.

"It all seems so shallow now...but I feared she was taking my mother's love away, Lorna thought she was trying to ruin her relationship with Greg, her boyfriend, and Joscelyn...she just didn't like her, I guess. I never understood her reason."

"And how are dey now?" *Are they as miserable and guilt-ridden as you?*

"They are doing amazing. Lorna's happily married and expecting her second child and Joscelyn was just featured in a major medical journal and is doing well, plus she helps our mother run a family business."

"Family business?"

"Yes, I don't mean to brag, but my stepfather was a genius in that department and his skin care company continues to rake in millions," she said with an indelicate hiccup.

Marie had clearly had more than she should have to drink, although she carried herself well, otherwise her tongue wouldn't be so loose, revealing such information. "She just bought her second home," Marie continued. Catherine didn't know who she was talking about and didn't care anymore. Marie's words felt like acid being poured into her ears. This was not what she wanted to hear. She wanted to hear that after her father's death they'd become destitute and had to beg on the streets. Instead, her father's death had provided them with a comfortable living and they'd gone on to live well—forgetting her.

"And what do you do?"

"Besides hate myself every day?" Marie said with a cynical laugh.

"Yes...if you were ever to see her again what would you say?"

"That I was sorry, that every day guilt has been my prison. That I didn't realize how much I'd miss her. I'd thought she was a nuisance, but then I liked the questions she used to ask me, the sound of her practicing at the piano, she was a natural. I remember how she used to make our parents laugh. Our mother has died a thousand deaths every year hoping that somehow she would come home. I wished we'd never given her hope and just told her that she was dead."

"What was your sister's name?"

"I can't say."

Yes, you can. "You should say it, you owe her dat much."

"Catherine, poor little Catherine."

"You pity yourself more than her."

Tears welled in her eyes. "No, that's not true. I hate myself every day."

She believed her, although she didn't want to. Her sister's sadness was real and her tears tugged on Catherine's heart. She wanted to shake her, she wanted to scream at her and she wanted to hate her, but she couldn't. Marie hated herself enough for both of them, but that wasn't enough.

Catherine lifted her hand and slapped her with such force that Marie had to grab the table to keep from falling out of her chair; her glasses clattered to the ground.

Marie blinked and stared at her, shocked. Before she could

speak, Faye rushed into the room, but Catherine held up a hand, giving her a signal that everything was fine. Faye cast a nervous glance at Marie, then closed the door.

"Wh—what was that?" Marie asked, rubbing her cheek.

"Punishment." Catherine came from around the table and picked up Marie's glasses from off the ground. She handed them to her. "Now go and live a good life."

Marie shoved the glasses back onto her face. "You think it's that easy?"

Catherine looked into the grief-stricken gaze of her stepsister, compassion and rage warring within her. *Your pity serves no one but yourself. You're throwing your life away. Remember your poor little Catherine in the eyes of every girl whose life needs to be changed. And use your fancy, expensive education to help them. Say her name to remind yourself that you cannot change your past, but you can alter your future.* She wanted to tell her all that and more, instead she said, "No," then watched her walk out of her life, only later realizing that she'd never heard Marie's dream.

25

"Did you hear what Marie's up to?"

"What?" Lorna said shifting in her seat. Although she was only seven months into her pregnancy, she was already starting to feel uncomfortable and her sister's fashionable chaise lounge seats made her back hurt, but she didn't want to say anything. She sipped her tea and nibbled on a tiny, triangle-shaped cucumber sandwich, although she felt ravenous and could have eaten her way through a large pizza, breadsticks, chicken wings, and a salad with room left over for dessert.

"Did you hear about Marie?" Joscelyn repeated.

Lorna set her tea cup down on the coffee table and finished her sandwich. She eyed another seat wondering if it would offer more comfort. "No."

"She's gone off the deep end."

She shifted again, discreetly rubbing her back. "How?"

"She decided to leave the cushy job Mom's connection got her and left it to work with some non-profit to help runaways."

Lorna grabbed a pillow to put behind her. It didn't help. "Really?"

"But not just any runaways."

Lorna removed the pillow and shifted again. "I see."

"What is wrong with you?" Joscelyn snapped. "You're hardly listening to a word I've said."

"I am listening," Lorna said, itching to move again when she felt a pinch in her side, but not daring to.

"Then why can't you keep still?"

"It's just this chair," she finally admitted. She didn't like criticizing her sister's stylish apartment, but she had no other excuse.

"There's nothing wrong with the chair. You've just gotten fat."

Lorna gritted her teeth. Her weight was a sore spot and Joscelyn knew it. Unlike their mother, who had been able to have four children and bounce back to her trim figure after each child, Lorna hadn't shed most of the baby weight from her daughter and now carried more weight than she wanted to into her second pregnancy. Fortunately, her doctor was pleased with her and Greg still loved her and that was all that mattered. "It's baby weight. But that's not something you would know about," she said, letting her gaze skim across an apartment that lacked any sign of a man or child.

Joscelyn nodded, undisturbed by her sister's words. She crossed her legs, something her sister couldn't do with ease, and tightened the belt on her form-fitting wrap dress, emphasizing her slender figure. "There's still time and I've had plenty of offers. Successful women aren't as frightening to men as people like to think."

Lorna reached for a cookie then thought better of it. "You can be such a bitch sometimes." She stood and sat in the other chair, which offered her a bit more comfort, but that didn't matter anymore when she felt like a fat, pale imitation of her glamorous older sister.

Joscelyn laughed. "Only sometimes?"

Lorna glanced up at a large abstract painting, ready to go home. At home she was the ruler and second to none. In her home she delighted in the sound of her daughter's laughter as she played with her nanny, the smell of her husband's cologne when he bent down to give her a kiss. She absently smiled as she thought of him. Her dear Greg. They had built the perfect life together.

"I'm sorry," Joscelyn said with a sigh. "You look great. You always do."

Lorna didn't quite believe her apology, but no longer cared. She liked hearing the words anyway. She touched the emerald earrings Greg had purchased for her, then smoothed down the ends of her shoulder-length hair. Her hair stylist had complimented her on her beautiful skin. "Thank you. Now what were you saying about Marie?"

"She's helping runaways involved in the sex trade."

Lorna reached for the cookie, she was hungry. "You can't be serious."

"I am. Mom's having a fit. But she's determined."

Lorna shrugged, quickly finishing the cookie before grabbing another. "If that's what she wants, so what? She'd always wanted to see the world."

"She's doing it here."

"Here?"

"Yes, that's what Mom told me. It seems some bleeding heart doctor at the clinic told Marie about the position. She said that Marie went on about how DC is one of the top destinations in the world for the illegal sex trade. In other words—slavery."

For a moment Lorna felt sick as she finally understood why

her sister had wanted to talk to her and the importance of Marie's change of careers. "Think she'll say anything?"

"I'm not sure. One of us should talk to her to make sure."

Lorna sat forward, resting a protective hand on her stomach. She had to keep her family safe. "But she won't talk to us," she said, feeling on edge as she thought about all that was at stake. "She hasn't been the same since…"

Joscelyn saw the look of panic on her sister's face and offered her a reassuring smile. "I didn't want to worry you, I just thought you should know."

Lorna took a deep breath. How could she not worry?

"Even if she speaks, there's no proof. It's her word against ours."

"Right," Lorna said eager to believe her. "And it's been so long."

"Exactly. I may be putting too much thought into this. She's always had a heart full of mush, maybe it would have happened anyway."

Lorna nodded.

"But don't worry, I'll stop by and talk to her, just to make sure she realizes that we're not the only ones with too much to lose."

26

____

She had no home to go to.

Catherine sat on her bed with her knees drawn up, tears spilling down her cheeks, but she made sure not to make a sound in case Robbie or Faye came to check in on her. It wouldn't be out of concern. And she didn't want to see their flaccid, insincere faces.

All these years she'd survived in order to see her family again. But she had no family. There were no loving arms to greet her. Her sisters had hated her so much that they'd lured her into the van to be taken away? They'd sold her into slavery?

Her sisters had condemned her to this soulless, horrible life. And now her father was dead. And her stepmother had a son she could pour all her love on. Her return wouldn't mean anything. Lorna and Joscelyn were doing well, better than well. They were thriving. They had education and families of their own. No one missed her. Marie spoke out of guilt and remorse, but had she ever loved her?

She had nothing to live for now. She'd worked with Robbie and Faye with the hope that she'd convince them to pay her and then she'd escape, but now she knew having a plan didn't matter. There was no place to go to. No place to run. She truly was a nobody. Nothing.

Which meant she had nothing to lose. That thought gave her a renewed strength. She wouldn't die like this. She would escape at all costs now. There was nothing to fear anymore. She didn't care that she didn't have any papers, that she had no one to trust, no money. Nothing mattered anymore except leaving this nonexistence behind.

Late that night, she gathered her few belongings and cautiously peeked into the hallway to make sure Robbie and Faye were nowhere about.

Unlike the Salako house, she knew the front door wasn't double locked. She was free to go. They knew she was dependent on them, so never feared her escape. She went to Faye's handbag and took whatever money she found—not much. After the first year they'd become lax about guarding her, so lax that she was able to walk out the front door without any trouble. No chains locked the door and when she opened it, no alarm bells sounded, although she moved slowly just in case she triggered something. When she realized nothing would happen—no loud noise would suddenly wake them up, no one would come out of the shadows and grab her—she closed the door and walked down the quiet hall into a new life.

But she didn't know what to do with that life. Her life had always belonged to someone else. She didn't know what decisions to make, what choices to take. She found her way to a bus depot and bought a ticket, asking the woman behind the booth how far the money she had would take her. The woman looked at the meager amount and gave her the name of a place she'd never heard of, but it didn't matter. Catherine just wanted to be away.

And an hour later, 'away' ended up being in the middle of nowhere. She saw no buildings or people. She'd debarked in the middle of a cross-section and all she saw were fields and the darkening sky above.

She started to walk, not knowing where she was going or caring. It started to rain and a chill wind plastered her wet clothes to her body, the muddy road soaking through her shoes. She silently hoped to catch a cold and die. As the miles stretched out behind her and in front of her, she remembered the last time she'd thought of death after Mrs. Salako had beaten her and she'd been in that cold room. But back then her anger had kept her warm. She didn't have that now. Just the cold chill of despair. She walked from the road and wandered into one of the fields. Soon she found a place where no one would see her then she lay on the ground, closed her eyes and waited for death.

27

———

Marie closed the door of the non-profit where she worked, pulling the door tight against the autumn wind that was sweeping through the city.

"Want to grab something to eat?" her colleague and roommate, Clara Park, suggested.

"That sounds good." She walked to her car in the nearly empty parking lot, then stopped when she saw her sister, Joscelyn, leaning against it. She took a deep breath, then approached her. "I have nothing to say to you."

Joscelyn didn't move, blocking Marie from unlocking the door to a car that had been manufactured in the previous century. "You're better than this. You could make so much more—"

"Move."

"You're punishing yourself for no reason."

"I like what I do. There's more to life than money."

Joscelyn smiled amused. "Who's been lying to you?"

"It's the truth," Clara said.

"I see you still have your Gay Best Friend. Is that still in fashion? I haven't been keeping up."

"She's not gay."

"She?" Joscelyn looked at Clara surprised. "You're a girl, I'm sorry I didn't know," she said casting a look over Clara's boy-like haircut, tie and trousers.

Clara folded her arms, used to the insult. She'd been mistaken for a man before, but didn't care because she found the attire more comfortable. "There's a difference between sexual orientation and gender identification. You—"

Joscelyn turned her attention back to Marie. "Why is she talking to me as if I would care?"

"What do you want?" Marie asked losing patience.

"It's been so long since we've spoken. I just wanted to make sure my little sister wasn't having a nervous breakdown or something."

Marie adjusted her glasses. "Because I want to do something worthwhile with my life and help people?"

Joscelyn looked at the old Toyota and small building with pity. "You can help a lot more people without taking a vow of poverty. Although we both know you're really not because of the money Emery left you—"

Marie tossed Clara the car keys, then motioned Joscelyn over to the side. "What do you really want? Are you worried I'll say something?"

"Lorna's mentioned it."

"I won't, so you can relax. I like it here. I wouldn't do anything to jeopardize that."

Joscelyn studied her for a long moment. Her sister was somehow better looking than she had been in the past. Her skin brighter and her eyes not as sad. She wasn't sure if that was good or bad. "There's something different about you. What happened in England?"

"I had an awakening."

Joscelyn stroked Marie's chin with her forefinger as if she were a kitten. "That's good."

"You should try it."

"That's cute," Joscelyn said, cupping her sister's chin. "So nice to see you finally have a spine." She tightened her grip until Marie winced. "Just don't forget that I can break it."

28

"**M**y goodness she's chilled to the bone, but I think she's coming 'round."

Voices? Why was she hearing voices?

"That's a good girl, Evelyn. Come on."

Evelyn? Who was Evelyn?

"What were you doing out there?"

Catherine slowly opened her eyes and saw a pale wrinkled face, wispy brown hair and sharp green eyes. "You gave us a fright, you did," the woman said, her voice high like a young girl's.

"What were you thinking, mucking about out there with a storm coming?" another more serious voice chided her.

Catherine shifted her gaze to the other woman, a lady with silver streaks in her black hair, dark brown eyes and olive toned skin.

"Evelyn, you must—"

"That's not Evelyn," the darker woman said. "I just spoke to her."

"You did?"

"Yes, she rang while you were looking after this one. Didn't you hear the phone?"

"No, my hearing isn't what it once was."

"Ah well, never mind."

"Are you sure she's not Evelyn?"

"I just told you—"

The high voice shook her head. "I know, it's just she looks so much like her."

"It's said everyone has a twin somewhere."

"You think she's Evelyn's twin?"

"No, it's just a saying. I...oh never mind." A thick, rough hand touched Catherine's shoulder. "What's your name, luv?"

Name? Did it matter anymore? But despite her serious voice, and rough hands there was tenderness in her tone and Catherine didn't know how to respond.

"She's just come 'round, don't pepper her with too many questions," High Voice said.

"We'll let you rest some more or would you like something to eat?"

Catherine shook her head and closed her eyes again.

She woke up to warmth. Catherine felt the warmth of the room, the warm smell of something cooking on the stove, the warmth of the quilted blanket on top of her and the warmth of... she paused when she looked around the room. It didn't suit the image of the two women. The walls were grey and one dark red with posters of women in bikinis and lingerie, another poster with a group of men and the name Wu-Tang Clan and another said NWA.

"Oh good you're awake," High Voice said, bustling into the

room. "You're looking much better than before. You looked like a right dog's dinner when we first found you."

Catherine sat up. "Thank you," she said, unable to avoid looking at another provocative image.

The woman noticed Catherine's glance. "This is my boy's room. I haven't had a chance to tidy it up yet. He's actually at uni, can you believe it?" She threw up a hand. "God the noise that used to come from this room. 'You call that singing?' my man used to say when he was still alive, God bless him and they'd get at it, but now with him gone the house feels too quiet."

Catherine nodded. She wasn't used to people talking to her. She didn't know the last conversation she'd had. She was usually behind a mask and offering help.

"Well, with you better, why don't you freshen up? Evelyn brought over a change of clothes, I apologize but what you had on isn't very suitable out here. Too flimsy."

Catherine took a shower. They'd cared for her. It was the first time in years someone had cared about her. Wondered about her health, talked to her like a person. Tears spilled down her cheeks as she dressed.

But when she joined them in the kitchen, none of her sorrow could be detected. She sat keeping her gaze lowered. Even when they presented her with a potatoes and leek casserole.

"I have nothing to give," she said. "But I work hard."

"Never mind that now," Dark Hair said with a wave of her hand. "We're just glad you're all right."

"Where were you heading?"

Catherine shook her head. "Nowhere."

"Then where are you from?"

"Nowhere."

"That can't be right, dear. Everyone's from somewhere."

"And to be honest there aren't many of the likes of you out here," Dark Hair said.

"Orla," High Voice said embarrassed.

"I'm being honest. You can count them on your hand. I bet your boy's got more of them on those posters in his room than we have in the entire village."

"But you're very welcome here," High Voice said with a smile.

"I didn't say she wasn't welcome, just that she's—"

"My name is Grace," she cut in, sending her companion a look. "And this is my sister Orla."

"Same father, different mothers in case you were wondering."

"I doubt she was wondering that."

Orla shrugged. "People do, might as well tell them."

"And what's your name, dear?" Grace said eager to change the subject.

"Catherine." She sipped her tea. She had no plan, no place to go if they could give her a place maybe that would give her time to figure things out. "I'm a good worker. I can clean your house."

"Oh, we already have help," Orla said.

"But," Grace added seeing the look of dejection on Catherine's face. "We can always use more."

"We can't pay you—"

"But you'll have room and board."

That was something. That's all she needed. "Thank you," Catherine said.

"Don't you have any family?" Grace asked.

"No."

"You still look worn out, go and have a lie down and we'll talk more later."

Catherine nodded and left the room, but as she climbed the stairs she heard Orla say, "Are you sure this is wise?"

"She needs help."

"She could be trouble."

"With a sweet face like that? Don't be stupid."

"Don't judge a book by its title."

"Cover. And I'm hardly doing that. I selected Evelyn, didn't I? And didn't she work out well?"

"You're right, but it's going to be strange to have two of them, don't you think?"

"The likeliness is striking. Let's hope they get along."

29

———

Evelyn Williams could have been her twin. Catherine could see why Grace and Orla had initially been confused. She looked as if she and their housekeeper could have been sisters. But that's where the similarities ended. Evelyn was more refined, carried herself as if she were mistress of the house and spoke flawlessly. She barely gave Catherine a glance and could be brusque and impatient when Catherine didn't do things to her exact specifications, but Catherine never took offense.

She'd learned about the other woman's life in bits and pieces from Grace and Orla. She'd learned that she was not much older than her and had once been married to a wealthy businessman who'd emigrated from Jamaica, but who had lost his fortune in a bad investment and his business soon went bankrupt. He died soon after. She had no one else and he had no family since he had no siblings and both parents were dead. She'd had an elderly aunt who'd raised her and passed on so she needed a way to make a living and offered her services as a maid.

Catherine learned to stay out of Evelyn's way as she admired her from a distance. She was too grateful to have a place to stay and work to do to be bothered by Evelyn's curt manners.

One early morning that changed. She'd overslept by five minutes and hurried to change, afraid that she'd meet Evelyn's wrath. She was pulling on her blouse when she heard a gasp behind her.

"Dear God what happened to you?"

Catherine spun around and saw the horror in Evelyn's face as she stood in the doorway. Catherine wasn't surprised to see her. She'd gotten into the habit of leaving the door of any room partially open. She didn't like locked rooms or closed doors and she'd never been granted privacy so didn't consider it. But for the first time she wished she had. She'd forgotten how ugly her body was—how it was marred by scars. She wanted to hide like an animal. The animal she'd been. The one kept in a cage, the one beaten, the one fed scraps and worked from morning until night.

Evelyn looked suddenly contrite. "I'm sorry I didn't mean." She held up another set of jeans and a pink shirt. "I thought you might want these."

Catherine nodded and took the items, setting them on the bed.

"Who did this to you?" She lowered her voice. "Are you running from a man? A husband or boyfriend?"

Catherine bit her lip and shook her head. For so long there had been no one to tell her story to, but now she had a chance and she wanted to. Needed to. So in a monotone voice, distancing herself from the ten year old she'd been in Lagos, the sixteen year old in the Salako household, the twenty year old who'd become Epic, she told Evelyn everything until she came to the present moment. Halfway through the story Evelyn had collapsed onto the bed as if her legs had given way, by the end tears had stained her cheeks.

She waited for Evelyn to say, 'I don't believe you' or 'That couldn't have happened', instead she stood up and hugged her and said, "I thought you may be using the kindness of the sisters, that's why I was a bit short with you. I had no idea you'd suffered so much. You poor thing." That's when the waterworks burst forth and Catherine sobbed and Evelyn cried with her and that's how Orla and Grace found them.

"What's going on here?"

"Can I tell them?" Evelyn whispered.

Catherine nodded.

So Evelyn told the sister's a condensed version of Catherine's story and soon they were in tears as well.

"You don't worry about anything like that," Grace said, wiping her eyes with a tissue as she sat on the bed. "We don't have any of that here."

Catherine nodded. She'd learned not to argue.

"But we still have to be careful," Orla said. "She's got no papers. She's not here legally."

"But we can't turn her out. She has no place to go."

"But aren't we just as bad as them, keeping her here when it isn't right and above board?"

Catherine pressed her hands together, understanding Orla's fears, but not wanting to be tossed out. "Please, mah." She rubbed her hands together. "I'll cause no trouble."

"Quiet, child," Grace said with a soft smile. "We know that."

Orla frowned. "It's not you we're worried about, it's—"

"Who's going to ask questions?" her sister cut in.

"Someone might."

"For now she'll just be a cousin of mine," Evelyn said. "No one will question that."

Two WEEKS LATER, Evelyn caught Catherine leaving the living room after dusting and stopped her.

"You must stop walking like that."

Catherine blinked. "Like what?"

"With your head down and stooped as if you don't want to be noticed."

"I don't wan' notice."

"Want," Evelyn said putting emphasis on the 't'. "And yes you do. You're a pretty girl. How you present yourself is essential. It tells people how to treat you. You're no longer in bondage. Come on. Chin up, back straight. Yes, now walk. Good, keep looking ahead. Eyes focused on the horizon. Good."

It was scary at first. Many times Catherine expected to get scolded by Grace or Orla for her new posture, but instead they'd inadvertently call her Evelyn and ask her to make their favorite pudding.

On their day off, Evelyn took Catherine to a pub in town and said, "Your speech is very different. You slide into a strange pidgin English and sometimes American expressions and British ones. When did you start doing that?" Before Catherine could reply, Evelyn shook her head. "Never mind. It doesn't matter. How you speak now will limit you. It's a mishmash of too many things. I'm not a snob, but the broken English just won't do. You must speak slowly, with purpose. Expect people to wait to hear what you have to say, that's how you control the conversation."

"Control? Why?"

"Why would you want to control a conversation?"

Catherine nodded.

"So that people don't waste your time and you're able to get your point across."

"Statements such as 'Is no good here' or 'sit down' becomes 'I don't like it here.' 'Please take a seat.' Now you try."

"Idon'tlikeithere, pleasetakeaseat."

Evelyn waved her hand. "No, that sounds like gibberish. You're talking too fast."

"People no listen, unless..." *I'm reading their dreams.*

"Unless what?"

"Nothing."

"They will. And you can't say 'dat' or 'dis', you must put your tongue between your teeth and say 'this' and 'that'. Round your vowels and pound your consonants. You must have more confidence in yourself."

"Dere's no point. I'm nobody."

"There," she corrected. "And how can you be a nobody, when you're somebody to me? To Miss Grace and Orla? If you want a better life than this, then you must study and work hard."

Catherine shrugged. She didn't believe her, but she wouldn't argue.

"There aren't many of us here. I think it was fate that brought us together. I'm not going to be here forever."

"You're leaving?" Catherine asked afraid that she'd soon lose her new friend.

"Not yet, but hopefully one day," Evelyn said with a mysterious grin, but didn't expand. "When I'm gone you need to be able to handle yourself."

Catherine nodded.

"Will you do as I say?"

Catherine nodded again.

"Don't just nod. Say it. Say yes."

"Yes."

"Good. Next time I want you to say it a little louder. Don't be afraid of the sound of your voice."

That night, Catherine went to sleep with a happy heart. She had someone who believed in her. A friend. She hadn't had a friend in so long...

And for the next year she did all that Evelyn told her to.

Studying gave her a purpose, something to do, something to aspire to. She didn't see all that Evelyn was determined to teach her doing her much good, but it made the days and weeks melt away. She read stories she'd never heard before. Children's stories she'd missed and then novels, and books on science and math, computers, music, history.

"What's the point of learning all that stuff?" Orla had asked her one day when she saw one of Catherine's books on Greek civilization left on the kitchen table. "You'll never use it."

Catherine just shrugged, but when she told Evelyn about Orla's comment, she said, "Pay her no mind. She has a good heart, but she doesn't see you the way I do. Or how you should see yourself. Her nephew's off to uni studying heaven knows what and no one will bat an eye, but someone like us picking up the Greeks, now that's a laugh, isn't it? We're just hired help. I say let them laugh. You must depend on yourself. I learned too late not to depend on a man for all my needs. I should have known a lot more than I did. Knowledge is important, but growth even more so. The mind must be used like a muscle or it goes limp. That's why most people's lives are unhappy. They let others do the thinking for them."

Catherine nearly wept at her words. Her mind. She had her mind, something that had been with her all this time. It was powerful, it was a tool, and it was something that could get her out of this one day. Someday. Evelyn was giving her permission to think again, to feel again. To be her own woman. Her sisters had tried to see her destroyed. She would disappoint them, but before seeing them again she had to plan. *My name is Catherine Ojo* she wanted to say, but kept her mouth shut. The time would come, but not yet. Not now. Now she still had a lot to learn. She wasn't clever like Marie and had to sometimes read things twice and take notes before grasping, but she did.

There was so much about life she didn't know. Her schooling

had stopped at the fifth grade and there was so much about technology she wasn't aware of. She learned about a new digital way to listen to music, how phones now acted like computers, and Evelyn patiently taught her,

extending her lessons from book learning to daily life.

"You dress for where you want to go, not where you are," Evelyn said when she'd taken Catherine shopping for a new outfit. "My aunty taught me that."

And Catherine soaked it all in for the following two years until Evelyn no longer had to correct her grammar. And although Catherine could never help them win quiz night at the local pub, she was able to manage the household expenses and also helped Grace make side money selling her delicious tea cakes and showed Orla how to cut her interest rate on a credit card. She'd perfected her new manner so well that soon the sisters were mistaking her for Evelyn even more.

"Oh there you are, Evelyn," Orla said from the couch when she saw Catherine walking past. She lay on her back with a towel across her forehead. "Could you go into town and get me something? I've got a headache."

"But I'm not—"

"I know you're busy, but I need it." She handed her the money, then closed her eyes. Catherine sighed. It wasn't any use telling her she wasn't Evelyn. She could do the errand anyway. But when she went into town, she was surprised by how many people mistook her for her friend and she didn't try to correct them. She accepted the smiles and waves with aplomb, perfecting her friend's gestures and voice. People addressed her with respect even though she was in service.

When she returned and handed Orla the pain medicine, she was actually shocked that no one had caught on to her little deception. When she told Evelyn later that day while in Evelyn's small kitchen, her friend laughed.

"They really thought you were me?" she said.

"Yes."

"Well, I can't blame them. We do look alike." The kettle boiled just as they heard the mail carrier slide the mail through the letterbox. "Go get that for me," she said, grabbing two cups from the cupboard.

Catherine got the mail and handed it to her.

Evelyn sorted through it then stopped and opened one letter. She read it, then paled.

"What is it?" Catherine asked.

She touched her mouth with trembling fingers. "I almost can't believe it."

"What?"

She fell into the chair. "I've found my family. But my grand-father's died. I knew he was sick, but I'd hoped to get a chance to meet him. I'd wanted to know him better. It says he's left me money in a trust. I don't know anything about money. Good manners and decorum sure, but trusts and annuities and equity are lost on me. "

"I can explain anything you need."

"Yes, you're clever with numbers, aren't you?"

Catherine flashed a quick smile, not feeling particular clever at all. She had learned that Evelyn had been raised by her aunt when her mother passed and that she'd never known her father or his side of the family, but Catherine hadn't known her friend had been searching for them.

"I got notice that someone was looking for me online. I'd signed up to a website for people looking for their birth parents. I didn't tell you because...I didn't want to be disappointed. I've been so before. I tentatively believed that I could be his daughter, but now this has confirmed it. The DNA results says there's a match."

Catherine hugged her. "I'm so happy for you." She sat back

down. "What happens now?"

"He and his wife want me to live with them. They live in the States, Virginia I think, and...my father's very well off." She hurried and got some pictures. "That's him and his wife. They didn't have any children so they really want to get to know me."

Catherine plastered on a smile. She'd be sad to see her friend go; she was a bright spot in her life. She envied her having a family that wanted her. "I'll miss you."

"Why?" She grinned. "Through emails I've told them about you...no, not everything," she quickly said when Catherine looked worried. "Just that you're a dear friend of mine. I plan to take you with me." She hesitated. "That's if you want to go."

"Of course, but I cannot go."

"Why not?"

"I don't have any legal papers."

"I already thought of your situation and spoke to Grace. She contacted her son for help and he told her of a friend who works with asylum seekers and could provide you with the necessary papers—for a price. I know with one word I can get my father to pay since I want to have you as my companion and plan to have him sponsor you."

"This is incredible."

"No, it's an opportunity. Are you ready to seize it?"

Catherine bit her lip. She'd return to America illegally, but she was willing to take the chance. "Yes."

"Then it's all settled. We're going to America!"

She could hardly sleep. She would be going to America again. And not just anywhere in America, but Virginia. A state right next to Maryland. Home was within reach. But then again, home didn't exist anymore. America wouldn't be what she'd remembered, and she wouldn't see her mother again or meet her half-brother, but it was still a chance to get closer to planning the best way to get back at her sisters. That desire burned brighter in her heart every day.

It was hard for Grace and Orla to lose them both, but to make it up to them, Evelyn treated them to a nice meal at a cozy restaurant hours before they were to leave for the airport. At the end of the meal, Catherine went to the toilet, not knowing how long the drive would be to the airport. When she returned to the table, she found it empty then spotted Evelyn's wallet on the seat. She'd clearly forgotten to return it to her handbag after paying. Catherine slipped it into her coat pocket, then met the three women in the front of the restaurant where Grace and Orla offered them a teary farewell, telling them to keep in touch. Catherine hugged both women, unable to tell them how dear they would be to her always. One day she hoped to repay their kindness.

Moments later, Evelyn and Catherine waved to them from the taxi as it took them to the airport and a brand new life.

30

———

Roberta Holloway hated the world and didn't care who knew it. She hated that she'd gotten fired from her job. She'd done her best, right? Could she help it that she'd missed a bunch of days? It's not like she did it on purpose, life just happened. Going to a doctor's visit was important, right? But noooo, her ass of a boss just wanted to get rid of her. And her parents kept at her because they thought she was shiftless. But she wasn't. She knew what she wanted, it was just hard to get it. Things weren't as easy for her as it had been for them.

Was it wrong to ask for their help? She said she'd pay them back. Okay, sure she hadn't been able to for the last several loans, but that wasn't her fault. Bloody hell. It wasn't easy to find a place or get a job and now she'd lost another one. But that wasn't the worse. Lance was a true git and she still loved him.

Roberta stumbled from the pub and got into her car. Sod the world. Why was it against her? She'd been a good student. One of the brightest and all her hard work had come to naught.

She pressed her foot hard on the gas, imagining it was Lance's slut of a fling—Veronica. Did he really expect her to believe there wasn't something going on between them? That cow. She knew she'd had eyes for her man, but she didn't think she'd go for it in the flat they shared.

Roberta drove blinded by rage, blinded by pain, blinded by alcohol. When she crashed into the taxi when she sped through a red light, she was blinded by the impact of the crash.

31

They were calling her Evelyn again. She needed to correct them, but her mouth wouldn't move. Catherine opened her eyes and saw a sterile white ceiling. What had happened? She remembered waving goodbye, laughing with Evelyn in the taxi as they made plans. She thought of how it would feel to be on an airplane again, to finally fly away from all her misery and then...and then...

Why couldn't she remember? What was she doing here? Why were they calling her Evelyn?

"Yes, yes, she's opening her eyes," someone said then the voice faded away.

Soon later, or was it days later, she wasn't sure, she heard someone talking to her softly, saw hazy figures in white before they drifted away as well.

When she opened her eyes again, the room seemed brighter than before and not as sterile.

"My dear, we were so worried," an older woman with cream colored skin and dangling gold earrings said holding her hand.

Where am I? she wanted to ask, but couldn't. The woman answered her silent question anyway.

"You're in the hospital. You've been unconscious. There was a terrible accident. A drink driver was going too fast. You were lucky to survive."

A terrible accident? Was Evelyn all right? She had to tell them.

"I'm afraid your little companion didn't make it."

Her little companion? She didn't have one...she was supposed to be Evelyn's companion, not...For a moment her mind stopped working as if it couldn't process information it didn't want to hear. They thought she was Evelyn so that meant Catherine was dead. But she was Catherine so that only meant...no there had to be a mistake. Only a moment ago they'd been so happy. Evelyn couldn't be dead. She was young, beautiful, but most of all her friend.

"Your father stopped in to see you, but had to travel back to the States for business. I've stayed behind to sort things out. Don't you worry. We'll take care and make sure she's buried properly since she meant so much to you."

The woman's voice was so soothing and kind, but the tenderness didn't belong to her. It belonged to Evelyn, who'd never get to feel this woman's touch. Never get to know the family that had searched so long to find her.

They thought she was Evelyn. Should she tell them the truth? If she did, then she'd have to go back to working for Grace and Orla. It wasn't a terrible life, but it would be harder without Evelyn. But it would be truthful. She shouldn't steal what wasn't hers. Catherine would never have such an elegant room, she would never have kind people by her side. But Evelyn did. Evelyn had a family and a future that Catherine didn't. Being Evelyn would be advantageous. But could she pull it off? Could she really fool them? If they found out about her deception, the penalty could be steep.

But this is your chance to be free! A little voice said. *This is your chance, your only chance don't waste it. They'll take you to America!*

"Evelyn, are you okay? Is there anything I can get you?"

Catherine slowly shook her head, a tear sliding down her face as she squeezed the woman's hand, grasping onto her new identity.

THEY BOTH DESERVED A BETTER GOODBYE.

Evelyn deserved a lot more tears at her passing. She didn't deserve the empty pews and scarce guests that came to the funeral in the village church. This was the end her sisters had wanted for her. They'd wanted her buried in foreign soil and forgotten. This was how they had wanted to destroy her.

And anger filled her heart until Catherine saw that Grace and Orla had shown up, and listened to the kind things they'd said. There had also been some regulars from the pub, the local librarian who'd helped her find plenty of books, and the grocer.

But in her mind she imagined a different kind of funeral. One where all of Evelyn's favorite songs where played, a poem read, *her* life remembered. She would not take it for granted. She silently vowed. She would live for both of them.

After she'd gotten retribution. But today she didn't want to think about the past. Just the bittersweet present and the reality that in all her small and simple ways, Catherine had mattered to those who had come out to say goodbye and it was a treasure to know that in a tiny pocket of the world she would be missed.

Catherine glanced up and saw Orla looking at her strangely, her dark gaze intent. When their eyes met, the older woman's widened a bit in recognition. Catherine felt her heart start to race. Maybe she'd imagined it. Orla couldn't know the difference. She'd never been able to tell before. Catherine had made sure to mimic Evelyn's manner and tone. But Orla had gotten to know them for more than two years. Did she really know? Catherine glanced at her new mother, Vera Doran, and her assistant. Her new father, Noah, had called to see if she was okay. Would Orla tell them? Even if she didn't mean to, would she accidentally slip and ruin everything? Would this opportunity slip through her fingers?

At the end of the service, Orla approached her outside the funeral home doors Catherine waited, not moving, barely breathing. Orla held out an earring. "You dropped this," she said.

Catherine touched her ear and realized that she had dropped it. "Oh thank you."

"No, let me do it," she said putting the earring back in place. "You were always so particular about your appearance."

Catherine just smiled, not knowing what move to make.

Orla hugged her, then whispered, "You also have pierced ears."

Catherine swallowed. Yes, that's right! She wore clip-ons while Evelyn didn't. She'd forgotten that.

Orla drew back and smiled. "Good bye and good luck."

PART III

FREEDOM

32

MARYLAND

He knew he was holding up the line, but he still couldn't move. Jason Redmon stared at the selection of choices before him in a state of panic, sweat glistening on his brow, his heart beating fast as he gripped the tray in his hands. He had to just answer one simple question: "What do you want?" but it felt monumental. In prison he never had that choice, he just took whatever was given to him. And he'd dreamed of a day like this when he could get anything he wanted, but he didn't know how to handle it. His mind blank, his tongue as heavy as lead in his mouth.

"Sir?"

"He'll have number three," an authoritative female voice said. "Correct?" she asked, turning to him. He nodded before glancing up at the choices and reading what number three was—roasted chicken and mashed potatoes. That sounded good and her question sounded more like a demand anyway. The black woman who had ordered for him was dressed in a striking dark suit and had black hair with golden brown highlights. She didn't look much younger than him, although for the past two years he felt he'd aged decades. She also ordered his side dishes and drink. With his tray now heavy with food, he released a sigh of relief. Now if he could just eat and not think—

"Sir, you have to pay for that," the cashier said, when Jason headed for the seats.

He nodded then went into the line, his heart pounding. He'd forgotten that he had to pay. He hoped they didn't think he was trying to steal anything. He checked around for a guard ready to take him aside and...

"That will be—" the cashier began.

"Add it to mine," the same authoritative voice interrupted.

"No, that's okay." He reached for his wallet, knowing exactly what was inside--two ten dollar bills, five quarters, six dimes, three pennies and a nickel.

"Put it away," she said without looking at him.

He hesitated, then did so.

Once she'd finished paying she said, "Follow me."

He didn't dare refuse her. He didn't want to cause trouble. He just wanted to eat and start feeling human again. He sat down and focused on his tray. "Thanks."

"You're welcome."

He lifted up his fork and ate, making sure to keep his gaze down. Even though he wouldn't mind looking at her some more, since she was pretty and he hadn't been with a woman in a while, but she wasn't to know that. No one was to know anything. Keep yourself to yourself. That's how he'd survived inside. He didn't make eye contact, he didn't make any fast movements, he didn't cause trouble.

"So how long has it been?" she said. "A day or two?"

He focused on his peas. He couldn't believe how green and fresh they were. Real green, not tin green. "What?"

"I know how hard it is. Decision fatigue is real, especially when you've been out only a few days."

He didn't move. *She knew.* How could she know? He'd spent the last couple days trying his best to appear normal. Although he'd bathed three times, never feeling clean enough, as if the stench of prison clung to his skin. He'd come to this office park to see how much money was left in his bank account. He didn't have much. Did she want something else from him?

"No," she said as if reading his mind.

He quickly glanced up in surprise then lowered his gaze again. "Almost three days."

"You're doing fine."

He felt his cheeks burning, but pretended he was in control. He sat a little straighter and glanced at her again, counting the seconds—one, two, three—before he lowered his gaze again. "You've been inside too?"

"Let's just say I've escaped a different type of prison."

He didn't ask. He'd learned early not to ask too many questions. You didn't ask why someone was in or anything about their past unless they told you.

"What's your name?" she asked.

For a second he almost gave her his prison number, then realized he wasn't that anymore. Damn, he actually had a name again. A name he could use. "Jason Redmon."

"I'm Evelyn Williams and I need you to do me a favor."

He knew it. She was after something. "What?"

"Look at me."

He pushed his peas around. "I'm sure you don't need me to do that."

"But I do."

"That's your only favor?"

"For right now."

He couldn't help a smile. He looked up then bit his lip and winked. "Is that better?"

He was hoping to make her smile, but she didn't. For a

moment he wondered if he'd lost his touch, usually women responded favorably to him. Unfortunately, this woman didn't appear to. He couldn't read her face. He sighed and lowered his gaze again.

She kicked him.

"Ow!" He stared at her stunned. "What was that for?"

"I told you to look at me."

"Does it matter?"

"Yes. Prison's behind you. Start keeping your head up. You can't look ahead with your eyes on the ground."

Jason blinked. His world seemed to tilt out of orbit as he looked at her solemn brown gaze, his eyes soaking in her pretty features as he suddenly realized that he was already falling in love with the woman he planned to marry.

33

"Are you going to see him again?" Vera Doran said with a smile when Catherine told them she wouldn't be available for dinner. She sat in the living room with a magazine, while her husband flipped through streaming options on their large TV.

"Yes," Catherine said.

"Isn't this the fourth time?"

"Yes."

"When are we going to get a chance to meet him?"

"Oh...leave her alone," Noah said. "She'll let us meet her young man when she's ready."

"I hope that doesn't take too long."

"At least she's not just focusing on us and work as she has the past few years. I was starting to worry."

Catherine only smiled, used to having them talk about her when she was still in the room. It was always affectionately done. Although it had taken getting used to at first since she was used to being talked about as if she wasn't there. 'What's the girl doing?'

someone would ask. 'Don't worry about her, she's too stupid to understand,' another would reply.

But her father and mother were very considerate of her, giving her space and helping her to adjust. "No, leave that for the maid, that's what she's there for," Vera had told her when she'd started to wash the dishes. Having staff had taken getting used to. Although she'd had them growing up, she'd never really paid attention before. Now she was fully aware that the meals didn't appear by magic, that the chandelier and silver gleamed, clothes washed, beds made, rooms dusted were due to someone's efforts. She'd never take that for granted again.

Her father delighted in showing her every aspect of his business, pleased when she asked certain questions. "Yes, you have a head for figures just like me." He was a boisterous man, with wide shoulders and ruddy brown skin, who loved to give big hugs. He wore his affection like a cape. There was no denying the pride he had in her. He liked to smoke thick cigars, laugh at dirty jokes and listen to ska music. Catherine wasn't sure Evelyn would have done well with him in the long term. She liked her quiet refined ways and Noah Doran made it very clear that he didn't have much time for education and what he called fine useless things. "If I was supposed to know Greek, I would have been born there," he'd said when Catherine had quoted a known scholar in the original text.

But although he didn't like academics, he was a smart man who'd built his wealth on savvy business skills. His wife, Vera, was more demure, many times being his good manners. A plump, pleasant and pretty woman born to a line of Irish steel workers who proudly proclaimed they'd helped build most of New York City. She'd grown up with a father and mother who loved her but didn't expect much from her. She'd proven them wrong by studying hard and becoming the first to attend college and becoming a doctor.

No children came from their union, which had been by choice as Vera once told her. "Noah makes a wonderful husband, but would have made a miserable father, for his business was his true baby." She'd told Catherine it was after a health scare and his father's failing health that had prompted Noah to look up the daughter he'd had from a youthful indiscretion. He wanted his life and business to mean something and have someone to pass it on to. He'd become determined that she would carry his business on when he passed away.

"Can't we just know a little bit more about him?" Vera asked, when she caught Catherine glancing at the clock.

"It's nothing serious."

"We don't even have a name."

"It's Jason."

"And what does he do?"

"He works in finance." *At least he did before he ended up in prison.* She didn't plan to tell them that. She wasn't even certain if what she was doing was wise. She'd helped him because he'd looked so lost and she knew the feeling.

She hadn't known what to do her first real day of freedom. Freedom to choose what to do with her time. For so long her life had been based on someone else's schedule. Now the choice was hers. Choice had felt so overwhelming in the early days. Where to go, what to do, what to say.

It had felt comforting to meet someone who understood that. If he'd been any other man, she would have said no when he asked to see her again to return the favor. But she'd found herself saying yes to lunch, then yes again to a museum, then dinner.

She couldn't tell them that she'd met him by design rather than accident. She'd already known his name and that he'd just been released on parole. He was to become an unwitting accomplice to her plans. She just hadn't expected to like him so much.

She'd heard about his story three years ago when she'd found one of the gardeners upset.

"My nephew's being set up and his stupid lawyer did nothing," the older man had said when Catherine had convinced him to tell her what was bothering him.

"What happened?"

And that's when she got the story, that he'd been charged with embezzling and been convicted. His nephew had been pressured to plead guilty, otherwise he was facing a long sentence if he'd lost, and the lawyer didn't feel confident he could win against the evidence the prosecution had. He'd been given an eight-year sentence and had been paroled after two. Catherine wasn't completely convinced of Jason's innocence or guilt, but that hadn't been what had interested her in his story—it was who he was as a man. If he was guilty, then he was the kind who could help her accomplish some tasks that may be on the outer shades of the law. If he was innocent, she hoped he was angry enough to want redemption, perhaps he'd be a cynical and angry young man. That would have been easier to manipulate. But he wasn't. That was only one of the many ways he continued to surprise her.

"Don't you want to clear your name?" she asked him on an early date as they walked along the Mall in Washington DC, after visiting the Air and Space Museum. He'd briefly shared how his lawyer had convinced him that accepting a plea deal was the best option but still confessed his innocence, 'But everyone says that, right?' he added. Now he walked beside her as if they were discussing the plot of a TV drama.

Jason squinted up at the sky. "Some day, but right now I just want to get my life back on track and eventually convince a beautiful woman to share it with me."

"I'm sure that won't be too difficult."

He looked down at her and smiled. "So you'll make it easy for me?"

Catherine didn't usually blush, but he had that effect on her. It was that smile, so guileless and genuine. "I'm serious."

"Good. Me too."

"I could help you."

"Why would you want to?" His smile disappeared. "Because you don't want to be with someone with a record?"

"No," Catherine said, quickly surprised how much she didn't like when he looked unhappy. "That's not it." *If you knew my past you may not want to be with me either.* "I just hate injustice. I've seen too much of it."

Jason reached out and took her hand. "Tell me who hurt you and I'll get them for you."

Don't worry, you will if everything goes as planned. "They're long gone."

He fell silent for a long moment, then said, "I don't think revenge is very useful, but I would like my reputation restored."

She remembered the shock of hearing the company, Sintex Inc, where Jason had worked before being blamed for embezzlement, provided computer security for companies, including her father's skin care company. Whether he was innocent or not—and she was beginning to think he was innocent—he could have crucial information about the business that she could exploit. Unfortunately, he didn't know why he'd been chosen as a scapegoat for the false charge.

But that wasn't forefront on Catherine's mind. The skin care company was very profitable, to her annoyance. When she'd seen Joscelyn's name as a member of the board she wanted to retch. Her stepsister had little interest in the business before and some of the recent changes to the business model had been surprisingly —if not miraculously—successful. But everything appeared above board and shareholders were happy. Catherine sensed something not right, but there wasn't any evidence and presently Jason could offer her no insight, but she'd be patient. Jason was important somehow, she just didn't know how yet. Once she did and had the right way to attack, she planned to do a lot of damage.

Jason didn't like to talk about his former job or about his life in prison and she didn't blame him, she didn't talk about her past—not that she could as Evelyn—and every day that passed she pushed it further from her mind.

But slowly he did open up and share his bewilderment about how incriminating evidence had shown up on his computer and how swift and complete his downfall had been.

As she listened to his story, Catherine felt angry on his behalf. It was so unfair. He was a rising star in the billing department and everything was snatched from him and yet he wasn't bitter. He could still laugh. He reminded her of Helen, the girl who'd first befriended her after she'd been sold. How people like them existed, she didn't know. How could they laugh and smile still? They may not dream of revenge, but it was what she lived for.

34

───────

"Are you doing this to hurt me?"

"Mom, I did my best."

"That's not an answer."

"It's the truth."

Maureen stared down at her nineteen year old son as he sat in his pristine room at his desk, looking miserable. She didn't care about that. She wanted him to be miserable so that he could improve. The C she'd seen on his report card was unacceptable.

"I know you think I'm pushing you hard," she said. "But it's for your own good. I will make sure you are the man your father never was. You will not become some woman's burden," she vowed, thinking of the man who'd left her to raise his son on her own because of his grief. His grief, as if she didn't grieve too. As if his grief was more important than hers. No, her son would be strong, he would make her proud. He wouldn't abandon his duty, his role. He would always do what was right no matter how much it hurt.

"Mom," he said in a quiet voice. "I'm just not good in science or math."

"With practice you will improve."

"But—"

"It doesn't come naturally, it's something that takes concerted effort and diligence to master."

"But I don't like it."

"You'll learn to like it. As a doctor—"

"I don't want to be a doctor. Joscelyn's already the doctor in the family. I want—"

"I don't care what you want. This is what you'll do. It's either this or business law so that you can help run and expand the business."

"I want to be a music teacher."

Maureen visibly shivered at the suggestion. "You don't know what you want yet. You may enjoy playing your little clarinet, but that's not real life. Next you'll want drums and to join a band."

Aaron shook his head, looking tired. "It's not the same. I'm really good."

"Teaching doesn't pay well. You're being given an opportunity to really prove yourself in this world. A chance your sister never had. Are you going to throw it all away?"

Aaron hung his head, tired of the ghost of his sainted sister Catherine. "I'm not her."

"You don't need to remind me of the obvious." Maureen sighed. She never told Aaron that Catherine hadn't been good in academics either. She didn't know why Emery's son hadn't gotten his smarts. "I know it's hard and you're young right now, but your path is set. It's a hard one, but the reward is worth it."

AARON STARED AT HIS BOOKS, wishing he could tear them up and burn them. Why wouldn't she let him be who he wanted to be? He loved music and kids. But he knew that wasn't a manly enough career for his mother. He wished she'd leave him alone instead of always reminding him of how much he disappointed her. Wasn't it enough that his sisters were all successful? Why did she have to push him so hard? He couldn't go out with his friends, he couldn't join sports. Or do anything. She never left him alone, but it had been that way since he'd been born.

"It's because of Catherine," Marie had told him when he was old enough to hear the story. He'd learned that his sister had been kidnapped and his mother seemed to blame herself and she'd make sure never to lose him.

But he felt suffocated. He craved just a little freedom without feeling his mother's eagle gaze on him. His friends laughed at him behind his back. It was so obvious how anxious she was and it was getting embarrassing. No, it was past embarrassing. It was downright humiliating. He was almost a man and he'd never gone out with a girl.

He was always the good and dutiful son. Always came home on time, did his work when told, gave her no cause for concern, but still it wasn't enough. He couldn't study at an out of state university or even live in the dorm like Marie. "Look how she turned out," his mother reminded him when he told her he wanted to live in the dorm like she had. He'd have to find a way around that.

He left his room and went to the kitchen for a snack, then turned on the TV and saw a popular teen-comedy. Soon he was laughing and his anger slipped away, and then he got an

idea.

An idea that would eventually send him to the emergency room.

35

"I saw a young man in the ER who looked so much like you he could have been your brother," Vera told Catherine at dinner. The two women were alone because Noah was away on a business trip.

"Really?" Catherine said cutting into her curried cauliflower. "Is he okay?"

"Yes," she said with a giggle. "He did some damage, but he'll heal."

"What happened?"

"He got cozy with a pie."

Catherine frowned, confused. "Cozy?"

"Intimate."

"How do you get intimate with a pie?"

"Let's just say when some young men get bored with using their hands, they find other things."

Catherine nodded, finally understanding. "Oh, what went wrong?"

"He didn't let the pie cool."

Catherine winced. "Ouch."

"Exactly. But not as bad as one guy who tried a bowl of steaming noodles." She shook her head. "Not a smart move."

"They should just stick with bottles."

"And make sure they're not too small. I could tell you stories about that."

Catherine couldn't help a laugh. "I guess anything can be dangerous. They should just stick with their hands."

"Poor kid was so embarrassed. His mother was the one who brought him in."

Catherine briefly closed her eyes. "He's scarred for life."

"Maybe literally," Vera said with another giggle.

"You shouldn't laugh."

"You would have if you'd seen this woman. She looked as if she'd stepped from a fashion magazine and was horrified by the incident, but kept her nose held high as if she smelled something distasteful."

Catherine paused. The description sounded familiar. Something her stepmother would have done. But that was impossible. Wasn't it?

"He'll recover," Vera continued.

"Why did you bring him up?" Catherine asked, wanting to focus on the important issue.

"Because he reminded me of you for some reason."

Catherine sent her a sharp look. "What reason?"

Vera sipped her wine. "He looked like you, that's all."

"Like me?"

"Yes, there was something about him that seemed familiar to me. He could have been your brother. He doesn't look like your father though, but neither do you. However, he definitely resembled you."

She licked her lip. "What was his name?"

"Sorry, can't tell you that."

"Is he still in the hospital?"

"He did a fair amount of damage so he'll need another day of recovery."

One day. She had time to see him and she planned to.

FINDING what room the young man was in was remarkably easy. People knew her at the hospital and she knew how to get the information she needed. Catherine walked to his room, but stopped outside his door when she heard voices.

"You should be more careful next time," a male voice said.

"This is why Mom told you not to play sports," a female voice added.

Catherine didn't recognize the voices.

The young man's voice was more mumbled, but she would imagine it would be. She could imagine his embarrassment. They spoke a few moments more, then she heard their footsteps. She stepped to the side and watched them exit. A woman who looked as if she were expecting and a man who looked older than he should with bent shoulders and thinning hair: Lorna and Greg! She knew they had two children, but didn't realize they were expecting another. She had to plan carefully. But that was for later. She waited until they'd turned the corner, then entered the room.

She saw the teenager staring out the window. When he turned to her, she saw her father as a young man. He had the same strong brow and full mouth.

"Yeah, I went," he said dismissively, confusing her for a nurse.

"I'm with hospital administration, making sure that your stay here is as comfortable as possible."

"Uh huh."

Gloomy, but she didn't know if that was his personality or

just the situation. Although she didn't expect to get much from him. She'd just wanted to see him.

"May I help you?"

That voice. Yes, that voice was still distinct. Clear. She'd never forget it. Catherine steeled herself before she turned and faced Joscelyn.

"I was just making sure the accommodations were adequate," she said.

"The room's a bit chilly," Joscelyn said.

"I like it," Aaron said.

Joscelyn walked over to his bed, resting her handbag on the chair. "That's because you settle for whatever comes."

"I don't care."

She tenderly touched his forehead. "You'll be out of here in no time."

Catherine gritted her teeth at the tender moment. She'd taken her place. She should be the one comforting her brother. She should be the one at his side. What right did she have to show a kindness she'd never shown to her? To anyone?

Joscelyn adjusted Aaron's bed sheets. "Is there a reason you're still here?" she said in a voice that made it clear she felt Catherine had overstayed her welcome.

Yes, I want to annoy you. I want to study your face and imagine seeing it crumble when I destroy you. "No, I'm glad things are fine."

"We didn't say they were fine," Joscelyn corrected her. "They're adequate, but that will do for now."

Catherine left the room with renewed vigor. She hadn't changed. Still cold. Something she hadn't noticed when she was younger. She'd found Joscelyn distant, but she'd always attributed it to their difference in age, but now she saw her in a new light. She saw the cruel touch of her jaw, the tightness of her lips. No warmth, she was the kind of woman who could hurt others and not flinch. She would enjoy making Joscelyn suffer.

CATHERINE WENT to the main floor of the hospital, surprised to still see Greg in the waiting room. She saw traces of the young man she'd known. He'd been kind to her, so how had he ended up marrying Lorna when they were such a poor match? That wasn't her problem anymore. She still remembered the dream he'd told her. Clearly he had hadn't followed any of the suggestions his dream had given him.

She went into the ladies room and saw Lorna washing her hands at the sink, but the way her dress fell was strange. She couldn't quite tell what it was, but it didn't fall naturally.

Lorna caught her staring in the mirror. "What is it?"

"That's a lovely dress," Catherine lied quickly recovering herself. "It's just the sash is coming undone."

"Oh dear," she said, looking down.

Catherine rushed forward. "Let me help you," she said grabbing the sash. As she tied the sash, she saw something underneath the dress that stunned her. She quickly made the adjustments then stepped back. "When are you due?" It was always a dangerous question to ask a woman so early in her pregnancy—or at all—but she needed to confirm her suspicions.

Lorna patted her stomach. "In the fall."

"Congratulations."

"Thank you."

Catherine went into one of the empty stalls, unable to stop a satisfied smile. A delicious opportunity had just fallen in her lap. Clearly there was tension in Lorna's marriage because she'd seen padding which meant one thing: Lorna wasn't pregnant.

36

———

"Do you have to flirt with every woman you see?" Lorna asked Greg as they drove home from the hospital.

"I wasn't flirting," Greg said with a sigh, tired of the same conversation. "I was just talking."

"I wasn't in the bathroom for a minute and you just *happen* to find a beautiful woman to talk to?"

"She was ordinary."

"She had a great figure or are you going to pretend not to notice that too?"

"Let's not do this."

"I know I haven't lost the baby weight from the last pregnancy and now with another on the way."

"One we hadn't planned for," he grumbled.

"Why do you act as if this is my fault."

"I didn't say that, I'm just...I thought we'd done enough."

"A vasectomy isn't 100%."

"Right, but it had been working and you were also supposed to—"

"There's no point going back. We're having another child and there's nothing we can do."

Greg ran a tired hand down his face. "It's just the wrong time."

"I don't know what you mean."

"You know things haven't been good between us for a while."

"No, I don't know that. I'm happy, the kids are happy. You're the one who's finding reasons to be unhappy."

"Why do you think I'm flirting with every woman I see?"

Lorna rested a hand on his thigh. "I'm sorry, I'm just feeling a little insecure right now. I don't mean to take it out on you. It's just the thought of ever losing you scares me."

Greg gripped the steering wheel. He couldn't tell her how many times he regretted his choice. How many times he wondered what his life would have been like if he had followed his heart and done something else. Instead he'd stayed with her. He'd told himself it would just be for a while. After Catherine's disappearance, she was so broken he couldn't imagine leaving her alone. It had taken her so long to get over it. By the time she did, they'd become comfortable together. A habit he'd gotten used to. He couldn't remember if he'd proposed to her or the other way around. He'd started to get cold feet and thought about calling it off. His father had even encouraged it.

"If you can't do this, then stop it now," he'd told him. "Marriage is a huge step."

"I know, but we've been together so long."

"You're still young. Five years is not a lifetime. Try fifty or sixty. Are you ready for that?"

No he wasn't ready and he had seriously considered calling off the wedding. He'd been practicing how he would do it when she'd shown up on his doorstep in tears.

"Emery's dead," she said, then fell into his arms and sobbed and he knew he couldn't abandon her now. Not when her stepfather had just died. He didn't remember the ceremony. Just felt the heaviness of the gold band as she slid it on his finger. He wondered if other men felt as if their world was coming to an end when they got married.

He dismissed his thoughts, thinking they were the result of the death of his single days that made him feel uneasy. Lorna had her good side and he could see them starting a family and he wanted that. They both did.

But after the birth of their first child, he knew it wasn't enough. As much as he loved his daughter, it didn't heal his relationship with her mother. She was still obsessive about his free time. Obsessed about his calls and texts.

He found himself staying later and later at work. And to his shame, he did think about other women, although he never acted on those thoughts. He'd never hurt her like that, but when he couldn't even talk to someone other than her, he felt tempted. What was the point of being a good husband when she never treated him like one?

And now they were having a third child. It had come unexpectedly. Although they were still intimate—she made sure of that—it wasn't as often as it had been in the beginning or even as much fun. Not that he'd admit that to anyone. His friends always joked about how their wives barely gave out, but his wife...sometimes he found her exhausting. Insatiable and demanding. He had to always perform and it was starting to feel like work. He couldn't remember the last time he'd call it making love.

He glanced at her. That was the biggest problem. He didn't love her anymore. Wondered if he ever did. He'd liked her a lot once, but even that had changed. They had a history together and a family, but that was all that kept them together. He wondered how long that would last.

Lorna rubbed his thigh, wondering what she should say to him. She hated when he got quiet. She didn't know how to reach him then. He was so successful and good looking she could understand why any woman would want to take him away from her. But she wouldn't let them. He was hers for life. They were meant to be together, although at times he seemed to forget that. They had a wonderful life. She loved cuddling with him on the couch as their girls watched a movie, having a date night every month and didn't he love when they'd taken salsa lessons? She remembered another time like this several months back when he'd been quiet as they finished a show, the girls asleep in bed.

"...Need to get away for a few days to think things through," she heard him say, his words shaking her out of her thoughts. He'd said he wanted to talk, but she hadn't been listening.

She turned to him. "Think what through?"

"Us."

"There's nothing wrong with us."

"We can't keep pretending that things aren't going wrong."

"I'm pregnant." She didn't know what made her say that—desperation, survival, fear or a combination of all three, but the words tumbled from her mouth.

Greg stared at her wide eyed. "What?"

"You heard me."

"But you can't be."

"I am."

"You're sure?"

"I wouldn't make this up." But of course she had. On the spot. But she had to. She didn't want him talking about needing space, moving out, reconsidering things. What they had was perfect. He was meant to be by her side--forever. After telling him the lie she'd hoped to get pregnant so that she could make it real, but to her horror his vasectomy held so she had to feign the pregnancy. She didn't know for how long. She would have to miscarry, but maybe after another month. She needed more time. A miscarriage should give her another year or two, but after that...

No, she wouldn't think that far. She couldn't imagine a life without him in it. He was her world. Her first and only love. A little deception wouldn't hurt anyone especially if it kept her family together. She needed him and so did their girls.

Later that evening, as she drifted off to sleep, she didn't know what made her think of the woman in the ladies' room who'd helped her with her sash. She'd seemed a little strange. When she'd first caught her staring, she'd felt chills, but then realized it was nothing. Other women generally envied her wedding ring, her home, her family, her looks so being the object of desire was nothing new, but the woman's look had been so intense, an expression she'd never seen before.

But then she'd explained that she just admired her dress and helped her with her sash. But for some reason when she congratulated her, she made Lorna uneasy, because her smile didn't reach her eyes.

37

Destroying Lorna's marriage wouldn't take much, but toppling Joscelyn would take more planning. Catherine sat in her room staring at the two files she'd created for her stepsisters. She had a smaller one for Marie. She closed Lorna's folder and stared at the one for Joscelyn. She tapped her pen against a recent article about Joscelyn published in the American Medical Journal, Catherine had to resist drawing a circle around her sister's face and stabbing the image as if she'd hit a bull's eye.

Joscelyn was not an easy target. She didn't have many weak spots. She'd remained single, had no children, was a stellar worker at her hospital and had a lucrative practice. She invested modestly and did nothing to excess—shopping, drinking, men.

The doorbell rang. Catherine quickly snapped the file closed and put it away. She walked downstairs as the maid led Jason to the conservatory where the table had been set for a light lunch. She'd invited him over when she knew both her parents were away visiting friends. She'd considered inviting Jason to her office, but she wanted to see how he'd respond to the wealth her father liked to display.

"You look beautiful," he said when he saw her, not seeming to pay attention to anything around him—the pool, the expanse of manicured land—except her. He held out the chair for her.

Catherine sat down, amazed at his unwavering interest. "Thank you. Did you bring what I asked?"

He sat down in front of her with a feigned look of hurt. "I feel like I'm being used."

Catherine motioned for the maid to start serving lunch. "You won't after you've eaten."

Jason handed her some documents. "I really don't have much. It's still going to be hard to prove."

"That's fine." Catherine said flipping through one manuscript. "I have time. I'll do whatever it takes."

"That's what I love about you."

Her head snapped up, alarmed. "Don't fall in love with me."

"You think I can help myself?"

"Jason—"

"It's okay if you don't feel the same about me yet, just don't tell me to stop."

"I do care for you, but..."

"You've been hurt and you're afraid to trust." He leaned back and placed his napkin on his lap when a plate of spicy collard greens with shrimp covering a mound of yellow rice was placed in front of him.

"Something like that," Catherine said.

He picked up his fork. "I'm patient."

Me too. I doubt you can wait that long. "I have to travel next week."

"I wish I could go with you."

"You sound as if you mean that."

"I do. More than you know, but my parole officer would have a fit."

"Oh yes, I forgot about that."

He fell silent and glanced out the window. "Are you sure that me being an ex-con doesn't—"

"How long before you can travel?" she interrupted, not wanting him to finish his thoughts.

"Two years."

"And where would you go first?"

He thought for a moment. "Andalucía, Spain."

"Okay, it's a date."

He grinned. "You shouldn't give me hope like that."

"I know, but making you smile is becoming regrettably important to me."

"When you come back, let's go to the theater. There's a new show coming to the district."

"I look forward to it," she said, both annoyed and amazed by how much she meant it.

HE WAS GOING to miss her when she was gone, Jason thought as he walked up his apartment stairs. Time with her was never enough. He sighed. Why did she have to travel now? Things were finally progressing between them. It was at times like these when he really hated being on parole, but it was better than being inside.

He turned the corner on the landing, then paused when he saw the tall lanky frame of a black man curled up on the stairwell. He nudged the man with his shoe. "Sleep off your hangover somewhere else, you're blocking the way."

The man stood up. "Jason, my man."

Jason looked him up and down in disdain, then continued up

the stairs. "I don't know who you are."

The man's mouth dropped open. "What the f—? It's me. Duane. We shared a cell together."

"A cell? You think we're related somehow?"

"What's wrong with you, man? Come on, Jason, it's me. You said I could look you up when I got out."

He opened the door to his floor and walked towards his apartment. "I don't know who you're talking about, but I hope you find him."

The man's face fell. "I can't believe you're gonna do a brotha like that."

Jason stopped in front of his apartment, opened the door, then turned to the man. "And I never would." He flashed a wide grin. "Come on."

"Damn!" Duane said grabbing his shirt as if he'd been shot. "You had me good, bro. I thought you were totally shittin' me."

"Never," Jason said, giving his old friend a hug. Duane had been his cellmate and protector. He'd been inside for a drug charge and had shown Jason tips to surviving inside. They'd formed a bond that could never be broken.

Duane stepped back and stared at him. "Damn, you look good." He looked around. "And this place." He let loose a stream of expletives, then said, "It's really yours?"

"Yep."

"You keep some of the money you stole?"

"I didn't steal anything."

"Oh yeah, you're innocent. That's right."

Jason knew Duane didn't believe him, but he didn't care. He'd met so many liars and those claiming their innocence, he could understand his attitude.

Duane lifted up a couch cushion. "Damn, look at that."

Jason came around and stared. "What?"

"No cockroaches. Man at my aunt's house they're setting up apartments." He put the cushion back. "Got anything to eat?"

"Yes, as long as you have some news."

"Not much yet. Still looking for work. I'll be honest with you, man. I didn't want to see you at first. I've got so much going wrong already."

Jason sat in front of him, concerned. "What do you mean?"

"No real place, no job, and I've got child support payments and debt so high I feel like I'm already drowning before I've even begun. You know what it's like paying for a kid I hardly get to see? I've been tempted to start my own little enterprise again."

"That's what got you locked up in the first place."

"How's a man supposed to make a living on minimum wage? He's not. I had to do something. I can try to go straight, but it would take me forever to get out from under this mess."

"I may be able to help you. As long as you're willing to work."

"I always am."

"Legally."

A wide smile spread on Duane's face. "As long as the pay's right, I'm your man."

38

"Someone's looking into the Jason Redmon issue."

Joscelyn had received the call as she was leaving the lecture hall where she'd finished giving a talk and signing books she'd paid her friend Gloria to ghost write for her. However, she hadn't signed as many books as she'd hoped, most people had taken out their cell phones and wanted to take pictures of themselves with her. She'd had to smile so much her cheeks hurt. But now that the event was over, she'd planned to relax with a game of tennis. She looked forward to slaughtering her volleying partner. "He can try to clear his name, but he's the one who pleaded guilty," she said, wondering why that was news. "Besides, there's nothing he can do."

"It seems that he has help," the voice continued.

"Who?"

"We're looking into it. He's dating someone named Evelyn Williams. Her family has connections and deep pockets."

Joscelyn shoved on her sunglasses before she stepped out the front doors. "Try to persuade him that it's not in his best interest to look into the past."

"He won't take money."

That was most annoying. He'd been the perfect one to clean up the mess they'd found themselves in. She'd built the business even bigger than Emery could have imagined, but there had been some eggs she'd had to break in the process to making her omelet. Fortunately, there was no way for anyone to tie her to what had happened.

"Try anyway," she said, her heels clicking against the new asphalt as she walked to her car. She wrinkled her nose at the smell. "And find out what you can on his new lady love."

"Will do. Mr. Carter called."

She stopped, surprised. "Why didn't you tell me that first?"

He hesitated. "I thought the other issue was more pressing."

Nothing was more pressing than the man she planned to have. She started walking again, ignoring a car that honked at her when she stepped into its path. "What did he say?"

"That he'd see you at the show."

She inwardly cheered. She knew the theater wasn't his interest, but she'd managed to convince him to go. It was a small step forward and though they wouldn't be going together, it was something.

There were few things she wanted that she couldn't have. Tytus Carter was one. He was magnificent, calculating, and just her type. Unfortunately, she hadn't been able to convince him of that yet. But she would.

39

______

His place smelled like Krispy Kreme donuts, but Jason knew his parole officer was anything but sweet. He had to see Jaime Perez every month as dictated by his probation. Every month he had to come to the sparse little room, sit in a chair that should have been tossed years ago, and stare at a carpet so threadbare he couldn't tell what color it was or had been or decipher the pattern on it. Perez sat behind his desk with the list of questions he was set to ask without variation. He had a buzz cut hair, square jaw and tiny pin prick eyes, which became eerily enlarged when he put on his glasses.

"How are you?"

Jason was certain he could say 'Right now my life is a steaming pile of dung' and that Perez would just nod and go to the next question, so he said what was expected, "Fine. And you?"

Perez nodded and went to the next question. "Do you have somewhere to live?"

"Yes."

"Where? A halfway house?"

"No, I have my own place."

"With family?"

"I have family, but I'm not staying with them. I have an apartment."

"Have you found a job yet?"

"Yes."

He looked up surprised. "Doing what?"

"Working for my brother."

"Doing what?"

Jason suppressed a smile at the suspicion. Did he think his brother was a criminal too? "Managing inventory. He owns a business that sells home goods." *It's not sexy, but it makes us money,* he remembered his father telling him when he wanted Jason to join the company.

"Okay, last question. Have you been tempted to commit the same offense that sent you to prison?"

Does wanting to steal a woman's heart, count? "No."

"Have you been taking any drugs?"

"No."

"Drawing unemployment?"

Considering I have a job, that would be stupid, right? Was the guy listening to anything he was saying? "No, because I'm working for my brother," he said slowly.

Perez nodded. "Yeah, that's right." He checked a box then made a note. "Have you had any contact with anyone from prison?"

So much for *one* more question unless he couldn't count. Or maybe he was new and read the script wrong. "Yes."

"Does he have employment?"

"I'm helping him look."

"And where is he staying?"

"With me for now."

"Is there enough room?"

"Yes."

"I may have to come by and inspect to make sure it's up to standards."

Jason shrugged. "Feel free."

For the first time, Perez smiled. "I always do."

HE WAS AN UNEXPECTED COMPLICATION.

Catherine looked through the series of pictures Jason had sent her via email. Images of him photoshopped into different scenes around the world. In front of the Eiffel Tower, the Taj Mahal, the London Eye, the Great Wall of China. He'd ended it with "All the places I want to see with you. Miss you."

Why did he have to make her so happy? Why did he have to be so wonderful?

She briefly closed her eyes and allowed herself to smile. She couldn't pretend that she didn't care about him and she missed him too.

Every day she thought about him more and more. She hated not being completely honest with him, but she couldn't. She'd planned to spend the rest of her life alone. She'd not expected to get close to anyone again. She even kept Noah and Vera at a safe distance. But he was slipping into her heart. When she returned home, he was the first person she called, and when he invited her to a local show she said yes as promised.

"Isn't this the eighth date?" Vera said as Catherine fixed her hair in the hallway mirror.

"You'll meet him."

"So you're ready to admit that this is serious?"

More serious than I want it to be. "It's getting close."

"But something about him worries you?"

"It's not him. It's me."

"There's nothing wrong with you."

"I'm not relationship material." At least not yet. She wasn't sure she'd ever be ready to trust, to love completely. He deserved more. She felt selfish, but being with him felt so good.

"I know your last marriage didn't work, but don't let that stop you."

Catherine blinked, then remember that Evelyn had been divorced. Yes, she could use that excuse, that would be helpful. She was afraid to marry again because her last one fell apart, she was afraid because her husband left her in debt. She'd have to remember to tell Jason, but for now she'd keep that to herself. "I'm trying."

"If you don't invite him to dinner soon, your father will."

"I will."

Jason was thrilled when she told him her parents wanted to meet him. They sat in the theater a few minutes before the show began. She'd started to read what the story was about, but stopped when Jason reached over and held her hand.

"Does this frighten you?" he said softly.

It shouldn't. "Why would you think that?"

"Because you stiffened and won't look at me."

She had to relax, this was normal. This was what couples did. "It's just—"

"I won't hurt you."

"I know."

"Do you want me to let go?"

She swallowed, then shook her head.

From the corner of her eyes she saw him flash his sexy grin before he kissed the back of her hand. "Good, because I wasn't going to." His grin widened when she turned to him. "I'm being serious."

That's what continued to amaze her. How he could be serious and smile at the same time. "I wish I could be more like you. I once..."

"You once what?"

Could laugh and smile as freely as you. But that Catherine had died long ago. So had the Catherine who would say whatever was on her mind. And the Catherine who could love easily. "Was a better companion," she finished.

"You're perfect for me. Don't change."

She wished she knew what he saw. She stared at the stage, glad she hadn't managed to scare him away with her quiet manner. She saw other women who were more lively and bubbly, and knew she was dour compared to them. At times she thought of how Evelyn would be, which was why she always presented her best...but after that she felt lost. She didn't know how Evelyn had been in her marriage, what kind of wife she'd been. Or the kind of wife she would be. So much pretending. Did Jason like the image of Evelyn? What would he think of her if he really knew her past?

"I've got some good news," he said.

"What?"

"We must be doing something right, I got a visit."

She turned sharply to him. "What?"

"Yes, they visited and offered me a sizable amount to keep things as they are."

"And you said?"

"No, of course."

"But were you tempted? I know you could use the money."

"Not as much as you think. Don't you think it's time you see my place?"

He'd asked her before, she'd always declined and each time felt guilty. She still felt that way. "It's just—"

"We'll watch a movie and order in, nothing more. I promise."

Catherine bit her lip. "Maybe this isn't good. I don't like them approaching you. Did they make any threats?"

He lifted a brow. "And if they did?"

"Maybe you should leave this to me."

"So that you'd become a target? Never."

Why were they targeting him? Why had they approached him? How could he be a threat? What were they hiding? There were still too many unknown variables. She may have inadvertently used him to poke a hornet's nest. Maybe involving him had been the wrong strategy. "Jason—"

"You're worried about me."

"Yes."

He gave her hand a warm squeeze. "Good."

"That's not funny."

"I know, it makes me feel good. Soon you'll start realizing you love me too."

Before she could reply, the lights dimmed and the show began.

40

The show was a flop.

"Well, that was twenty thousand down the drain," Joscelyn said with a sigh.

Tytus shook his head in sympathy and looked at her, amused. "You invested in this?"

"It's not something I'll admit to in public."

"Good idea," he said, standing up from his seat. "Let's pretend we didn't even come here." He held out her coat. Then led her to the exit. Joscelyn Payton wasn't really his type, but he'd been bored and she was persistent enough. Maybe he'd give her a chance to be more persuasive. He was halfway up the aisle when a voice caused him to pause.

"What is it?" Joscelyn asked, when she'd crashed into his back.

He couldn't reply. He knew that voice. Why did he know that voice? Why did it seem to rise above all the others? The voice reminded him of a small, candlelit room in England and a woman behind a mask who'd disappeared. After all these years, could it be her?

"Excuse me," he said, then followed the voice, his heart picking up speed the closer he got to it. Then he was upon it. He only saw the back of her. A long honey brown neck, hair twisted up. She was the right size and height. He waited for her to finish and the other people to move away before he said, "Excuse me, Miss?"

She turned around and the world stood still. Her eyes met his. He knew those eyes. He knew that mouth. He'd searched for her and here she was. For a moment he felt lightheaded and breathless.

"Yes?" she said.

"We've met before," he managed, his tongue feeling heavy in his mouth.

"No, I don't think so," she said politely.

"Years ago, you read my dreams and—"

"I'm sorry, but you must have me confused with someone else."

"No, I know—"

"And I know that I don't know what you're talking about. I'm sorry." She grabbed her handbag and jacket then left.

He stared at her back, stunned. Could he be wrong? He'd been so certain. All these years he hadn't heard a voice like hers. But...she was right there. There was something different about the cadence of her words and her word choices, but...no, that voice. That voice was hers and those eyes... he'd know them anywhere. Why would she pretend not to know him?

CATHERINE HURRIED out of the theater. Jason had gone to use the restroom and she'd stayed behind to chat with some people who'd been just as baffled by the performance as she had been, but that had been a mistake. She should have waited for him outside the theater. She stood near the men's room, trying not to appear too anxious. What was taking him so long? She had to get away before Tytus spotted her again. Tytus! How could this be?

"Are you okay?" Jason said when he saw her.

"I'm fine. I was just getting hot in there."

"Well, let's get you..." His words trailed off when he saw something behind her. "I don't believe this." His face spread into a broad grin and he raised his hand.

Catherine turned to see who he was signaling and froze. It was *him*. Again!! But this time he wasn't alone. Joscelyn stood almost possessively by his side. That was interesting. Joscelyn never seemed very interested in others before. Especially men. What made Tytus special to her? What was he doing with her? Or better yet, what was she doing with him? Joscelyn and Tytus, what a horrible yet appealing mix. She'd thought the play was bad, but this was worse. She considered feigning illness, but seeing Joscelyn's eagle glare, she decided against it. She didn't want to show any weakness in front of her.

"Haven't we met before?" Joscelyn said.

"No," Catherine said, surprised. Joscelyn had barely glanced at her in the hospital, but she wasn't worried. She'd worn a suitable disguise. Unless her sister thought she seemed familiar because she recognized who she really was. But so many years had passed and if Catherine dismissed the idea, Joscelyn wasn't one to press a topic. Catherine shifted her gaze to Tytus. "I guess I have that kind of face."

"I wanted to offer my apologies," Tytus said. "I didn't mean to frighten you."

Yes, she remembered telling him he'd frightened her all those years ago, but she wouldn't fall for the bait. "There's no reason to apologize. It's understandable."

"You two already know each other?" Jason said.

"No, it's just that she reminded me of someone I'd met a long time ago," Tytus said holding her gaze, daring her to look away. "Someone who changed my life."

Catherine offered a thin smile, trying not to be mesmerized by his dark eyes. "I didn't take you for a romantic."

"A romantic?"

His gaze had grown even more intense over the years, she could feel goose bumps on her arms, but didn't dare look away. "Yes, making such an exaggerated claim."

"It's not. I meant every word."

Joscelyn slipped her arm through his. "Tytus always says what he means."

"I don't doubt it," Catherine said, noticing the gesture. Her stepsister was feeling insecure. That was rare. Joscelyn usually didn't have to stake a claim. Tytus meant a lot to her. That was good to know. Maybe this unexpected reunion would prove useful.

Jason shoved his hands in his pockets. "Yes, my brother always speaks his mind."

"Brother?" Joscelyn and Catherine said in startled unison.

"Yes," Jason said with an embarrassed grin. "Sorry, I didn't make introductions."

"Allow me," Tytus said holding out his hand to Catherine. "I'm Tytus Carter."

She didn't want to touch him, didn't want to remember cupping his hand in hers and pretending to read his palm, but had no choice. "Evelyn Williams," she said, taking his large hand in hers, steeling herself against the same electrical current that seemed to happen every time they touched. Part of her hoped it wouldn't happen, but it did. Even more forceful than it had in the past. His gaze sharpened and his eyes narrowed, but she kept her features neutral, pretending not to feel anything. "And your lovely date?" she urged him.

He blinked, not releasing her hand, his palm hot against

hers. "What?"

Jason playfully hit him on the arm. "Wake up, bro. Are you in a trance or something?"

"Excuse me," Tytus said, quickly recovering himself before he motioned to the woman beside him. "Joscelyn Payton."

"A pleasure," Catherine said, shaking her hand. *It's been a long time.*

"Thank you," Joscelyn said, sending her a look of cool disinterest, which she'd perfected. But Catherine knew the look meant the exact opposite. She saw Evelyn as a possible threat and that wasn't good. She hadn't planned to be an enemy of Joscelyn this soon in the game. She wouldn't be able to get her in a vulnerable spot if she had her defense up.

Catherine took Jason's hand and kissed him lightly on the cheek. "Come on, I'm starving and I know just where I want to treat you."

He looked so delighted at her unexpected display of affection that she felt guilty for using him just to ease Joscelyn's concerns. But she had no choice. She would make it up to him.

"I won't say no to that," Jason said, giving her hand a tender squeeze. He nodded at Tytus and Joscelyn. "See you both."

As they walked to the exit, Catherine made sure not to look back, although she wondered if her diversion had worked. Was Tytus or Joscelyn watching them leave? Would Tytus believe her lie and forget her? This was getting more and more complicated. Jason's brother was dating the woman she wanted to destroy.

Joscelyn seemed genuinely surprised they were related. Did that mean she knew who Jason was? And did his connection to Tytus worry her? If so, why?

If Joscelyn was really serious about Tytus, she'd be afraid to lose him. That would be a good soft spot to exploit, but she wasn't sure how yet. Catherine knew she had to tread carefully because if Tytus tied her to her past, everything could fall apart.

41
___

He had to find out more about her.

"I didn't know you had a brother," Joscelyn said as Tytus walked her to her car. "Why do you have different last names?"

"It was our parents' idea. My father gave his surname to Jason and my mother gave me her surname," he said, then fell silent.

Joscelyn sighed, annoyed. She could tell his mind was far away. "I know that look. What are you thinking?"

He shook his head. "Not sure."

"You seemed taken by your brother's date." *And you should be thinking about me.*

"Just curious."

"She seems very taken with him and they make a great couple, don't you think? They look so happy together."

A muscle twitched in his jaw. "Yes. I don't know much about her."

"She seems to have an interesting history. She's the long lost daughter of Noah Doran, the serial entrepreneur."

"Hmm."

"But you're spoiling my already horrible evening."

He stopped and stared at her. "Really?"

"Yes, I don't like you thinking about another woman when you're with me," she said, trailing a finger down his shirt. "So I expect you to make it up to me."

He wrapped his hand around hers, a slow smile spreading over his face. "It's not like you to be jealous."

"I can be very jealous," she warned in a low voice. She pulled him close and kissed him. "Do you need a better reason to follow me home tonight?"

He licked his lips. "Tempting."

She frowned sensing his hesitation. "But not tempting enough?"

He straightened, taking a step back. "Another time."

"I won't wait forever."

"I don't expect you to." He walked to her car, then held out his hand for her keys. When she handed them to him, he opened the door and waited. "A beautiful woman like you should never go to waste."

Joscelyn slid into the driver's seat, frustrated that she'd ended up empty-handed again. She'd hoped to spend the evening with him. She didn't want another man. She wanted him. But he was determined to stay out of reach. Maybe she was making it too easy for him, perhaps she needed to offer him some competition.

He'd found out more about her, but it still didn't feel like enough. "That's it?" he asked his assistant, Ralph Gaston, who'd offered him the report about Evelyn Williams he'd requested.

"Yes, as Joscelyn told you, she's the long lost daughter of Noah Doran. Over the past several years she's helped his business—"

"I don't care about the business. I care about her...I mean, I'm interested in her," he said quickly correcting himself. "For my brother's sake."

Ralph nodded. He'd worked for Tytus long enough to know that was the best response. "Of course. Your brother is still vulnerable, but she has her own money, so I don't see her wanting to use him that way."

True. He wasn't really concerned about that. His brother usually chose women well. Their family had dubbed him the sensible one, which was why his prison conviction had come as such a shock. He'd begged Jason to fight the charge, but his brother hadn't listened. It had been one of the worst years of Tytus's life. The business was in trouble and he'd been forced to take over from his father, who'd started making erratic decisions that harmed the business, before his brain tumor was diagnosed. His grandfather had emigrated from Barbados and started a small furniture restoration business, his father had expanded the original business concept to selling home goods, and it was expected that Tytus would take over from there. He'd initially rejected the position, not wanting to feel that his destiny had been dictated without his consent. But he'd fought a losing battle.

A mountain of sugar...he remembered his dream and Epic's interpretation. He had taken the reins with reluctance, but discovered he was better suited than he'd expected. However, it had still been a struggle to keep it afloat and then his brother was sentenced to eight years for embezzlement.

Now Jason was getting his life back and had met someone. *They look so happy together.* Joscelyn's words echoed in his mind. Yes, they did look happy and he should leave things. But he couldn't. He had to know.

"What about her life before finding her family?" he asked Ralph.

"She lived with an aunt and cared for her before her passing.

She was married briefly to a man whose death left her with lots of debt. She briefly was in service for two sisters. It's hinted that her life was hard and is rarely discussed."

'In service', but no mention of her making money interpreting dreams. Was that a secret she didn't want her new family knowing about? Maybe she'd needed the money desperately then. It was possible. "She had a harrowing journey here. It's said they'd nearly lost her. She survived a major car accident, but her companion didn't."

Tytus rubbed his chin and started to smile. *Now that was very interesting.*

42

H e'd found something he shouldn't have.

Jason stared at the screen, his heart racing. After weeks of digging, he'd finally hit something interesting. Something that wouldn't exonerate him, but could even the playing field. Something that had initially bothered him, but that he'd dismissed. He'd never made the connection before about telling his boss about a minor computer glitch and weeks later being charged with embezzlement. He couldn't dismiss the possible connection now. Fortunately, he knew someone who could help him.

"I need to talk to you," he said when he caught Joscelyn leaving her tennis club.

"I'm afraid I'm busy. You'll have to make an appointment."

"There's something you need to know. I think your company may be a victim of fraud."

She stopped. "Okay, tell me what you know."

Moments later they sat at a private table. Jason took out a file with the Sintex logo prominently displayed and slid it across the table. "Does this look familiar? It should."

She barely glanced at it. "Of course."

"I think we can help each other. Your skin care company has been using Sintex for your computer security and protection. It's possible they fleeced your business and when I noticed a small discrepancy, thinking it was just a computer error, I was charged with embezzlement."

"You have proof?"

"No, my suspicions are still just speculative, but these charts I discovered reveal some questionable business transactions."

"How did you get these?"

Jason just smiled.

"Right, it's best for me not to know." Joscelyn sighed. "But without more evidence what do you expect me to do?"

"You might know who was responsible for sending me to prison. You're in a better position to figure out what's going on there."

Joscelyn looked at the file. "Why not let this alone? You're out now."

"With two years of my life taken and a prison record."

"I'm not trying to be cruel, but I think you should forget those years and move on."

He frowned, surprised by her disinterest. He'd assumed that she would feel the same outrage he felt. His brother usually dated women who cared about integrity and ethics. Maybe he hadn't presented his information well. "But this is bigger than me. I thought you'd want to know that—"

"I'm very glad you told me about this, but it may be larger than both of us." She sat back and crossed her legs. "Does your girlfriend know what you've found?"

"I haven't really found anything, it will still take some time to connect more dots. I thought we could do a fair exchange. You help me and I put in a good word with my brother." He smiled. "I can be very persuasive."

"You think he needs persuasion when it comes to me?"

"He can be...slow to move."

"I'll think about it and see what I can do."

Jason felt his tension ebb. He hadn't misjudged her. "Thanks."

"But until I know more this must stay between us." She put her hand on the file and lifted a questioning brow. "May I take this?"

"Of course."

"You're dealing with powerful people," she said when Jason rose to leave.

"I know, but everyone has a weakness."

43

She'd stared at him without blinking for what seemed like an age. When Joscelyn had called him into her office, her voice had given nothing away. It was only when he stepped inside and felt the chill in the air that Jack Miller knew something was wrong. He'd closed the door and walked up to her desk, waiting for her to give him instructions. Instead she just stared at him. A cold, blank stare. He didn't dare move or take a seat, he just stood and waited, hoping the silent torture would soon end.

Finally she leaned back and clasped her hands together. "Are you coming or going?"

He took a seat. "You wanted to see me?"

"I'm furious with you right now," she said in a low voice.

He felt chills race up his spine. It was worse than he thought.

"I discovered something disturbing."

"What?"

"It's in my desk drawer. Come and see."

Had a rodent gotten in? That was odd. He approached the desk with care.

"It's the lower top one."

Jack pulled it open. He saw a file and froze.

"Yes, that's it. Take it out."

He reached for it, but before he could get it, she slammed the drawer shut, trapping his fingers.

"I'm so angry right now," Joscelyn said in the same detached tone.

Jack fell to his knees, swallowing hard. "I'm so sorry."

"That doesn't help."

Tears of pain gathered in his eyes. "I can fix this."

She pushed the drawer even more. "Really?"

He bit his lip and nodded.

"You're always so good to me. Why disappoint me like this?"

"I'm sorry."

She released the drawer.

Jack opened it, then cradled his hand.

Joscelyn pulled out the folder, then tossed it on the ground next to him. "How did he get this!"

"I don't know," he said, his voice higher than usual.

"I thought you said you were careful, everything had been covered."

"I thought it had been."

"You thought wrong. I have enough I have to worry about with Edmund Cristo buying up shares of my stepfather's company. Do you know what's at stake?"

He could hardly think for the pain, but knew he had to. "Yes."

"I want him taken care of, discreetly. Make sure he's no longer a problem to me. Or the company. Understood?"

He nodded.

"Good. You may go."

Jack scurried out of the room, enraged. Fortunately, he knew who to blame.

44

Catherine hadn't want to attend the charity function, but her stepmother had been unable to come and begged Catherine to appear in her place. She'd asked Jason to join her, but he too had other plans. She smiled at the other guests, but felt awkward and out of place. She'd perfected her new identity in small groups, but larger groups always proved a challenge.

"I can't have you standing here by yourself," the hostess Lelia O'Connell said when she found Catherine alone in a corner. She'd been a runner up in the Miss America pageant in the 70s, but carried herself as if she'd won the crown and a kingdom.

"I'm having a wonderful time," Catherine said, smiling warmly. *Remember to be Evelyn.*

"Liar," Lelia said with an affectionate laugh. "You look miserable."

"It's just my face," Catherine said, making an attempt at humor.

"No, let me see if I can find a suitable companion to brighten your mood." She searched the crowd. "Oh yes, I see one. He's perfect." She waved him over. "Tytus."

Catherine looked up in a panic. "Oh no, please don't..."

But it was too late. Within seconds he stood in front of her.

"Would you mind keeping her company for a while?" Lelia said to him, missing Catherine's thunderstruck expression.

"No," he said in a dark, smooth voice. "I wouldn't mind at all. We've met before."

Lelia looked both surprised and pleased. "Really? When?"

His eyes sent her a private message. "I'm still trying to figure that out."

Catherine sipped her champagne. "We met at the theater several weeks ago."

"Yes, that's right. The theater. I don't know why I keep thinking we've met before that."

"Because you don't like changing your mind?"

He smiled. "You know someone did tell me that before. That change is hard for me."

Lelia clapped her hands together delighted. "I'll let you two catch up then," she said before she left.

"Yes, let's do that," he said.

"What?"

"Catch up. What have you been doing these last several *weeks*?" he asked making sure to emphasis the last word.

"Working."

"How did you and my brother meet?"

"Why don't you ask your brother that?"

"I will, but I want to hear it first from you."

Catherine took another sip searching the room for a reason to escape. "To make sure we keep our story straight?"

"Something like that."

She shifted her gaze back to him. "You don't trust me, do you?"

"No, I don't trust myself."

She didn't want to dig further so decided to change the subject. "I met him in a cafeteria. I noticed him looking lost."

"And took pity on him?"

"Something like that."

"And now?"

"I think he's wonderful."

To her relief that silenced him for a long moment. But when the silence continued she hazard to look at him again. She saw him staring at the ground, his brows drawn, his jaw clenched.

She sighed. He was clearly upset, that dark, brooding energy she'd sensed before swirling around him. Just like his brother, his unhappiness tugged at her heart, but unlike Jason, his displeasure was harder to understand. Did he not like her that much because she wouldn't confess? Why did the past have to mean so much to him? "I don't know who you think I am, but for Jason's sake I don't want to be enemies."

A sour grin touched his mouth. "Just Jason's?"

"For some reason you dislike me—"

His eyes caught and held hers. "You know I feel the exact opposite."

Something intense flared through her, causing her pulse to pound. Why did he always have this effect on her? Before she could come up with something to say, he snatched her champagne and finished the contents. "My brother's been talking about introducing you to Mom and Dad. Are you ready for that?"

No. I'm not ready for any of this. I don't even know what 'this' is. "That's a discussion for us, not you."

Tytus handed her the champagne glass, his brown gaze dark with emotion. "At last something we can agree on."

~

"I THINK we have another ally to help us," Jason said a week later as he and Catherine lazed on his couch after watching a comedy, a half-eaten pizza on the coffee table littered with soda cans.

"Who?"

He stroked her neck. "Let me see if it works out first, then you'll know. Otherwise, I'll look like a fool."

Catherine moved away from his touch. "No, please tell me."

"No."

"Even if I beg?"

"No."

"And plead?"

He frowned. "Isn't that the same thing?"

"No. Please."

He shook his head.

She stared at him for a moment then tickled him. When he responded a mischievous grin spread on her face. He saw the look, jumped up and ran. And she chased him around the apartment.

"This is cruelty," he said, darting into the kitchen, then out again.

"Just give me a hint."

"No."

"At least let me guess."

He vaulted over his couch. "No."

On the other side of the couch, Catherine wiggled her fingers as if they were a menacing object. "Then you must pay," she said then crawled over the sofa and lunged towards him.

He held out his hand. "Okay, I'll tell you."

She paused, letting her hands fall. "Go on."

"It's—" He grabbed her, pinning her hands behind her. "Never mind."

"You cheat!"

He lifted a sly brow. "Yes, I'm also a thief," he said and bent his head to kiss her.

The sound of the doorbell interrupted him. He swore.

Catherine laughed. "Serves you right."

"We'll finish this later," he said, releasing her. He opened the door and saw his brother.

Tytus stepped inside then halted. "Oh, I didn't realize you had company."

"That's okay," Jason said opening the door wider. "We were just torturing each other."

Catherine sat on the edge of the couch. "Maybe we should torture him too."

"It's no use," Jason said with regret. "He's not ticklish. Just one more difference between us."

"One of many, no doubt," Catherine said.

Tytus shot her a look, but didn't reply.

"Why did you come?" Jason asked him.

Tytus shoved his hands in his jeans pockets, looking uncomfortable. "It can wait." He jerked his thumb towards the door. "I should go."

"You don't have to go." Catherine said, grabbing her handbag and keys. "I will." She pointed at Jason. "And when I see you again. I'll get you to talk about your contact." She wiggled her fingers in a threatening gesture.

He winked. "You can put your hands on me any time."

Catherine walked past Tytus, wondering why Jason's teasing made her feel embarrassed or why Tytus's gaze made her heart hammer in her ears.

Jason said something to his brother, then followed her to the elevators. "You really don't have to go. I know my brother makes you nervous, but he's really not a bad guy once you get to know him."

"It's not him."

"Yes, it is, but didn't I tell you I wouldn't let anyone hurt you?"

Catherine stopped walking. She spun around and wrapped her arms around his waist. "You're so good to me."

Jason stiffened, surprised, then wrapped his arms around her. "I told you I'm good at being patient."

Tears filled her eyes because she knew he was. She knew he understood that time was an illusion—that going fast or slow was all a matter of choice. They both knew the sweet taste of freedom and didn't need to gobble it whole. Every bite was a gift. But something about what he ignited in her—joy, fun, play, dare she call it happiness?—frightened her. She wanted to keep him safe. She knew how cruel life could be.

He wiped a tear away. "I didn't mean to make you cry."

"I'm happy," she said, releasing him. "I didn't think I'd get to be happy again."

"Come over tomorrow evening. I'll cook you dinner."

"I'll be there." She stepped into the elevator. "And you'll tell me about your contact. I don't want any secrets between us," she said, although she knew she had many.

"I will."

The doors closed as he blew her a kiss.

45

"That took you long enough," Tytus said when Jason returned to the apartment. "Did you walk her to her car?"

"Hands off," Jason said, closing the door.

"What?"

He walked over to the couch and picked up the pizza box on the coffee table. "It's my first and last warning."

"I didn't realize I needed a warning."

"Now you do," he said, taking the pizza box into the kitchen. "She's mine."

Tytus leaned against the counter. "I know that, does she?"

"Yes." He opened the refrigerator and placed the pizza box inside.

"How long have you known her? Are you sure she's all that she seems?"

"I don't care." He pulled out a can of beer and held it out.

Tytus shook his head, declining the offer. "You're serious."

He opened the can then took a long swallow. "I plan to marry her, is that serious enough for you?"

Tytus glanced around. "Where's your new roommate?"

"I paid him to stay away for awhile."

"Has he met her yet?"

"No, but he will."

"Taking your time because you're afraid he might scare her off?"

"No, besides if she's afraid of anything, I've made it quite clear that she should run to me."

"She seems like a hard woman to win over."

Jason grinned and returned to the couch. "Fortunately, I know her soft spots," he said, taking a seat.

Tytus stood in front of him. "You sound confident."

"Because I am. She just needs time and tenderness."

"And you plan to be the man who gives it to her."

"I don't plan to, I am." He took another swallow of his beer then set it down. "So look elsewhere."

"Of course." Tytus rubbed the back of his neck and sat down beside him. "I don't know why you think—"

"I've seen the way you look at her."

"It's just curiosity."

"It's more than curiosity."

Damn, he was caught. "You're right. It's just she reminds me of someone."

"Someone you slept with?"

"No." He shook his head. "Just someone."

"Fine, but don't make her pay for it."

Tytus frowned. "Pay?"

"You go out of your way to make her nervous. She's been hurt and I won't see her hurt again by anyone—especially you. I love her."

I loved her first. If it is her and I think it is, even though I don't have proof. I wanted her before you even knew she existed. Not that it mattered. She belonged to his brother now. He didn't know how he would stand having her in his life and not be able to… He inwardly groaned. He'd fought hard to forget her and now he didn't have that option. But for his brother's sake he would let it go. He'd pushed down what he felt. "Fine," Tytus said, holding up his hands in an act of surrender. He didn't know if he'd be able to stop thinking about her, stop wondering about her. In his dreams he saw her eyes, the shape of her neck, felt the feel of her fingers, smelled her faint unique scent.

This wasn't good. He had to get away, travel to get over this feeling. A feeling he'd never had for anyone before or since. He didn't know why she affected him so strongly, but clearly she had his brother under the same spell.

"How's Joscelyn?"

He blinked. "Who?"

Jason laughed. "The woman who wants you more than a desert wants water."

"She's fine."

"You don't sound very interested."

"I have a lot on my mind right now."

"Still not ready to settle down?"

Tytus forced a grin. "You'll do it for me and get Mom off my back. She thinks I work too much."

"You do, but you managed to save the company. You can take a break now." He patted him on the back. "Don't worry, big brother, the right woman is out there for you."

Tytus watched his brother go into the kitchen and let his smile fall. *I know and you're determined to marry her.*

Tytus considered getting drunk when he left his brother's place, but decided to go to work instead. *He had to get over Evelyn. His brother's happiness meant everything to him.*

He worked through the night into the next morning, not caring that it was the weekend. When he finally made it home, he crashed on the couch and went to sleep. He woke up to his cell phone ringing. Groggily, he reached out and answered it. "Hello?"

"Were you sleeping?" Joscelyn asked.

He rubbed his eyes, the light from the setting sun bathing the room in a reddish haze. He hadn't expected to sleep as long as he had. He glanced at the clock and saw it was late afternoon. "Yeah."

"Alone?"

He couldn't help a smile. "Do you want to change that?"

"I have a new bottle of wine and no one to share it with."

A beautiful woman who wanted to be with him. It was an enviable position to be in. A night with Joscelyn would be a lot better than getting drunk and trying not to think about Evelyn. He sat up.

"I'll be right there."

46

She'd never done something like this, Marie thought, looking over the investment opportunity sitting in front of her. She adjusted her glasses, absently tapping her forefinger on the worn desk in her office. It was an opportunity of a lifetime. A way to save her organization, which was in desperate need of funding—the girls they helped depended on it. Ericka Dantes had been a godsend to her. She was one of the few people who really cared about the plight of the girls they served. Most people just talked, but over the past two years Ericka had volunteered at fundraising drives, donated clothes for the girls and, most of all, donated money. At times Ericka reminded her of someone, but Marie couldn't remember who.

"And you think this is good for us?" Marie asked her.

"Yes," Ericka said, smiling at Marie in a way that made her feel reassured. "The organization is sustainable the way it's presently structured. However, if you buy this property, you not only will be able to use it but it can be leased and bring in a sizeable revenue for you.

She was right. They did need a new building.

"As I said," Ericka continued. "I'll put up half the money and you the other half. Do we have a deal?"

At least she was risking money too, that meant they were in this together. It would be tight and she'd have to scramble to get all the funds she needed, but worth it. Marie held out her hand to the woman she'd come to see as a friend. She smiled. "We have a deal."

MAN, she needed something so bad she couldn't keep still. Yvette Walker surveyed the entrance of the university student hub, hoping her target would come out soon. She wanted to do what she had to, then get a fix.

She shifted and scratched her arms, wishing it didn't feel like ants were crawling over her. Damn, she hated being like this. She knew Ms. Payton would be pissed, but she'd just needed something to get the memories to stop. The memories of the men and what they did to her. Yvette chewed on her nails. Maybe he wouldn't show up and she'd have to tell them she'd try tomorrow, hopefully he'd still give her what she needed. He'd been so sweet the other times, telling her she didn't owe him anything.

Yvette started to turn, then saw the guy she was supposed to target. Not her type at all, but tall and good looking with reddish brown skin and short cropped black hair. She looked down at the picture on her phone. Yep, that was him. She hurried over and bumped into him dropping her bag in a way so that its contents would spill out.

"Oh, sorry," she said.

"That's okay," he said, helping her pick up her books and wallet and a lipstick that had rolled away near a bush.

She waited until his back was turned before she slipped a packet into his backpack. "Thanks," she said when he turned and handed her the items he'd gathered.

He just nodded and walked away.

Yvette sighed in relief then called her dealer. "It's done."

47

———

S*he hoped he could cook*, Catherine thought with amusement as she rode the elevator to Jason's apartment for the dinner he'd promised her. If he couldn't cook, she'd just pretend to enjoy the meal.

A whisper of warning coursed through her when she approached his door and saw it was partially opened. "Jason?" Catherine said slowly pushing the door open further. She saw the place clouded in dark and cloaked in quiet. She didn't smell anything cooking on the stove. "Jason?" she called again.

When she walked further into the apartment, she turned on a lamp and saw the place in disarray—pillows thrown to the ground, a lamp broken on the floor. She pulled out her cell phone and called the police. "It may not be anything," she said when the dispatcher picked up. "But my boyfriend's place has been burglarized and I can't find him," she continued, searching around the place. She stopped when she saw a foot by the couch. She raced forward and saw Jason laying on the ground, blood seeping from his chest.

A startled cry ripped from her throat as she rushed over to him. "No, no, no," she said, falling on her knees beside him.

"Ma'am? What's wrong, ma'am?"

"I found him! I need an ambulance."

"What happened?"

"He's been shot. Please hurry!"

"Stay on the line with me."

But she couldn't. She had to stop the bleeding. She set the phone aside and got a throw cover from his couch and pressed it against the wound. "Stay with me," she pleaded, wishing he'd open his eyes. "The police are coming."

"Warn...Tytus."

He was still alive! "I will," Catherine said not knowing what he meant and not caring. All that mattered was that he held on until the EMTs arrived. "Don't worry and don't speak, you must conserve your strength."

"They warned me," he said, his eyes remaining closed as if he didn't have the strength to open them. "They warned me to leave things alone."

"You can't leave me. Hold on, please. Please."

"I didn't listen. Now Tytus..."

"Tytus can take care of himself."

"She's...dangerous. Tell him."

"I will. Just hold on. The ambulance is coming. Dear God, this is all my fault. I shouldn't have told you to—"

His eyes fluttered open. "You are the best thing to ever happen to me. I don't regret a thing. Not one moment."

"And we'll have more time together. We'll do whatever you want to do when you come out of the hospital."

"Marry me?"

"Yes, yes. I will marry you. Just stay with me a little longer."

"We'll be free together."

"Yes."

"Hold me just a little. I feel so cold."

She gathered him close, pressing her body to his. "Please stay with me."

"I love you, Evelyn. In your arms I'm always free," he said, then sighed his last breath. His body going limp. She held him tighter, tears burning her eyes. "No, no, don't go." Her gaze settled on the dining table where he'd set the place with a vase of red roses, candles and china for the dinner they'd planned to share. It was cruelly pristine and untouched in the chaos. A stark symbol of what would never be.

48

R

alph rarely hated his job. For the seven years he'd worked for Tytus Carter, he'd only had two times when he'd wished he were doing something else. Today would make a third. He took a deep breath and entered the office. "Carter?"

"Yes?" Tytus said his back to him as he stared out the window at the street outside his office. He knew his boss needed time alone—Ralph sensed something was bothering him, but didn't know exactly what. Now it didn't matter.

He cleared his throat. "It's about your brother."

Tytus spun around—sharp, quick, which was rare for a man who made sure to move slowly and methodically. "What about him?"

"He's dead."

Tytus shook his head and took a step forward. "No, I didn't hear you."

Ralph felt tears gather in his eyes and swallowed. "Yes, you did."

Tytus blinked quickly. "No, I didn't because that's impossible."

"I'm sorry. Your mother was too distraught to tell you herself."

He took a deep breath. "My brother is not...How is that possible? I just spoke to him yesterday. Yesterday he was fine."

"It appears there was a burglary that went wrong. The police are still looking into it."

Tytus didn't move. He wasn't even sure he breathed. He just stood there looking at nothing in particular.

"And you're sure...?" he finally said.

"His girlfriend was with him until the end."

Tytus paused. "Evelyn was there? Did she see anything? Was she attacked too?"

"We don't have all the particulars, but she's helping the police. It seems she was the one who found him. She comforted him through his last breath."

His last breath. Tytus couldn't process the words. How could his little brother be dead? Not when he'd been so alive. Not when he'd made so many plans. He saw them riding their bikes together, covering up a dent when he'd scratched their dad's car, when he'd won his soccer trophy, wearing his college gown. He even remembered visiting him in prison, when he'd kept his smile, although he knew every day behind bars was hell. He remembered hugging him when he'd finally gotten released. He'd just gotten his life back. It couldn't be taken like this. Tytus swore. He'd spent the night with Joscelyn as a great diversion so he wouldn't think about the future.

He'd never imagined a future without his brother in it.

Ralph took a step back and grabbed the door handle, afraid he could no longer keep his tears at bay. The devastation and misery on Tytus's face was worse than the news he'd had to share and the sound of Jason's mother's crying. "I'll leave you," he said fighting to keep his voice in check. "Let me know if you need anything."

"I do," he said in a soft voice, his gaze fixed on the ground.

"Yes?"

Tytus raised his eyes, which glistened with unshed tears of rage. "I need answers. Now."

49

He'd risk going back to prison.

Duane watched Jason's killer struggle against the restraints around his wrists and ankles. Only minutes ago, his captive had been leaving a convenience store. He hadn't heard Duane approach and couldn't fight the taser that left him immobile. And now he couldn't do much except curse against the blindfold around his eyes, and squirm in the metal chair fastened to the ground.

"What the hell do you want?"

Duane didn't speak. He just walked around the man as if he were strolling around a park, his sneakers hardly making a sound on the concrete, the chill of the abandoned warehouse dancing along his skin. But he didn't feel cold, he was too angry to feel anything.

He and the man weren't strangers, which was why when Duane saw Hampton leaving Jason's building that night, he knew he shouldn't have been there. The middle-class apartment complex wasn't his kind of place. He took his nickname from the place where the rich liked to vacation. He liked to say he made one's life easy for a price. Hampton always brought bad news at the end of a gun.

Duane hadn't made the connection until he heard about Jason's murder. He'd returned home from visiting his aunt to crime tape and neighbors talking. The police would look at the CCTV but Duane knew they wouldn't find anything. Hampton was like a ghost. He never appeared on film and if he'd been paid to do a job no one would be able to connect it to him. The police had closed the case quickly—a burglary gone wrong—and he wouldn't be able to convince them otherwise.

Duane knew the courts wouldn't be able to prove anything, so he'd have to deliver his own kind of justice.

"I said what the hell do you want?"

He had seen a lot of people die in his life. He'd had an uncle shot, a sister murdered, a cousin who thought kissing a gun was the best way to go. But when he'd heard about Jason's death, he'd cried like he hadn't since he was nine years old and his beloved grandmother died of cancer.

A guy like Jason was supposed to live to a ripe old age and then die. He wasn't supposed to be taken out like this. Duane had lived his life in shades of grey, he'd learned early that life wasn't black and white. Good and bad. But Jason had been one of the first people that made Duane believe that there was actual good in the world. Good people. And someone had him killed. He'd had to protect him inside, but he'd never thought he would have to protect him outside. Even though he knew Jason was asking some questions about the company that put him away. He hadn't thought his friend was in real trouble.

He'd live with that regret forever, but he'd make amends.

"Jason Redmon," Duane said. "Tell me what you know."

Hampton smiled. "I don't know who you're talking about."

Duane pulled out his gun. "Do you want to lose a knee or a foot?"

"I don't—"

Duane pointed at Hampton's big toe and fired.

Hampton screamed, then let out a string of expletives.

"I saw you there. Of course you can pretend that you don't know anything and I can pretend I don't know where your little girl goes to school."

"I don't like threats."

Duane fired again, hitting Hampton's second toe. "Does that sound like a threat?"

"I don't—"

Duane fired a third time, this time hitting Hampton in the shoulder. "I bet you thought I'd go for another toe, but I like to mix things up."

"You crazy son of a—"

"Tell me what you know or the next one will hit your heart."

50

______

S he had to find out who Jason's contact was.

Catherine knew what she was doing was illegal, but she didn't have a choice. If picking the lock to Jason's apartment would help her get the information she needed to catch his killer, she'd do it. *Jason.* She still couldn't believe he was gone. Couldn't believe that the last time she was here she'd been so happy.

She'd always remember him blowing her a kiss. She wouldn't remember how she'd found him. Everything had gone so drastically wrong. But she didn't know how. She knew it hadn't been a burglary, but that was only instinct, she had no proof. She knew that he'd found something she only wished he'd told her what. With a soft click, the lock disengaged and she slipped into the apartment. She flicked her flashlight on and swept the room, trying to push from her mind the scene from before. It had been dark then too and when she'd turned on the lights and found Jason...

"You might as well put that away and turn on the lights."

Catherine froze, her stomach twisting in knots. She knew that deep, gritty voice and it seemed to reach out to her in the darkness. What was he doing there? Why did he have to be there? What could she tell him?

She heard him sigh and then a table light turned on. Tytus looked at her from the couch. "Nice of you to drop in."

His words were a little slurred and when she stepped closer she noticed the beer cans that littered the floor and table. Maybe that was a good thing, then he wouldn't ask too many questions.

"I'd left something here," she said, trying to sound nonchalant though her pounding heart made her feel breathless. "I have a key," she said making a motion of putting something in her jacket pocket, hoping he wouldn't ask to see it.

"Took you long enough to use it."

Did that mean he heard her picking the lock? She gripped her hands into fists. She didn't have time for him or his strange comments. "Excuse me," she said then went into Jason's bedroom, but his laptop was gone and so were some papers and several flash drives. She swore. This changed everything.

She returned to the living room.

Tytus hadn't moved. "Did you find what you were looking for?" he asked.

"No," she said unsure whether he cared or not.

"Shame."

Catherine made a noncommittal sound. She hadn't found what she needed and she didn't want to be alone with him. She headed for the door.

"Just for one night pretend to be her."

She halted with her hand on the door. *Why did he have to bring that up now?* She swallowed. "Who?"

"The other one. The one I met before. The one who reads dreams."

"You're drunk."

He shook his head. "Not enough."

Catherine slowly turned to face him, ready to say no. Ready to escape a room that both repelled and drew her and the man who did the same. But when she finally looked at him, he looked so miserable—anguished, devastated, distraught—that the sight of him briefly brought tears to her eyes. She'd remembered his eulogy at Jason's funeral, how his voice broke, how he held his mother who could barely stand. Her heart couldn't refuse him, although her mind screamed no. It was risky to pretend, but they'd both lost so much and she knew she may be the cause of Jason's death—if she hadn't encouraged him to look into his case he might still be alive— she felt that she owed Tytus somehow. She glanced at the littered beer cans and doubted he'd even remember the evening.

"You should—"

He held out his hand. "Please, just once."

She took his hand, her skin tingling when she touched him, and sat down beside him. She cleared her throat, hoping to keep her voice steady. "I probably won't do it right since I don't know how she did it."

Tytus bit his lip and shook his head. "I don't care."

"Close your eyes."

"I'm afraid to," he said, closing his fingers and trapping her hand in his.

She didn't move, not sure how to read him. "Are the dreams fierce?"

"I wished they'd warned me. I would have protected him. I could have done something."

"No, you couldn't."

"You sound certain of that. She was certain of things too."

Catherine glanced down at their hands. "Did you hold her hand like this?"

"I wanted to," he said, his voice deepening. "There was so much I wanted to say to her, but she disappeared."

"I'm sure she had a reason. And now you must forget her."

"Or try to find her again," he countered.

She had to change the subject. "If you want to pretend, you have to tell me your dream."

Tytus fell silent then said, "I'm at a large banquet where all the food is wax. But everyone else is eating it and they are happy and I'm starving."

"Are you really starving or does it just appear that way?"

He paused. "You're right. I feel fine, but I feel like I should be eating too. My brother is a little boy and he keeps his hand on my shirt, tugging on me every time I go towards the table."

"Your brother visited you in the dream?"

"It only felt like that, I'm sure it wasn't real."

But she knew it was very real. His brother wanted to warn him. *Warn Tytus*, he'd said before he died. But from what? She still didn't know. She envied Tytus's connection with Jason. She'd hoped he'd visit her too, but her dreams were no longer remarkable, except for the one when she was a child and she wasn't sure that would ever come true. But she couldn't focus on her pain, when Tytus's pain was so clear. She could offer him comfort. Perhaps he'd even forget her words and imagine it was a dream too.

"You must be very careful about the people surrounding you," she said. "There will be a major opportunity that you must resist. It will be tempting but you must turn away."

"Must I turn away from every temptation?" he asked holding her gaze.

"I don't understand."

"I think you do. What step should I take?"

She pulled her hand away and stood. "I can't help you."

"What about another dream I have? A dream where I'm in

this big bed and I like it, no...that's wrong. I love it. It's perfect for me, but then I lose the bed and it ends up in my brother's house and he loves it as much as I do. I don't have the heart to tell him the bed had once been mine so I let him have it until...one day my brother's no longer around and I want the bed back. Should I take it?"

"You and your brother may have loved the bed, but was the bed ever yours to claim?"

"Good question."

"You can always get a new bed. Property can always be replaced." She should know, she'd been property for years.

"Why did you disappear?"

She turned. "I'm going home."

"Make up a reason, I don't care."

"We've pretended enough."

"Not enough for me. I want to pretend that my brother's still alive. That he'll come through that door or send me a text. I want to pretend that my mother..." his words fell away.

Catherine turned back and knelt in front of him, remembering how lost she'd felt after Evelyn died. "I know."

"It hurts so much I'm afraid I'll never stop missing him."

"I know."

"Did you know I'm a selfish bastard?" He nodded at the look of surprise on her face. "I wanted him out of the way so I could have you to myself. But not like this. I would change places with him in an instant."

"He wouldn't have wanted that."

He studied her for a long moment. "You're not angry at me."

"You can't stop how you feel."

"No. Can you?" he asked his dark, gritty voice low with meaning.

Catherine swallowed unable to read him. Something had changed. Suddenly his words didn't appear to be as slurred.

Suddenly his gaze seemed clear—more intense. She saw a quiet fury simmering in his eyes.

"I should—"

"Tell me what happened."

Now she could read him. She could see his fury, but it was controlled. Too controlled. She didn't know how to proceed. There was so much she couldn't tell him. He'd tricked her, he'd gotten her to let her guard down. "I don't know what to tell you."

"Yes you do."

"The police said—"

"I know what the police think. That's not why I'm here and you know that. Why is my brother dead?"

"I don't—"

She stopped when he lifted his hand. He frowned. "Why did you flinch like that? Did you think I was going to hit you?"

Yes. "No."

"I don't hit women." Tytus folded his arms. "I just don't want you to confuse me for a patient man. I want answers not lies."

"I'm not—"

He let his arms fall to his sides and leaned forward. "We both know he wasn't killed by a burglar."

She paused wondering why he would think that. What made him suspect? Did he know something she didn't?

"Am I right?"

There was no point in denying it. "Yes."

"My brother was keeping secrets. Jason never used to, until he met you," he said sending her a cutting stare. "But you're good with secrets I imagine."

She blinked. She wouldn't be provoked. That would give him the upper hand. "Do you have a question?"

"What was he hiding? I overheard him mention a 'contact'?"

Catherine shook her head. "I never got to hear who he'd spoken to. I can't—"

Tytus hung his head. "Did you love him at all?"

"With all my heart."

"You admit to having one?" he said with a cynical twist of his lips. "My brother had the biggest heart of anyone I'd ever known and he'd fallen hard for you. He would have done anything for you. Walked over hot coals, run into a burning building, taken a bullet for you. Wait, he already did that."

"I didn't kill him!"

"Then who did?"

He had her. He'd stabbed her with his accusations and caused her to lose her composure--again. Now he was twisting the knife. "I don't know."

"But you have an idea," he pressed, his eyes studying her.

"I couldn't stop him and..."

"You couldn't stop him from what?"

Catherine sighed defeated. "We were investigating the company that charged him with embezzlement."

"You think they're behind this?"

"Yes, but I don't have proof. Don't worry I'll find it. Your brother will be revenged."

"Why didn't he tell me? There's nothing wrong with him trying to clear his name."

"He didn't want you or your mother to know. He—I was afraid it was dangerous."

"But he trusted you."

"Yes."

"Why?"

Because I gave him the idea. "I don't know."

Tytus folded his arms. "Another lie, but I'll let that slide for now."

"All you need to know is that—"

He wagged a finger. "No, don't tell me what I need to know.

I'm not going anywhere until I get the answers I need. The answers I deserve."

"Yes, you're right." She clasped her hands together, choosing her words carefully. "I didn't realize it would be so dangerous or I would have done everything to stop him. In the end he was worried about you."

"Me?"

"Yes."

"Why?"

"That's what I am trying to figure out."

"So that's what you're hoping to find on his laptop?" When Catherine hesitated, he continued. "It was one of the things our 'burglar' decided to steal."

"Of course."

"I think we should work together."

"And why should I trust you?"

"You don't have to trust me, but if you want to avenge my brother's death, you'd better consider it."

"Why would I do that?"

His dark eyes flashed with promise. "Because when it comes to revenge, I plan to get it first."

No, you won't. "Goodbye," she said.

"Until we meet again," he said as she walked out the door.

Moments later, Catherine sat in her car contemplating her next steps. She couldn't work with Tytus. She couldn't continue to play Evelyn with him when he was determined to treat her like Catherine. She had too much to do. She'd have to find the truth on her own.

Her cell phone rang just as she started the ignition. She glanced down and she saw a familiar number. "Hello?"

"Evelyn?"

"Yes," she said, surprised to hear Duane's voice. She'd gotten to know Jason's former cellmate without Jason knowing about it.

She knew a man with Duane's background could prove useful. So far he'd proved loyal and trustworthy.

"I've got some information," he said.

"I'm listening."

"I know who Jason's contact was."

PART IV

REVENGE

51

———

A RE YOU SURE THE BABY IS YOURS? C

Greg looked at the note then looked at his wife with new suspicion as she sat on the other end of the couch. Who was 'C' and why had they left the note on his desk at his office? Was it a prank? If it was real, what did they suspect?

"Is there something you want to tell me?" he asked her, hoping to sound nonchalant.

"Why would there be anything?"

He handed her the note.

Lorna looked at it, her lip trembling a fraction before she frowned. "Well, this is clearly a joke."

"I missed the punch line. This isn't the first."

"What do you mean?"

"I've gotten other notes like this. All one sentence. All like this."

"Then someone's stalking you."

"What are you hiding from me?"

"Nothing."

He nodded at her stomach. "We both know this mistake shouldn't have happened."

"The baby is yours, I haven't been with anyone else. I can't believe what you're accusing me of."

He couldn't either. He never would have suspected this, but now... "I want to make sure."

"You can't be serious. I haven't been with anyone. When would I have the time?"

Her outrage didn't bother him, but made him more determined. "We'll make an appointment."

"I won't go."

"Because the child isn't mine?"

"Because this is insulting."

"You know this isn't even the worst of them."

"I don't care."

He went over to a desk drawer and pulled out a slip of paper. "No, you'll like this one. It said 'Are you sure your wife's pregnant?' I wonder why they'd say that?"

"Because they're crazy."

"You haven't let me see you these past several months."

"I just haven't been in the mood."

"Remember when we took a shower together when you were pregnant with—"

Lorna stood. "I'm going to bed," she said, heading for the hallway.

"Are you planning on having a miscarriage?"

She halted, but didn't dare to turn around.

"That's what another note said. 'Be careful, she might miscarry.' Isn't that strange for someone to say?"

"Yes."

"What are you hiding?"

"Nothing."

"Then why have you made doctor's visits that you haven't

gone to?" He slowly stood and approached her. "Isn't that strange."

"Please don't do this. Trust me. I—"

"Why are you backing away from me? Isn't it right for a father to touch his unborn child?"

Lorna searched her mind in a panic. What should she do? Who was sending him notes and why? Why were they doing this to them?

"Greg," Lorna said taking another step back. "Let's talk about this."

"There's nothing to talk about. Do as I say or this marriage is over."

MARIE HURRIED to the apartment number left on her phone. She'd gotten a frantic call from one of the girls, but she wouldn't explain what was wrong. She knocked on the door, hoping she could be heard over the loud rock music coming from down the hall.

A well-dressed woman answered.

Marie took a step back. "Ericka, what are you doing here? I must have the wrong number."

Ericka opened the door wider. "No, I've been expecting you."

Marie looked around the dimly lit room, but didn't step inside. What was going on? Why was her friend here? "Where's—"

"You'll find out in a minute."

She hesitated then entered. She stopped when she saw the girl who'd called her, Yvette Walker, sitting on the bed looking scared. But she wasn't alone. Aaron sat next to her looking just as terrified.

Marie spun around to Ericka. "What's going on here?"

"That's what I need to find out," another voice said. Marie turned and saw a tall, thin black man step out from another room.

"Ms. Payton, I'm sorry," Yvette said.

"It's okay." But she wasn't sure. Had Ericka come to intervene? What did this man want? He pointed to Yvette. "This one owes me and this one," he nodded at Aaron, " stole from me."

Marie swallowed. She knew Yvette had a substance abuse problem, but after four years in the trade that wasn't unusual. However that didn't explain why her brother was there. What would he be doing with a drug dealer?

"But I didn't, I swear," Aaron said.

The man emptied Aaron's backpack and uncovered a packet of white powder. "Do you still want to argue?"

Aaron blinked quickly, stunned. "I don't know how that got there."

Marie adjusted her glasses, trying to look more confident than she felt. "How much does she owe you?"

"Three thousand."

That much? Fortunately, she could easily cover it. "I'll write you a check."

He laughed, then looked at Ericka, who hadn't moved, but her eyes continued to watch them. "A check? She's adorable," he said.

"I can go to the bank," Marie corrected.

"That's better."

She nodded to the packet. "And you got that back so let's just pretend—"

"Do I look like a kid to you? I don't play make-believe and I don't like thieves."

"How much more do you want?'

"I don't want your money. I want to know the best way to punish him. I thought he should work it off."

"No, let me take the blame, he's just getting his life started."

"You'll take his place?" Ericka said.

"Yes."

"Even if it means your life?"

"Yes."

"No, Marie," Aaron said.

"Shut up."

Ericka folded her arms. "You love your brother very much."

"Yes," Marie said, wondering why her friend suddenly seemed so cold and distant. She'd told her how proud she was of him and how well he was doing in his studies at the university. She hadn't mentioned how miserable Aaron was or how worried they both were about their mother's health, which had become fragile recently.

Ericka whispered something to the man, who nodded before saying, "You can all go. You have a week, I'll contact you again."

Marie looked at Ericka, relieved her friend had come to help them. She'd been worried for a moment. She ushered Yvette and Aaron into the hallway.

"I swear I didn't do anything," Aaron said.

"I'm so sorry," Yvette said at the same time.

"We'll talk about this later," Marie said. At least she'd gotten her and Aaron away from that man—for now. She'd have to find out how her brother had gotten mixed up with him. Before she could ask the sullen figure beside her, her cell phone rang. She looked at the number then answered. "Clara, I can't talk right now, but—"

"We're in trouble," Clara interrupted her.

"What?"

"The investment money is gone."

Marie gripped the phone, her hands suddenly feeling clammy. "How?"

"It was all a sham. There was no building."

Marie felt sick. She'd borrowed and used all her savings to get the building. Her finances had been stretched to the limit. Now she wouldn't have the three thousand to pay Yvette's debt. There had to be a mistake. She had to talk to Ericka.

Marie raced back to the room, relieved when the door easily opened when she tried the knob. Her heart crashed to her feet when she found the room empty and realized she'd been scammed.

"THERE SEEMS to be concerns about your involvement with the incident about—"

"I was cleared," Joscelyn interrupted, not wanting Dr. Swartz to bring up a long ago malpractice suit. Why was that being brought up now? She'd come to his office expecting good news about her promotion.

"Yes, we've had an anonymous contact," he said, resting his hairy forearms on the desk. "New questions are coming to light."

"Questions?"

"I'm sure they can be answered, but there are concerns about your business's relationship with Sintex and a young man named Jason Redmon."

"That incident has nothing to do with me."

"You're dating his brother now, correct?"

It was impossible. How could anyone make a connection between her and Jason's case? She hadn't meant for Jason to die. She'd hoped Jack would make sure Jason got a good scare. Instead the idiot had hired someone to take him out. At least it had given her a chance to get closer to Tytus. He was determined to find his brother's killer and she'd help him find the perfect scapegoat. "My private life is none of your business or anyone's."

"Unfortunately, there seems to be information to the contrary."

She hated when people used mealy-mouse words. Why couldn't he come to the point and tell her what he knew? But she couldn't be direct either. Feigning innocence had become an art for her. "What information?"

He held out a file. "Perhaps you should read this," he said.

Joscelyn stared at a file she thought had disappeared for good, but seemed to have risen from the dead.

52

Catherine watched Joscelyn enter the ballroom with Tytus on her arm, looking as if she held the world in her hand. Fortunately, Catherine knew it was all a façade. But she knew she'd have to do a lot more damage to get her to crack. She had Marie scrambling to save her brother, Yvette and her business; Lorna was trying to save her marriage and way of life, and Joscelyn's chance of being the head of her department was looking like a distant dream as she dealt with the legal issue surrounding the embezzlement case, but Catherine knew her eldest stepsister would need a stronger push to send her over the edge.

She'd had no desire to attend the fundraiser for the hospital, but she had to if she wanted to put the second part of her plan into play. She waited for Joscelyn to be distracted and Tytus moved to the side to talk to other guests. It had only been two weeks since she'd spoken to him in Jason's apartment, but it felt like ages. He said he wanted to work together, and now she could use him. Catherine quickly checked her reflection, then approached him.

"Hello," she said.

He turned. "You've ignored my calls and texts."

"I've been busy."

"And you're not busy anymore?"

"No," she said, glancing to the side to see if Joscelyn was paying attention to them. Just as she hoped, her sister's gaze had focused in on them. Catherine smiled up at Tytus, then brushed something from his cheek.

He grabbed her wrist. "What was that?"

She shivered, wishing his touch didn't always affect her so strongly. "You had something on your cheek," she said, keeping her smile in place so that her sister could misinterpret his gesture.

Tytus narrowed his eyes. "Don't make me part of your game."

"You don't like playing games?" Catherine asked, struggling to keep her smile in place.

"Not when I'm the toy."

"I'd never toy with you." She glanced at Joscelyn. "Please let me go."

He glanced at Joscelyn, then returned his gaze to her. "No," he said, then covered her mouth with his.

For a moment the world stopped and just as suddenly started spinning again. She stared up at him, wondering if she'd just imagined it all, but his heated gaze told her it had all been very real. She bit her lip, panicked. He shouldn't have kissed her, no matter how briefly. He'd raised the stakes higher than she'd planned to. "You shouldn't have done that."

"Why not?"

She glanced at Joscelyn and saw the cool mask in place, but knew not to be fooled. Her sister was boiling. She'd made an enemy. But so had he.

His gaze searched her face. "What aren't you telling me?"

So much. How could she protect him now? "Go to her now and tell her that I made you kiss me."

He raised a brow. "And why would I do that?"

Because she's more dangerous than you realize. "She cares about you."

"I can't help that."

"And you care about her."

He shrugged. "We're not exclusive." He narrowed his gaze. "But you didn't answer my question."

"Please go to her."

"You're trembling. Tell me—"

"I'll explain later."

He shook his head. "No, you'll explain now," he said, then led her outside the ballroom. Once they were alone in the hallway, he said, "What has gotten you so frightened?"

"I wish you hadn't kissed me. What did you do that for?"

"What do you want to ignore more—my question or how I feel about you?"

Both. "You don't know me."

"You're making that very hard. What are you keeping back or should I ask Joscelyn?" He turned.

She grabbed his arm. "No," she said, quickly releasing him when he faced her. She took a step back as if she'd just happened upon a lion.

"What is it between you two?" he asked, his compelling eyes holding her still.

"Your brother met with her."

"So what?"

"I believe that Joscelyn is responsible for what happened to him."

The corner of his mouth kicked up in a cynical smirk. "You think Joscelyn's a killer? Impossible."

No, it's not. You don't know her as well as I do. She's capable of anything. "She may—"

"She didn't kill my brother."

"How do you know? She—"

"She couldn't have."

"Why not?"

"Because she spent that night with me."

His words hit her like shards of ice. He was her alibi! She had meant to tell him what she'd discovered about Joscelyn, but now knew that would be useless. She didn't know why the thought of Joscelyn being with Tytus made her heart sink. She knew they were close, but hadn't thought they'd become intimate. She looked at him through new eyes, seeing a stranger.

What kind of man was this? How could he sleep with one woman and kiss another? He'd been toying with her about his dream of the bed, of his feelings for the woman in the past. She'd learned there were few people she could trust, and she was glad she hadn't completely trusted him and knew she never would. Her heart bled a little, but her steely resolve helped to fuse it close, wrapping her heart in iron. She had no claim on him now, or ever.

He was in bed with the enemy and that made him an enemy too.

"But I haven't been with her since—"

"It doesn't matter," Catherine said, wishing that were true. Wishing the iron around her heart didn't melt a bit. She wanted to hate him or feel neutral, but she couldn't. Her emotions weren't important, it was defeating Joscelyn. "There are a few things you don't know—"

"Can I join or is this a private party?" Joscelyn said, approaching them.

"I was just sharing memories about Jason," Catherine said, not surprised that Joscelyn had made an appearance. She'd expected her sooner.

Joscelyn wrapped an arm around Tytus's arm. "I know you're

heartbroken because you lost one brother, but don't expect to get the other."

A cold and callous remark. Her stepsister so wanted to hurt her that she didn't notice how Tytus flinched or the expression of pain that briefly crossed his face. "You sound jealous," Catherine said. "Don't you trust your man?"

Tytus pulled his arm away. "I'm nobody's—"

"I'm a very jealous woman," Joscelyn said in a cool tone.

Catherine winked at her. "That's good to know." She turned. "Don't mess with me, Ms. Williams."

Catherine walked away, unable to stop a smile. *I already have.*

53

―――――

"What were you two talking about?" Joscelyn demanded once Evelyn was out of hearing.

"She told you," Tytus said, watching Evelyn return to the ballroom. "Jason."

Joscelyn studied his face for a long moment. "But she bothers you."

"Yes." She bothered him more and more every day. And now he wondered if she was more connected to his brother's murder than she let on. She seemed determined to use him to get at Joscelyn. He didn't like being used. His brother was a true innocent, but Evelyn definitely wasn't and she was starting to make him angry. No, he was already angry. "She's not all that she seems."

"What makes you say that?"

"I know I've met her before."

"I had that same feeling."

He looked at her curious. "Where do you think you've met her?"

"I don't know."

He rested his hands on his hips. "I do," he said in a grave tone.

Joscelyn's tone sharpened. "Where?"

"A long time ago in England, but her name wasn't Evelyn."

"It was something else? What?"

"She was just called Epic."

Joscelyn frowned. "That's strange."

"It was a stage name. She worked with two other people. They seemed shady but she was the real thing."

"What did she do?"

"She read dreams."

~

SHE READ DREAMS!

Joscelyn sat in her Jacuzzi as the soft sound of a string quarter came through the speakers. She had to be calm and rational. She scooped up water and watched it slip through her fingers. She hadn't been able to convince Tytus to spend the night with her again. He'd been a magnificent lover and she was eager to repeat their time together, but he kept turning her down. At first she'd blamed his brother's death and that was understandable, but now she was growing impatient. They were perfect for each other and it was time that he saw that.

She read dreams.

Joscelyn briefly closed her eyes and took a deep breath. Evelyn was trying to anger her, but it wouldn't work. She'd underestimated Tytus. Joscelyn remembered the look of annoyance on his face when Evelyn left. He may have kissed her, but the moment had been fleeting and meaningless. She'd chosen him for a reason and although he didn't know why, Joscelyn was beginning to suspect the reason.

Was she...? She hadn't thought of her in so long and didn't

want to say her name. She was supposed to have disappeared from their lives for good.

But there was something very familiar about Evelyn that she couldn't deny, but after all these years, how had she managed to escape and set herself up so well? She wasn't that bright. A scheme like this would take cunning that her stepsister hadn't possessed. It could just be a coincidence.

But she wouldn't leave anything to chance, she had to find out more. If what she suspected was true, she could understand why their lives seemed suddenly under attack. Lorna's marriage had broken up, Marie's business was on the brink of financial ruin and she'd asked for an emergency loan of three thousand dollars, not telling her what the money was for, when Marie had hardly spoken to her for years. She hadn't gone to her mother for the loan because of their mother's declining health.

Joscelyn ran her hand over the surface of the water. She had to find out if her suspicions were correct. She could let Evelyn know about their mother's health and see how it affected her. Her stepsister always had a soft spot for their mother and that would give her the upper hand.

"THIS IS VERY GENEROUS OF YOU," Vera said when Joscelyn arrived in Vera's office and handed her a check to support the charity Vera supported. She looked at the large amount then back up at the younger woman. "What made you decide to help us?"

Joscelyn took a seat in front of her. "Evelyn told me about it."

"Evelyn didn't tell me that she knew you, but then again, I don't know all of her friends."

And I'm certainly not one of them. "Yes, well, she told me all about you."

"Oh she's been such a blessing to me and her father."

"Is it true that you found her after searching for many years?"

"Yes, it's no secret. Although she's only been in our life for a few years, it feels as if I've known her all my life."

"But do you know much about her life before?"

Vera put the check away in a drawer. "She doesn't like to talk about her past. Especially Catherine."

Joscelyn froze. No, it couldn't be. "Who?"

"Catherine. Her dear friend. They met in England and were together for at least three years. Everyone in the village thought they were sisters because they looked so much alike."

They looked alike? Her name was Catherine? Catherine!!

"How did she meet this Catherine?" she asked, her fingers tensed in her lap.

"The women she worked for found her. She told Evelyn that she'd run away, saying she'd been enslaved for years. Can you imagine such a thing still exists?"

Enslaved? She was free? It was her? "Yes," Joscelyn said, no longer focusing on the conversation as blood-chilling anger slithered over her skin. She would make Catherine regret setting foot back on American soil.

54

"I know the reason for all our recent trouble," Joscelyn said.

It had been years since the three sisters had been in the same room. Today they sat in Joscelyn's sitting room. Outside a bright moon hung in the sky, inside a tense energy filled the air. Marie refused to eat any of the elaborate snacks laid out on the table and Lorna couldn't stop.

"Trouble?" Lorna said, munching on a carrot, wiping tears from her eyes. "You call the destruction of my marriage a bit of trouble?"

"You think that's anything?" Marie said. "I've lost all my money, I had to beg a drug dealer not to force Aaron to work for him and pay off a debt one of the girls I help owed."

"It's because we're under attack," Joscelyn said. "We have to be extra careful."

"Attack?" Lorna asked.

"Why?" Marie asked.

"Someone doesn't like us very much," Joscelyn said.

"Who?" Marie said outraged. "I haven't done anything. I've spent the last several years trying to help people and—"

"And you think you deserve a gold star or something?" Joscelyn said with a sneer.

Marie folded her arms. "Why are we here?"

"Do you want me to charge interest on the loan?"

Marie let her arms fall. "I shouldn't have asked you."

"But you did," Joscelyn said in a low voice, then pinned her sister with a fierce look. "Some things cannot be changed."

Marie let her gaze fall.

"He took my girls," Lorna said. "I can't believe Greg left me and took the girls with him. They need their mother. How could he do this?"

Joscelyn crossed her legs and leaned forward. "I may be able to get them back for you."

"How?"

"You said we're under attack," Marie said impatient. "By who?"

Joscelyn leaned back with a satisfied smile of triumph. "If I'm correct, you'll find out very soon."

55

―――――

The sight of three dozen yellow roses in her bedroom was a surprise. Catherine walked up to one bouquet and read the note:

TO MY DARLING DAUGHTER EVELYN. MUCH LOVE, MOM

Catherine took the card and found Vera in the kitchen washing out a tea cup.

"What's this?" she asked holding up the card.

Vera turned to her and beamed. "Because you're so wonderful."

"But I didn't do anything."

Vera wagged a finger at her. "It's just like you to be so humble."

What was she talking about? "I really don't—"

"Okay, okay. We'll pretend that you didn't convince one of your friends to come by my office today and make a generous donation."

An icy prickle of fear coursed through her. She didn't have friends. She couldn't afford to. "Friend?"

"Yes, Joscelyn Payton."

Joscelyn had gotten to her? "She saw you?"

"Yes." She hugged her. "You don't have to pretend that you didn't put her up to it. She's not known as the most generous woman. But I guess her mother's sickness has changed her."

Catherine started. "Her mother's sick?"

"She didn't tell you?"

Catherine could only manage to shake her head.

"Yes, cancer. It's terminal. She seemed very distraught, which is understandable, but I didn't think she'd share so much with me."

"How long does her mother have?"

"Months."

Mummy was sick? The ten year old who still lived inside her raged against the thought. How could she be sick? In her mind her mother had seemed invincible. She couldn't be sick. She couldn't die. Not yet. She was supposed to live a long life. She may never see her again. She hadn't realized how much she wanted that, until now. She wanted to see her stepmother's face again and say 'Mummy, I'm home' and be held in her embrace. But would she care? Was it best to leave things alone?

How was she taking all that was happening to her daughters? Was that making her illness worse? She'd hoped to punish her sisters, not her mother. Catherine stopped her rapid thoughts. Why had Joscelyn told Vera about her mother? She knew her sister was usually a very private person. Had she told her on purpose. And why?

Why had Joscelyn given Vera a check? What was she up to? What was her plan? She knew she'd made an enemy, but hadn't expected the next move to be this. What game was she playing?

Catherine knew the answer didn't matter. The fact that Joscelyn had approached Vera was a sinister sign. She knew her sister wasn't above hurting others and she wanted to keep Vera and Noah safe. Now the clock was ticking. Her mother was dying.

She didn't have the time she needed to put together a grand plan, she had to face her now and she needed help.

DESPERATION. That was the only reason she'd contacted Tytus. She had to expose Joscelyn's true nature and tell him the truth. She leaned against a column in the atrium of the National Museum of Natural History in the rotunda where a giant elephant looked as if it were ready to roar.

She'd sent him a text and he'd replied, but she wasn't sure he'd show up. He could change his mind at the last minute. He hadn't been convinced the last time she'd hinted at Joscelyn's nature and she may not be able to convince him now, but she had to try. She straightened from the column when she saw him enter the museum, his big, powerful form making its way easily through the crowd of people. *Don't make me part of your game.* He was right, she'd selfishly brought people into her quest for vengeance—Jason, him, Noah and Vera—and she had to stop before someone else got hurt.

"So what's this about?" he asked, looming over her.

She headed down one of the corridors not having the courage to look up at him. "I need to tell you all that I know. I—"

"Wait," he said taking her hand and stopping her. "Why do you look terrified?"

Because I am.

"What's happened?"

She bit her lip. *Too much.*

"No matter what you tell me, I won't hurt you. You're safe with me."

Safe. When was the last time she felt truly safe? She glanced down at his hand for the first time not frightened by the feelings he ignited in her. She wouldn't run anymore. "You're right," she said in a low voice. "We did meet before. I was a slave for over ten years when I met you."

"A slave to what?"

"People. I was property."

He shook his head. "I don't understand."

She lifted her gaze, a wry grin on her face. "Yes, you do. You just don't want to."

"You were a slave? A real slave?"

Are there fake ones? She nodded.

"Where?"

"Many places. Nigeria, Germany, England. That's where you met me. I'd recently escaped from my last mistress and was being held by Robbie and Faye. I finally left them and was found by two kind women. That's where I met Evelyn. She worked for them."

Tytus rubbed his forehead, glancing down the corridor before looking at her again. "Wait, you mean you were an actual slave?"

Catherine sighed. If he couldn't get past that, how could she tell him the rest? "Yes."

"I knew you were in trouble. You looked so scared. You said I frightened you."

"You did. When you've seen what I have, you learn to be frightened."

"I could have helped you."

"I wouldn't have trusted you."

"How did it happen?"

"I was sold as a little girl. When I saw your brother, I felt a connection to him. I could tell he'd been enslaved too, in another way. That was our bond. I wanted to help clear his name," she said, knowing she'd never tell him she'd initially just meant to use him. "And now I am a slave again. Because you hold the key to my freedom."

"Don't talk like that."

"It's true." Tears fell down her cheeks.

"Why won't you believe me when I say I won't hurt you? You know how I feel about you."

"You don't know me." She tugged on her shirt. "These clothes hide a body deformed by scars and marred by beatings. But they are nothing compared to the scars that have mutilated my heart. I didn't love your brother enough to protect and care for him as I should have. He was too good for me. I warned him not to love me and I'm giving you the same warning. What you see before you is not a woman. I am a ghost, wandering through life and haunting others. That's my only true existence."

He cupped the side of her face, his gaze tender. "No, it's not."

Catherine held herself still to stop herself from leaning into his touch. His words stirred up hope in her, hope she's buried long ago. But she wasn't here to feel human again, she'd come for one reason only. "Joscelyn is dangerous." She held up a hand. "Just hear me out before you argue."

He let his hand fall. "I wasn't going to," he said, then continued down the corridor.

She took a deep breath and followed him, glad she didn't have to hold his gaze anymore. "I believe Joscelyn is responsible for your brother going to prison. I had an investigator help me look into her affairs. Her skin care company was doing poorly, so she devised a scam. Sintex was a ghost corporation, which she secretly bought several years back under another name. Owners remain unknown and individuals face little risk of being investigated because of this. Once she owned it, she used this company to infect the files of several large hospital systems nationally so that they would have to pay Sintex exorbitant fees to fix the problem. She then funneled money made from the scam into her skin care company to make it look profitable although it wasn't.

"Your brother, while working at Sintex, unwittingly found out about the scam and reported it to one of his directors, and they needed a scapegoat to cover their tracks and he was selected. Everything was fine until he looked deeper into it when he got out of prison and discovered that the scam was larger than anyone suspected. He went to Joscelyn, not knowing she was involved, hoping she'd help him."

"And you think she hired someone to kill him?"

"I don't think. I know. A friend of Jason's discovered who had been hired and got the man to talk."

He clasped his hands behind his back and kept his tone neutral. "Is this friend willing to talk in court?"

"No, but I was able to get a key document and send it to influential people who will make life a little more difficult for her."

He shook his head. "This won't work."

"But—"

"She's clever and she's clean. No one can link her to my brother's death or this scam. She'll fire the CEO or CFO and claim ignorance. It will take too much time and money to make any charges stick. Trust me, I've considered every option."

"But how could you...?" She sighed as a thought came to her. "You had his laptop, didn't you?"

"No, but I did find the flash drives."

"And you didn't tell me?"

"I told you we should work together," he said without apology. "And from the digging I've done we can make her nervous, she may get a suspension or reprimand, but nothing serious. We can't touch her."

Catherine could feel herself trembling. *She'd come this far and Joscelyn would remain untouched? There was nothing she could do?*

"But even if we could," he continued. "I don't think Joscelyn would go that far. Do you think she'd be with me while she hired someone to kill my brother?"

He didn't believe her, he wouldn't help her. She was on her own again. "She's capable of anything." She spun away.

Tytus grabbed her arm then immediately let go when she flinched. "What is this personal vendetta you have against her?"

Catherine stared at him for a long moment, knowing the moment would come, but still surprised how hard it was to say the words. "I know her better than you do."

"How?"

"Because she's my eldest stepsister and she was the one who sold me."

Tytus stared at her for a long moment, stunned. Then his expression clouded in anger and regret. "Shit."

"What?"

"I think I helped Joscelyn figure out who you are."

56

T he angry sound of a fly trapped in a spider's web buzzed in his ear as he sat on the orange vinyl-covered chair and added sugar to a cup of coffee he'd probably not drink.

Tytus glanced up at the corner where the large spider's web hung, then let his gaze fall to a faded photograph of the Lincoln Memorial. The out of the way diner wasn't one of the nicest places to eat, but he hadn't chosen it for the food. He wanted a place to talk to Catherine without being seen and he needed to think. He was still trying to absorb all that she'd told him. She and Joscelyn were stepsisters? On a trip abroad she'd been lured into a van and sold? She thought Joscelyn may have gotten Jason killed? How could he have misjudged her so much?

"You can stay with me," he said.

"I won't hide from her," Catherine said, using her fork to poke the large slice of chocolate cake he'd ordered for her.

"I'm not asking you to hide, but...I feel responsible."

"I'm not running either. She's made a move and she'll wait to see how I respond."

"Or she might not. You don't have much time."

She set her fork down hard, splattering some chocolate flakes on the table. "I know." She grabbed a napkin to clean up the mess. "Excuse me," she said, then went up to the counter to grab some extra napkins. On her return to the table, she bumped into the maid cleaning the floor. "Excuse me," she said.

"Sorry, mah," the woman replied.

Catherine paused, recognizing the accent, then slowly turned and looked at the young woman. The woman had a round face with a stocky figure and pretty West African features. She seemed familiar.

"How long have you worked here?"

"Not long, mah," she looking nervous, fear clear on her face. "I'm sorry."

"It's okay, you're not in trouble," Catherine said quickly, recognizing the fear. "The floor is spotless. Keep up the good work."

The woman smiled. "Thank you, mah. Your words are kind."

The smile was hers. That smile that seemed to make the clouds drift away. Catherine stared at her, speechless, shock leaving her mute. But could it be? After all these years? She'd survived too? Or was this just a foolish hope? She had to be sure. She made a simple gesture of twisting her wrist in a request for water. One she'd made many times when trapped in the cage.

The woman's eyes widened, then she dropped to her knees and covered her eyes.

Catherine knelt down and wrapped her arms around her. "It is you."

Helen continued to weep.

"All these years," Catherine said, tears streaming down her face. "I wondered."

"Me same," she said in a whisper. "I no think you'd live."

Catherine touched her face. "Is this a dream?"

The owner approached them. A stick figure of a man with frizzy hair and a matching mustache. "What is going on here? Has she insulted you?"

Catherine stood, lifting Helen up with her. "No," she told him before looking at Helen again. "How much do you get paid?"

Her hesitation told Catherine everything she needed to know: She was still property. Catherine looked at the man, daring him to challenge her. "She is leaving with me."

"I can't," Helen said her voice rising in panic. "I have to—"

"You're not working in this place anymore."

"I must," she said in an urgent whisper. "I have a son."

Catherine paused. That made things more complicated, but not impossible. Before she could say more, Tytus approached them. "Is there a problem?"

"That depends on him," Catherine said nodding to the man. "Where is her son?"

The man sent Tytus a wary look, then his shoulders drooped in defeat. "Working in the back."

"I'll get him," Tytus said, leaving no room for argument.

Catherine wrote a check, then handed it to the man. "You don't know where she is. Understood?"

The man folded the check and stuffed it into his shirt pocket. "Clearly."

Moments later, Tytus returned carrying a little boy, his face like thunder. He walked past the man and said in a low voice. "Let's go."

In the car, he swore. "That child is barely five years old and that bastard had him in a hot kitchen peeling pots of potatoes nearly as high as him."

"That is not unusual," Catherine said.

"But it doesn't make it right," Tytus said. "What do you plan to do with them?"

She inwardly groaned. Just as she had as a child, she'd behaved recklessly.

"You need to deal with your situation first," he continued when she didn't reply. "And that means Joscelyn. If she reveals your real identity and your parents file charges—"

He was right. What would happen to Helen and her son? "I haven't thought that far."

"Don't worry, I have."

57

Unlike many Georgian-style homes, Tytus's home appeared to grow more impressive the closer they got to it, although its wide and relatively shallow architecture had been designed to complement the grand landscape and strike guests with its remarkable size at a distance. But it was not the home's size or design that most shocked Catherine, it was its familiarity. Although she knew she'd never been there before, she felt an eerie sense of recognition. And as Tytus took them to the guest house where Helen and her son would stay, the recognition seemed to grow stronger. But she pushed her feelings aside determined to make sure that Helen felt okay.

Despite the luxury around her, Catherine sensed Helen's anxiety even as they settled her son in bed for a nap.

"Please don't leave here," Helen said once she and Catherine were alone in the kitchen after Tytus had given her a tour and told her how to reach him. "Let me come with you. I can work for you. I am good. Please."

"You'll be all right."

She clasped her hands together. "I am not a fine lady like you. I may anger him. Please, please, mah, I don't know how to do dis."

"There's nothing you have to do," Catherine said, not understanding her friend's distress.

"You are dat man's lady, no?"

Slowly, realization set in. Helen thought she was there to be the sexual property of Tytus. "No, I am not. And neither are you. You are here as a guest."

Helen looked at her, uncertain. "In dis fine house? Me?"

"Yes, your days of servitude are over. You are safe now. His name is Tytus Carter and he is a good man. I wouldn't leave you here otherwise."

"You are a fine lady now."

"Not yet. I nearly cost you your life before."

"It was no your fault and de one who gave me baby, his end was bad-bad."

"What happened?"

"His brother got in trouble again-again. Dey both gone soon after. Poof! Like smoke. Only a bottle of acid left. I heard a whisper that Chief took care."

Catherine nodded, remembering Booker's dream about a snake and the premonition that a terrible misfortune would befall him. The bastard was dead and Helen was free. That was justice and now she hoped to have a taste of some of her own.

58

———

The second time Joscelyn Payton showed up in her office, Vera was more confused than surprised. She greeted the younger woman feeling a sense of unease as she sat behind her desk and watched her. She wondered how close Evelyn was to her and why Joscelyn had decided to see her again. She wore a designer suit and an expression of deep concern. "I'm sorry to barge in on you like this," she said.

"That's okay," Vera replied, wondering why her apology didn't sound sincere.

"It's just that something has been bothering me and I thought you should be the first to know about it."

"Go on," she pressed when Joscelyn paused.

"It's about Evelyn."

Icy fear swept through her as she remembered the phone called she'd received years ago that Evelyn had been in an accident. She remembered taking the first flight available. The long anxious journey. "What about Evelyn? Has something happened to her?"

"No, no," Joscelyn said quickly. "It's nothing like that."

"Then what is it?"

"I'm afraid that Evelyn may be an imposter."

"An imposter?"

"Yes, it's possible that she really is a con artist named Catherine. Catherine lived off of others using her invented story of modern-day slavery or other disguises. I am not alone in my suspicions. Tytus Carter the man I'm seeing also believes she's a woman he met in England who used to interpret dreams for money. It may be in your best interest to get another DNA test to make sure that she's truly your daughter."

"Someone has been wondering about Evelyn," Vera told her husband over the phone the moment Joscelyn had left her office.

"Who?"

"Joscelyn Payton."

"And why would it interest her?"

Vera gripped the phone. She was a doctor, used to acting calm and rational, but she felt neither at the moment. "I don't know. She said she wanted to warn us."

"Warn us?"

"She thinks Evelyn is a fraud. She even suggested we do another DNA test."

"Do you think she'll cause trouble?" Noah asked after a long pause.

"I don't know. She's never been particularly friendly with me before but said she was a friend of Evelyn and now she's casting doubts about her and—"

"It's going to be okay."

"What if she confronts Evelyn? She might scare her away, make her start to doubt that she belongs to us and we could lose her."

"Don't worry my darling. I won't let that happen."

59

—————

They knew.

Catherine had that sense the moment she entered the house and felt the tense overcast that filled the marbled halls. When she stepped into the sitting room and saw Vera and Noah speaking in low voices—Vera looking anxious and Noah resolute—Catherine knew something was wrong and could guess the reason why. They'd discovered the truth.

Joscelyn had gotten to them.

The fact that she hadn't seen police cars waiting outside had to be a good omen. Perhaps they wanted to handle her deception quietly. She wouldn't embarrass them, she would own up to her actions. They looked up at her with caution.

"Evelyn, please take a seat," Noah said.

She knelt in front of them. "There's no need. I have done you a great wrong."

Noah leapt to his feet. "What are you doing? Get up. No daughter of mine—"

Daughter? He still thought she was his daughter? Joscelyn hadn't gotten to them yet? Then why did they look so upset?

Vera walked up to her and helped Catherine to her feet. "We know you haven't been yourself since Jason died."

Catherine searched her mind wondering how to proceed. Should she tell them the truth before Joscelyn had a chance to?

"Has anyone spoken to you about us?" Noah asked.

So Joscelyn had gotten to them, at least that much was certain. She just didn't know what she'd shared. "Yes, and clearly she's spoken to you too. So you know I'm not—"

"Thinking rationally because you must be confused. So please don't say another word." His eyes begged her to stay silent. He knew what she was going to say, but didn't want to hear the words. Refused to accept the truth.

She hung her head. She wouldn't say the words, but she couldn't stay. Those she cared about always suffered. "I must leave you and make my own way."

"No."

"I can't take anything more from you."

"You've taken nothing from us."

"Your money, your home—"

"Is nothing compared to what you give us. You were there when I put my back out and helped me when the business had some hits, you were there when Vera's mother came to visit and made her stay one of the best she's had. You've given us so much."

"Do you want to leave us?" Vera asked in a soft voice.

"No, but—"

"Then you will stay."

"But—"

"Joscelyn Payton is a petty woman who we will ignore."

But Joscelyn could still reveal the truth and then all that he'd given her would be taken away. It was all a lie. "We can't do that," Catherine said, taking a seat. "Because I'm not—"

"Remembering what you put in your will," he interrupted.

"My will?"

"Yes, you wrote and notarized that if anything were to happen to you that Catherine was to inherit your entire estate and all that you owned. Fortunately, you didn't need to."

Evelyn had left all that she owned to her? The money was hers? She was truly rich? So even if the truth came out she couldn't be charged as a thief. But that still didn't solve her other problem. "Joscelyn may hurt you to get to me and I can't allow that," Catherine said.

"I've lived a lot longer than you. I can protect you better than you can protect me."

"No, you—"

"We lied to you," Vera said in a rush.

"What?"

"Vera, don't."

"Noah, she needs to know. She has the right."

He hung his head. "All right."

"What is it?" Catherine asked, her gaze darting between them.

"We never had a natural child, neither together or apart," Vera said. "When we put out the notice, we didn't expect much. When you responded and we corresponded we knew you were the right one for us. After the accident we couldn't imagine not having you part of our lives no matter what that may mean. We wanted you no matter who you were."

"You gave my life new meaning," Noah said lifting his head with tears in his eyes. "Can you forgive us?"

She saw pain and fear swimming in his watery gaze. The fear that she'd reject them, that she'd leave them, that the life they'd built together would crumble in one moment. Pain that Joscelyn had caused. She would no longer let her stepsister use others to get to her. It was time to face Joscelyn. Catherine slowly rose to her feet and held open her arms.

60

─────

Joscelyn checked her reflection in her compact mirror. She knew she looked perfect but she wanted to make sure. She'd dressed with extra care for her dinner with Tytus. He'd invited her and her two sisters to his house, something he'd never done before. She closed the compact and put it away in her handbag, then sat back and glanced around the sitting room, noting the minor changes she'd make when she moved in. After they were married, the maroon-colored walls would become a more uniform cream white, the wood flooring would be a lighter color and the amount of foliage would be greatly reduced and she'd give the fireplace a new mantel.

"Why does your boyfriend want to see us?" Marie said with annoyance, sending a look at the maid watering the plants.

Boyfriend. He wasn't quite that yet, but she wouldn't correct her. "I told you. He wants to help your organization. He has the money and key contacts that will serve you well."

"I don't know why he needs to see me," Lorna said with a sniff. "He can't get me my husband back."

"But he may have a position for you."

Marie looked at the time. "What's taking him so long?"

Joscelyn also glanced at the time. It wasn't like Tytus to keep her waiting. Before she could call out to the maid to find out what was holding him up, they heard footsteps—high heels. Her heartbeat kicked up in anticipation. Was he going to introduce her to his mother? She smoothed down her hair then looked towards the entrance. Evelyn appeared, dressed in a gossamer blue dress as if she were something from another world.

"So glad you could come," she said with a smile. "Sorry I've kept you waiting."

Marie surged to her feet. "Ericka, what are you doing here? Is this some sort of trick?"

"No, I wanted to formally introduce myself." She looked at Joscelyn. "Or maybe I should let you do that, since you already know who I am."

Joscelyn glared at her with burning eyes. "Where is Tytus?"

"He'll be here later."

"What's going on?" Marie asked her sister. "Do you know her too?"

"We all do," Joscelyn said in a low voice, her angry gaze never leaving Catherine's face.

"I don't know her," Lorna said.

"She's Ericka Dantes," Marie said.

Catherine folded her arms. "That's one name I've used."

Marie folded her arms in disgust. "Because you're a con artist."

Lorna squinted her eyes at her. "You look a little familiar. Did we meet at a party or something?"

Catherine swept her hand through the air in large arc. "I am going to live in a big house one day and have lots of riches," she said, recalling the dream she'd told them. She rested her hands on her hips and slowly let her gaze rest on each sister. "And you will remember my name."

Lorna screamed.

Marie fell to her knees. "Dear God, forgive me."

Joscelyn sat stiff in cool fury. "What do you want?"

"Not much anymore." She looked at Lorna, who'd regained herself and stared at her with a look of horror. "You lost a man you never deserved to have." She shifted her gaze to Marie. "Your conscience has kept you prisoner for years." She finally looked at Joscelyn. "And I haven't completely finished with you yet."

"Please don't tell Mom the truth," Marie begged, gripping her hands together. "She's ill and doesn't have much longer to live."

Catherine's lip trembled before she recovered herself. "I'm sorry to hear that."

"If you loved her at all, let her die in peace," Marie said, tears streaming down her face. "Please, I'll do anything."

"Your sisters don't seem as willing," she said, casting a glanced at Lorna who'd covered her eyes as if she couldn't bear to look at Catherine, and then Joscelyn, whose gaze hadn't wavered —challenge in her eyes.

"It would destroy her," Marie continued. "We're the ones to blame, not her or our brother. He's suffered the most. Our mother hardly lets him out of her sight and has demanded more from him than any of us. He—"

"You've begged for him before, I don't need to see a repeat of that. I will leave him alone and I will also help your company. I have no intention of telling our mother anything."

Marie's shoulders drooped in relief. "Thank you."

"Don't thank her yet," Joscelyn said in a cutting tone. "I'm sure that's not the end of it."

"That's true," Catherine said with a bright smile as if Joscelyn were a clever pupil in her class. "I also have another name, with which you've become familiar. Edmund Cristo, the new majority owner of your stepfather's business."

Joscelyn narrowed her eyes. "It was you," she said in a low voice filled with venom. "But you can't—"

"I can't what? Own my late father's business? A business you completely mismanaged? Do you plan to stop me? You were very clever with Jason's embezzlement case. I can't make you pay for that, but I'll win this time."

"Ericka Dantes? Edmund Cristo?" Joscelyn said with a sniff. "How very droll."

"Yes," Catherine said, pleased her sister had made the connection. "The vengeful character Edmund Dantes of *The Count of Monte Cristo* was a particular favorite of mine."

Joscelyn leaned back, unfazed. "I don't care, you can have the company." She glanced around the grand room. "Do you think this means anything? You're still nothing to me. Do you think we care about your new fake parentage while our dear mother is dying? Do you think it matters to us that you'll take off our hands a business we never really cared about? Lorna will find someone else, Marie would have found an investor and I certainly don't want anything that you have."

"Sorry I'm late," Tytus said, walking into the room. He walked up to Catherine and placed an affectionate kiss on her cheek.

Catherine measured her sister, seeing the cool mask of fury settle in place, as she finally realized why Tytus's house had seemed so familiar to her. It had been in her dream. "You were saying?" she pressed.

Joscelyn gripped her hands into fists, incensed—she'd been tricked and betrayed. She slowly rose to her feet. "Fine, you can have everything," she said and walked towards the exit then she grabbed a fire poker, spun around and ran towards Catherine. "But you can't have him."

"Joscelyn, don't!" Lorna said, blocking her. She gasped in

pain when the poker went through her. She stumbled back and fell.

"No!" Marie rushed forward and fell to her knees beside her fallen sister, watching in terror as blood spurted from the wound. She pressed her hand over it, the blood seeping through her fingers. "Oh God, Joscelyn, what have you done!"

Joscelyn stood paralyzed, horrified by what she'd done, then she looked at Catherine with renewed rage. "It's her fault! She made me do it! Everything is her fault."

"Don't move it," Tytus said quickly when Marie reached for the poker. But they both knew that keeping the poker in place didn't matter, the blood continued to flow with steady frequency indicating that a major vessel had been hit. He dialed 911 then said, "Yes, I need an ambulance," when he finally connected.

"Catherine?" Lorna said.

Catherine hurried over to her. "What is it?"

"I'm sorry," she said tears streaming down her face. "So sorry."

Catherine grabbed her hand and kissed the back of it, all her anger dissipating like smoke and love and compassion filled it. "I forgive you." She held her sister's hand tighter. "Now hold on. You can survive this."

Marie shot Joscelyn a look of disgust as her eldest sister still stood immobile and hadn't made a move to assist them. "You're the doctor," she said. "What should we do?"

I don't know! Joscelyn wanted to say. Why were they looking at her like that? Why did they think she should be blamed? Catherine was always so charmed. She'd come into their lives and had been given so much, while Joscelyn had to struggle and fight for everything. Even now the Dorans had forgiven her deceit. She would get the business? Joscelyn briefly looked at Tytus. No, Catherine couldn't have him. She wouldn't let her. Joscelyn looked at the back of Catherine's head, her stomach twisting. She hated her to the very core of her being. "It's not my fault," she said in a distant voice. "None of this is my fault."

Lorna looked up at her beloved sister—the beautiful, successful sister she'd always looked up to and had wanted to please and emulate. "Yes, it is," she said her words growing faint. "Now you have to pay..."

PART V

REDEMPTION

61

Maureen lay in her hospital bed, assailed with regrets as she looked out at the summer evening, knowing it would soon be the last time. She closed her eyes.

She wished she'd been a better wife and a more caring mother to Aaron, who she knew she'd pushed too hard. He'd rarely laughed as a child and as a man he had a grim visage much older than a man his age. There were so many things in her life she would change, although she'd never admit it aloud. She wouldn't give her mother the satisfaction. Her mother. To think she wouldn't outlast her. Her mother would think it was suitable punishment. But that didn't matter now. She wouldn't have to hear her acid tongue again.

Her funeral would be exquisite. She'd already made arrangements. Her sister Robin had broken down in tears when Maureen had asked her to organize it. Her sister had held her hand mumbling nonsense about needing forgiveness for what she'd done. Maureen didn't know what she was talking about and didn't much care. She just hoped Robin did he job well with the funeral. Maureen knew exactly how she wanted everything to be

—from the casket to bouquets. She could imagine her son and daughters sitting in the front row dabbing away tears. They'd all be together, except for one.

"Mummy?"

She hadn't been called that in so long.

"Mummy?"

And the voice...there was something familiar about it. But it was that of a woman, not a child.

"You're the most beautiful woman I know."

Her weak heart began to race. Yes, she'd told her that. Her dear little Catherine. Could it be? Maureen let her eyes flutter open and looked up at the woman bent over her. She saw Emery's eyes and Catherine's mouth. But was it just a dream? She reached her hand out to her. "Yes, I'm here," Catherine said, taking her stepmother's hand.

Maureen marveled at how real and solid the woman felt. And she smelled the faint scent of lilacs. It wasn't a dream! Tears of joy and sorrow gathered in her eyes. "I knew you'd come back to me. I knew you were alive."

"Yes, Mummy. I'm home and I'll take care of Aaron. I'll make sure he has a good life. I always wanted to be a big sister."

She had so many things to ask her, so many questions, but she didn't have the strength or the time.

"How did you—?"

Catherine adjusted the bed sheets. She wouldn't tell her stepmother the truth—where she'd been, how she'd escaped or what she'd done to her sisters. She wouldn't tell her that Lorna had died, that Joscelyn would be charged for her murder and that Marie had suffered a nervous breakdown. She didn't have the words to tell her mother about another dream she'd had. A dream where Aaron had become a popular, award-winning music teacher and lived his life with joy. A dream where she reconnected with Marie and healed their relationship. A dream where her friend Helen helped Marie expand her non-profit so that it provided services for people freed from all types of modern-day slavery—from the sex trade to domestic servitude. She didn't have the words to tell her that she saw them all with long full lives.

So she said, "Don't worry about anything, Mummy. You can rest now."

Rest. Maureen clung to the word. She didn't have to fight anymore. Her daughter was finally home. Maureen closed her eyes and a soft smile spread on her lips as her final breath left her body.

62

____

The dark figure rose to his feet as Catherine drove her car up the drive, the black sky scattered with stars, hung low overhead. She briefly caught the figure in her headlights before she turned and parked. She took a few deep breaths before she got out of the car and approached him.

"Your father told me you went to the hospital," Tytus said.

"How long have you been waiting?"

He shrugged. "How is she?"

Catherine stared at him for a moment, wanting to tell him that he shouldn't have waited for her, that he shouldn't care so much. She'd done what she had to and didn't need him. She'd made Joscelyn tremble with rage, Lorna weep with sorrow and Marie beg for mercy. But an acute sense of loss made words impossible and she burst into tears. She didn't pull away when she felt his arms around her. She knew he was strong enough to carry the weight of her sorrow and the pain that tore her heart.

"I'm sorry," he said, holding her tight, but it didn't feel tight enough. She wanted to melt away, she wanted to stop breathing so that the pain would stop too.

"You made her final moments happy," he said.

Yes, she had done that. And he held her as she wept for her mother, the ten year old who'd been betrayed, the sister who wouldn't see her children grow, the father who'd never seen his daughter return, and the pain of nearly twenty years threatened to drown her in a sea of despair, but somehow in his embrace she wasn't submerged by the waves. And slowly his quiet power helped her to remember all those who'd been kind to her like Orla and Grace, Evelyn, Noah, Vera, Helen, and Jason.

Those memories of compassion, caring and love slowly calmed the waves.

"What are you going to do now?"

It seemed like a simple question, but she hadn't thought that far. Her life had been consumed with facing her sisters again and making them pay for the pain they'd put her through. "What is a ghost to do but fade away?"

He brushed his lips against her forehead. "You don't feel like a ghost."

She didn't feel like one either, her skin tingling where his lips had touched her skin. He made her feel human. He always had, his touch always making her feel alive, a sensation she wouldn't fight anymore. "Thank you for everything," she said, drawing away to look up at him.

"You know I don't want your thanks."

"Tytus—"

"I'm not my brother," he said with feeling, his gaze filled with regret and yearning. "I may not be able to make you laugh and smile as he did, but I love you. I have since the first moment. Please give me the chance to make you happy."

Catherine glanced away and in the distance saw a slice of yellow in the horizon as the sun rose, pushing away the night to make room for morning. She lowered her gaze and sighed. "Give me your hand."

He hesitated, then did.

She kissed her two fingers then pressed them in his palm. "I don't need you to make me happy." She looked up at him, her gaze shining with love. "Because now I'm free and that's all the happiness I need."

The End

ABOUT THE AUTHOR

Dara Girard, an award-winning, national bestselling author of more than forty novels, from romance to suspense, loves telling stories.

Born in the US to immigrant parents, Dara enjoys pulling from her Jamaican, British, Nigerian heritage and exposure to various cultures to bring what reviewers and fans call "vivid emotional stories" to life. She is best known for her popular Henson Series, the mysterious Clifton Sisters, and the fun Black Stockings Society.

You can write her at:
contactdara@daragirard.com
or
P.O. Box 10345
Silver Spring, MD 20914
If you'd like to receive a reply, please send a self-addressed stamped envelope.

Visit her website to sign up for her newsletter and get sneak peeks, monthly updates on new releases, and special offers.

For more information visit
www.daragirard.com

9 781949 764215